THE TORTURED KINGDOM

BRYAN ASHER

Also, by Bryan Asher

Novels

The Assassin of Malcozé

The Treasure of Lor-Rev

The Fear of Moncroix

Comic Books

Soulless City

(Featured in Anvil Magazine #2)

INTERCONT
PRESS

This book is a work of fiction. Everything within this book is a product of the author's imagination. Any resemblance to actual people, events, or locations, is entirely coincidental.

The Tortured Kingdom

Copyright © 2025 by Bryan Asher

Illustrations Copyright © by Bryan Asher

Written by Bryan Asher

Cover Illustration by Batsky Starman

Character Illustrations by Batsky Starman

Cover Design by Elizabeth Mackey

Chapter Header Illustrations by Arief Rachmad

This book is published through Intercont Press, all rights reserved. No part of this publication may be reproduced, distributed, or transmitted in any form or by any means, including photocopying, recording, or other electronic or mechanical methods, without the prior written permission of the publisher, Intercont Press, except in the case of brief quotations embodied in critical reviews and certain other noncommercial uses permitted by copyright law. For permission requests, write to the publisher at intercont.novels@protonmail.com.

ISBN 978-1-7357628-6-9 (Paperback)

ISBN 978-1-7357628-7-6 (eBook)

www.ashernovel.com

To Cody,

The adventurous son I always wanted.

THE TORTURED KINGDOM

BRYAN ASHER

CHAPTER ONE

THE UNDEAD CHAMPION

WATER SLOSHED around Evan's metal-plated boots with every step. A dry sting, like scraping nettles, rubbed the insides of his lungs. His body begged him to turn and flee. To go back to his cottage, where he'd be greeted by a thick fur blanket and warm, dancing flames. He compromised instead, ducking into a stone alcove to rest. Finally catching his breath, he began ascending a nearby staircase. After reaching the landing, he finally escaped the ankle-deep water covering the first floor of the Colosseum.

He squinted, staring carefully down the wide hallway ahead. After ensuring there weren't any more monsters lurking about, he unhooked the chin strap on his helmet and lifted it free. Holding it in both hands, he observed his reflection on its onyx-colored surface. His wavy brown hair was tattered and matted from the sweat of battle. His shaved down horns, resting atop his head, were littered with small scratches. Fresh scrapes and tiny bits of black dirt speckled the thin features of his young face.

Closing his eyes, he slumped to the floor and rested against the smooth marble wall.

'I've only reached the first hall,' he thought, *'and I already look as though I've fought the entire army of Herrgal.'*

While he hadn't faced the *entire* nation's army, he'd slashed his way through a hefty contingent of the zombified soldiers in the capital city. Sadly, he even recognized a few of them. His consciousness flashed a sudden memory of a particular undead face he'd felled upon entering the front courtyard. As he impaled the ghoulish knight, its teal, watery eyes met his. A pitiful empty stare from a gaunt, soulless face. A face that, regardless of its condition, he knew once.

'Those weren't the men I stood beside,' Evan told himself, steeling his resolve. *'Not anymore.'*

Sunlight seeped through a circular window overhead, glinting off the outstretched legs of his black armor. Before the Cataclysm, this colosseum was his place of occupation, patrolling the grounds as one of its guardsmen.

He took a heavy breath, shoving down the rising knot in his belly. The world he knew was stolen, and the memories of his dead friends wouldn't bring it back. Gazing over his shoulder, he observed the next corridor through the nearest arched opening. After fighting past a horde of armor-clad zombies in the courtyard, he'd only reached the first rim of the circular building. Three more layers of hallways stood between him and the central pit.

Evan gathered himself, climbing to his feet. Never too careful, he unsheathed his sword before striding purposefully across the fifty-foot-wide hall. Even in the world's apocalyptic state, the Colosseum still held its grandeur. A massive arched ceiling decorated with bright paintings of different rulers, battles, and famous figures spanned the overhead space. After crossing the stone threshold to the next hallway, another one of equally exquisite architecture sat above.

Evan remained on-guard despite being met with more emptiness. He knew better than to trust his environment. In the entire continent of Yohme, you could only trust yourself now.

'I wonder if the lands beyond Yohme met the same fate?' Evan asked himself.

It had been only one month since the meteor struck the land bridge connecting Yohme to the others, sending it spinning away from its neighbors. Word of the other Intercontinents' fate hadn't returned to his city.

Evan sighed, *'Hopefully, their magic wasn't tainted as well.'*

THWOK!

As the clank of metal rang out one room over, Evan readied his sword. Shuffling footsteps followed as another armor-clad skeleton appeared. It ambled towards him, dragging a hefty longsword it could no longer lift. What was once a proud commander, capable of wielding a massive blade and wearing the heftiest plate, now stood as a dismal stack of bones. Thankfully, its skin, muscles, and tendons had melted away, making it easier to kill than the ones outside.

Evan sidestepped the clumsy creature and swung his sword through the opening between the skeletal knight's helm and breastplate. His weapon connected perfectly with the spongy disc between two vertebrae, making a ripe sound like a butcher chopping raw chicken. The helmet-bedecked skull clunked across the marble floor as Evan returned his sword to the sheath at his side.

'Only two more halls 'till the center,' he thought, continuing forward.

Briskly crossing the third hall, he was met by a massive set of marble stairs spanning the entire length of the room. After ascending them to the fourth and final circle, he crept to the other side and hid behind a column at the arena entrance. His eyes grew wide at what he saw beyond the rows of marble benches. There, in the middle of the raised platform, he finally found what he'd fought so hard to reach.

'The champion,' Evan thought.

However, it wasn't the same fighter from before the cataclysm. Its former sun-kissed, bronze skin now resembled the color of wet mold. The once dashing green eyes were replaced with small emerald flames, curling from the sockets to the middle of its forehead.

The corruption of the champion's body hadn't affected its attire. It still wore a tricorn hat, thick leather armor, and spiked gauntlets. He watched the hulking monster aimlessly stomp around the center platform; mangled corpses strewn about its feet.

'There!' Evan told himself.

Hanging from the champion's right hip was a clear flask containing a red liquid. A small silver shield was stamped on one side.

'Once I find an opening, I'll snatch it and run,' Evan decided.

"*Greeeeeawwwww!*" a raspy voice shrieked behind him.

He turned, yanking his sword free to face whatever lurked at his back, but he was too slow. Sprinting towards him, something snatched his shoulders before he could square up to it. The force sent them tumbling down the steps between the stone bench seating. After rolling past several rows, they slammed onto a square landing halfway down the aisles. Evan grimaced as sharp pain surged down both legs. His eyes darted about in search of what ambushed him. He found it one row down, slowly pulling itself upright. It didn't have features like his own, instead sporting furry skin, a small snout, and pointed ears.

"A Rehnarian," Evan wondered aloud, "That explains its speed."

A guttural growl pulled his attention from the fox-faced zombie. Looking past it, he saw the champion's flaming eyes harshly observing them. He reached for his sword, but it was gone.

'Dammit!' he cursed, eyes searching frantically for it.

"*GRAAA!*" Another shout from the champion echoed as it leaped off the combat stage. It bound ahead in hulking steps toward them.

Evan glanced back to the Rehnarian, noticing its attention was also averted by the massive monster. Scrambling to his feet, he shoved his shoulder into its back, sending it tumbling down the stairs. Bones snapping like twigs announced the end of its descent. It lay limply in front of the wall between the first row and the arena. Two large spiked gloves grasped the tip of the wall above the fallen creature.

'It can jump high enough to reach us!?' Evan's gut clenched at the thought. He'd hoped the ten feet of wall was too difficult for the massive thing to traverse.

Unfortunately, he was wrong.

"Where's my sword," Evan grunted angrily, scanning his surroundings.

A deep huff caught his ear. Turning toward it, he saw the champion standing on the wall, glowering at him. Despite its appetite to kill, it seemed in no rush, either by choice or due to its current physical state. Watching it reach over its back with a bony hand, bits of decaying flesh dangling loosely from its fingers, Evan assumed the latter. As it slowly pulled its blade overhead, a glint just a few rows over caught his attention. He ran for the speckle of light, hoping to find his sword.

"It's not mine, but it'll do," Evan announced, observing the object that caught his eye.

He snatched the black leather hilt of the bright silver blade and immediately dove behind a nearby aisle. A thunderous clang shook the ground as the champion's immense weapon slammed into the spot Evan once occupied.

"His blade still has the same magic," Evan thought, noticing tiny sparks flicker off his enemy's weapon.

The champion groaned angrily and yanked the sword free from the divot it created in the marble floor. The action caused its decomposing body to stagger backward.

"I better not regret this," Evan said, gritted his teeth and charging forward.

He had a second, maybe two before the monster would recover its footing. As he closed in, its flaming eyes locked on him, and it swung for his head. Ducking his chin and pulling his metal-plated arm up, he barely blocked the strike. The force of the blow sent him toppling over a bench into the next row.

Scrunching his eyes, he tried his best to ward off the combination of blurring vision and ringing ears. More grunts and lumbering steps followed as it stomped toward him. Feeling the heat of flame and the stench of rotting breath, he knew it was closing in.

In desperation, Evan thrust his newly acquired sword upward. A clang of metal connecting with bone told him that his stab was successful. He peered through watery eyes and saw it had fallen to one hip, its lower mandible dangling from its jaw. Scraping together his last ounce of energy, he snatched the bench and yanked himself upright.

A few dancing sparks caught his attention, noticing the champion's lightning blade was leaning against nearby seating.

"My lucky day," Evan noted aloud, a smirk crossing his lips as he snatched the weapon's blue hilt.

His adversary growled, slowly climbing to one knee.

"I won't let you stand again," Evan announced, lifting the sword high overhead in both hands.

Swinging down ferociously, the glowing blade sliced through the champion's outstretched hand and cleaved his skull down the middle. Guttural whisps of air came from what remained of its throat as it slumped onto its knees. Evan yanked back the sword, and the monster toppled face-first onto the smooth marble. A few heavy breaths later, his nerves returned to normal. After scanning the arena and seeing no other enemies, he sighed and took a seat on the closest bench.

Once the sparks subsided on his sword, he laid it across his knees, noticing how the corruption of magic within the living hadn't extended to the inanimate.

The Burnished Blade, once wielded by Herrgal's arena champion,' Evan thought, *'After countless victories against the best warriors in our country, I own this prized weapon now.'*

Another silver object caught his attention near his boots.

"Well, that's where you've been hiding," Evan laughed, leaning over and collecting his old sword.

After a careful moment comparing its scraped and weathered state to the beautiful weapon resting on his knees, he tossed it away.

"I think I'll keep this one instead."

CHAPTER TWO

THE ONLY
MERCHANT AROUND

JULIEN STARED OUT the square window while cleaning a glass container with a spare rag. His eyes narrowed, observing a thin fog curl past the glass pane. Even with the lantern hung outside to illuminate the darkness, he couldn't see through it.

"Never a good sign when the smog's light," Julien thought aloud, "if the weather can't choose to stay or go, we won't see summer for at least another month."

"Everything changed after the impact," a husky patron grumbled, rubbing his thick blonde beard, "Why should the weather be any different."

Julien huffed, setting the container down before selecting another one to clean. He and Gillium were the only ones occupying his shop, which he'd kept running after the Cataclysm.

Gillium's ability with magic became invaluable to their town, as he was one of the few nearby who wielded with a staff instead of his own body. So, he hadn't turned into a flesh-eating undead corpse. A week after the comet struck, the two had bartered a deal where he'd protect Julien's shop.

Gillium leaned his elbow on the wood countertop, pointing a finger at Julien. "Don't get sour on me. You can get back to having all the answers soon enough."

"I'm not wrong about this," Julien retorted, "The warlocks and mages powers were perverted, but you and I, we still stand the same as ever," he set the glass container down and grabbed a jug to clean, "Not everything corrupted after Yohme was dislodged."

Gillium grunted nonchalantly. "I guess… But we've only heard from those within our city. Who knows what's happened to the rest of Herrgal, let alone the neighboring kingdoms."

The shop's front door creaked open, causing Gillium to swivel on his stool. Julien held an inquisitive gaze on the dark-haired figure stepping through the threshold.

"I saw a Rehnarian," Evan said, approaching the countertop, "And its body was decayed. Like many of our soldiers."

Julien cocked an eyebrow. "Was it wearing cleric robes?"

Evan took a seat at the counter and shrugged. "It ambushed me, so I wasn't concerned with its clothing." He plopped a glass bottle emblazoned with a silver shield on the counter. "You have the coin to buy this off me?"

Julien chuckled. "You place a high value on coin even after the world's come to an end."

Evan eyed him skeptically. "Guessing you want to barter instead."

"No, no," Julien started, waving a hand before reaching for a shelf under the countertop. "I'm happy to give you coin, just thought you might be more interested in something another Traveler brought me." The shopkeep dropped a small beige coin purse on the counter in front of Evan. "Go ahead and count it; there are twenty-five pieces as the reward offered."

Evan pried open the purse and dug one finger through it, then lifted his eyes to Julien. "Good to see you're still a man of your word."

"How could I keep this village running if I weren't?" he replied smugly, hands on his hips.

Evan grinned and set the pouch back down. "Typical merchant, overstating his value. If it weren't for men like Gillium and I providing protection, I don't think this shop would last through the night."

Julien huffed. "Typical soldier, only seeing combat as the answer. Now," he held a finger aloft, "considering you set that pouch back down, I gather you're interested in the item I mentioned earlier?"

Turning on his heel, Julien walked through a single door behind the U-shaped counter. A few loud clangs and thumps of boxes and items being tossed around made Evan and Gillium eye each other nervously.

"You're the one that put him up to it," Gillium said flatly, leaning over the counter to find a brown corked bottle.

"Oh, it's my fault now," Evan laughed.

Gillium nodded before extending a second bottle to Evan. "Want one?"

"Why not," Evan replied, taking the drink from his friend before uncorking it and downing a hearty swig. "That's not bad ale," he remarked, taking a moment to observe the wax seal stamped on the side.

"It better be, considering I aged it in the cellar for all of spring," Julien interjected. He set a heavy cloak on the counter. It was covered in feathers that were a mixture of deep blue and black. "I thought you'd appreciate this."

Evan eyed him quizzically. "The Cataclysm has turned you mad if you think I'd take clothes over coin."

Julien's weathered face wrinkled into a wry smile. "It's much more than that, young Traveler," he stated while running his hand along it, inviting him to take a closer look.

Evan pinched a section between two fingers and drew his eyes closer. Upon inspecting further, he noticed the colors change. It now resembled a hue between his tan skin and the dark walnut counter.

"Here, try this as well," Julien said proudly, extending a dagger to Evan, hilt first.

He took the short blade and ran the tip over it, trying his best to slice the feathers in two. When they didn't, he held a section upright and stabbed, but the dagger wouldn't puncture through.

"Who would trade this to you?!" Evan exclaimed in bewilderment.

"Hunger is a powerful calling," Julien answered, "I'd also assume the Traveler who exchanged this has more powerful tools available."

"Why save it for me?" Evan asked, turning a suspicious eye to the elder shopkeep.

Julien lifted his chin in a quick jut, aiming his gesture at Evan's sheath. "If you're going to keep the Champion's Burnished Blade, I thought you might want something to conceal it from covetous eyes."

Evan instinctively placed a hand on the hilt, glancing at the emerald sphere inset at its base.

"Don't worry," Julien said, "I don't plan to take it unless you'd like to trade that as well?"

Evan slid the coin purse back to Julien, then lifted the cloak and slung it around his shoulders. It returned to the black and blue mixture as he fastened the metal clasps on the neck tie. Reaching over his shoulder, he threw the hood overhead.

Gillium grinned. "Has a nice look to it."

"So, it doesn't fully cloak me then," Evan stated, removing the hood.

"Of course not," Julien replied sternly, "It's not meant to make you invisible. It just provides a nice disguise should you need it."

Evan rubbed his chin before extending a hand to his friend. "Gillium, pass me your staff."

He obliged, tossing his spell-wielding weapon to Evan before leaning against the counter and crossing his arms, his brow furrowing curiously. Holding the wood staff in one hand, Evan wrapped his other in some of the cloak before placing it at the opposite end. The light yellow and beige color of the pine that comprised Gillium's staff bled across the cloak.

"So, it bonds with nature for its disguise," Evan said, tossing the staff back.

Gillium caught it and nodded approvingly. "Healing potion for the veil of your terrain sounds like a fair deal to me."

Julien plucked the potion from the counter and took it back through the single door, stashing it in his stock room. As Evan took his seat back on the stool, Gillium slid another bottle across the counter towards him. Evan uncorked it and lifted it towards his friend.

"To Yohme's Champion," Evan said, "May his excellent service deliver his soul to the heavens."

"Aye, and may his sword keep your hide firmly attached," Gillium replied, raising his bottle in kind, clinking it off Evan's.

The entrance door creaked open, and the two friends turned on their stools. Evan slid his arm behind the cloak and wrapped four fingers around his sword's hilt, his thumb resting on the smooth emerald. He was never too careful in the newly dangerous state of their decayed world.

Three men briskly entered from the night into the lamplit room. Upon noticing the men made no furtive movements and kept customary distance, Evan exhaled, relinquishing some – but not all – of his guard.

The man in the center slowly raised a hand. "We come looking for a Traveler to take up our cause. The townspeople informed us we could hire the best ones here."

CHAPTER THREE

SWORD FOR HIRE

Evan tilted his head, surveying the three men. Each had well-kept auburn hair tied back in a neat braid. Their facial features as pointed as the tips of their ears. They wore thick armor comprised of leather and fur with few signs of wear.

'Likely Hiroyan nobles,' Evan thought, *'Considering there's not a scratch among them, I'd assume they employ guardsmen. Probably watching the front door as we speak.'*

"Are you native to Herrgal?" Evan asked, testing their truthfulness.

The one to the right, wearing dark green armor, shook his head. "We've traveled here from the north, chasing a thief. We saw him just outside your village, crossing the stone bridge on horseback. However, we lost his trail soon after that."

Their town within the massive nation of Herrgal was quite intense to traverse, as it held a litany of towers that mostly fell when the comet struck. So, Evan wasn't surprised they'd lost someone in the rubble littering the streets.

Gillium hopped from his seat and took a step forward. His Koln heritage meant he barely stood above the hips of the tall Hiroyans. Koln were the shortest race in Yohme, but easily the most vocal and opinionated.

"You're the first we've met outside our country. Has your magic been tainted as well?" Gillium asked.

The one in the center nodded. "Everyone we knew who could wield Aura with their hands is cursed. I had hoped it was only our region; sadly, I was wrong…"

Evan sighed heavily. "At least we know. I'm assuming our vantage points were similar when the comet struck the High Bridge."

"Yes. Thankfully, we live in Maishi, which is further inland. Our city wasn't completely ravaged like those closer to the western border," the Hiroyan in the center replied. He stepped forward, extending his hand to Evan. "Apologies, this talk of destruction made me forget my formalities. I'm Aethin."

Evan removed his right hand from his weapon's hilt and shook Aethin's. "Evan," he answered, "And if you're looking for a Traveler to catch your thief, I can help."

The Hiroyan on the left stepped forward eagerly, shaking hands with Gillium. "I'm Edgar. We're very thankful you'd take our cause."

Gillium thumbed to his right. "He'll be taking your request. I stay here and protect the shop."

"He really stays to protect the ale," Julien chided, slapping Evan on the shoulder.

Evan laughed, turning to Gillium, who only replied with pursed lips and a solitary grunt.

"You weren't corrupted?" Edgar asked.

Gillium shook his head, holding his staff aloft. "Since I channel, I had no Aura in my bones that could be poisoned."

The three Hiroyans shared intrigued glances.

Evan broke the brief silence. "I hate to sell myself out of work, but is there a reason you need me to assist you? Considering you made it this far; I can't imagine why you'd need to spend coin on a Traveler."

The Hiroyan on the right, who'd remained silent until this point, stepped forward. "We didn't need a hired sword initially. However, the deeper south we venture, the closer we are to Rehnarian territory. And we both know they aren't welcoming to our people. Thankfully, you're Kah'zyin," he finished, nodding to Evan.

Evan touched a finger to one of the short horns on top of his head, then shot a knowing glance to Gillium, who shrugged in agreement. While he'd filed his to a nub, most let theirs grow in a curl around their head. Eventually finishing at a point underneath their ear, like Julien. Being part of the Coliseum guard meant he had to shave his down to wear a helmet, a habit he hadn't broken after the Cataclysm.

"I guess you're right," Evan answered, still running a finger over the stub.

Edgar reached under his dark green cloak and rummaged through a pocket. After retrieving a coin pouch, he extended his hand towards Evan. "We'll offer the first half now, then the second once we collect the thief."

Evan politely took the pouch and skimmed a finger through the contents. His eyes widened.

'They're offering fifty silvers for this!' he thought, fighting to keep his cool.

Evan swallowed, concealing his eagerness. "I'll take the job, but you'll need to take me to the southern border in your carriage. Then we'll part, and I'll track him alone."

Aethin and Edgar looked to the mostly silent Hiroyan, wordlessly asking for approval. Turning an eye to his companions, he briefly bit his inner cheek, contemplating the request. "If you're seen with us, word might spread…"

Evan raised a hand. "I'll stay hooded; I just need more information from you. And considering the rate at which this thief fled, I don't want to waste any more time talking here. I'd rather have you catch me up once we're off. I hope to catch him before he reaches the first city in Rehnarian territory."

The Hiroyan's eyes narrowed, clearly perturbed at the interruption. "Fine. I'll trust you, Traveler."

Bumping over rugged terrain, the carriage jostled the four men in their seats. There was already thick tension weighing down the mood, mostly from the Hiroyan who'd yet to introduce himself. Evan's intuition told him it was better that he didn't know the man's name. He took a moment to survey the beautiful interior once more, noticing how the walls were intricately engraved in the swirling patterns of Hiroyan writing.

He turned his eyes to Edgar, directing his questions to the friendliest of the three. "So, you mentioned a Chyterian stole several riches from you. How did he gain access to your wealth?"

Edgar sighed. "He was a servant of ours. Once the Cataclysm occurred, it gave him the opportunity to reach our vault. Unfortunately, it had been cracked open after much of our castle was torn apart."

Evan rubbed his chin thoughtfully. "When did you discover the burglary?"

"It was the next day. Guards were pulled from their duty to assist in more needed areas of the manor. When they returned, several of our most valuable pieces were gone," Edgar answered.

"And you're sure it was the servant?" Evan asked.

Edgar nodded. "Yes. But he was much more than a servant. He was one of our cartographers, giving him access and understanding to more areas than most."

Evan ran a tongue across his inner cheek, contemplating Edgar's answer. Chyterians were the best at traversing and mapping routes since their rodent-like bodies made them capable of trekking every terrain in the kingdom. Their people mainly occupied caves and tunnels in the western mountains because their eyes saw in the dark better than most human-formed races during daylight.

'I can see why they offered so much,' Evan thought, *'Trying to catch a Chyterian won't be easy.'*

Another question came to him, and he quickly turned his eyes towards Edgar. "Why didn't he flee to the caves?"

The silent Hiroyan shot a harsh glance at the other two. They were clearly subordinates or younger relatives, and he didn't take kindly to them being questioned thoroughly.

Aethin swallowed a lump back upon seeing the disapproval, then turned to Evan. "Our guard cut his path off, knowing he'd head that way, which sent him southbound. If he'd reached the caves, we knew we'd never see our heirlooms returned."

Evan wished to press further but thought better of it. His time in the guard academy had taught him when to keep his mouth shut. He'd also noticed two daggers on either side of the nameless leader's waist and didn't want to provoke him. Hiroyans of his status were known to have excellent combat training, and he could finish Evan off in such close quarters. Suddenly, the Champion he'd fought a day ago didn't seem so dangerous. At least he had room to maneuver and no political courtesies to navigate.

Evan winced as he straightened his posture, stretching his back. While the Champion might have been a simpler foe, he'd left him with some lingering wounds. Questioning the nobles wasn't the only reason he'd requested a ride. In truth, he needed the rest but worried showing any fatigue would lead them to hire someone else, and he couldn't lose his chance at their generous reward.

"Well, Traveler," the nameless Hiroyan said, interrupting his thoughts, "We've reached our destination. Care to inform us of your plan from this point on?"

Evan's eyes met his harsh stare. "From the map you showed me, I'll take the uphill road that circles the edge of town. You'll continue heading straight."

"You hope he scurries out from his hiding place at the sight of us then," the Hiroyan leader stated.

Evan nodded.

The leader looked to Edgar, who immediately rose from his seat and opened the carriage door for Evan. "Alright, we'll see you on the other side, Traveler."

CHAPTER FOUR

THIEF AT THE EDGE OF TOWN

'I can't believe he understood my plan so easily.' Evan thought, *'Maybe he was involved with military strategy before society collapsed.'*

He gingerly climbed over a fallen marble column in the drizzly daytime rain, keeping a quiet trail. Taking a few steps off the dirt road, he knelt in a grass patch close to the cliff's edge. The column he'd climbed over belonged to a temple, whose other remains had tumbled downhill, crushing several houses and shops at the base of the cliff.

'Most likely fled south to the larger city... or died. Hopefully, the ones here dealt with any tainted corpses.'

Throwing his hood overhead, the feathered cloak ruffled, matching itself to the grass underneath. Peering to the small town in the valley below, he observed the carriage and its guard. Horseback knights surrounded the vehicle; some carried bows, while others had short swords strapped to their backs. Two bannermen marched at the front of the party. Before their world was struck by a comet, it was the customary arrival for a traveling foreign noble. In the post-collapse they currently inhabited, cold water running down your spine was less jarring. Of the twenty or so people lingering in the streets, none could peel their eyes from the display.

'If the thief is still here, surely he'll notice the caravan coming or catch on from the commotion.'

Fishing on his belt, Evan unclasped a pouch and retrieved a small spyglass. Closing one eye, he peered through the device for a better look. Surveying the crowd, his eyes narrowed on one particular woman. She was standing on her porch, anxiously leaning against a railing. Looking to the upstairs windows of her home, he noticed only one of them had cloth covering the inside. Many homes had boarded or covered windows for safety in this dangerous age. However, most homes barricaded every opening. This appeared like an attempt to conceal something at the last minute.

'If the thief is hiding there, she likely took him in the night before. Maybe to tend to his wounds,' he thought, rising to a crouch before moving further uphill, *'Let's send a signal and see what crawls out.'*

Reaching to his belt, he retrieved an eight-inch metal cylinder from his hip. Thankfully, he'd built enough goodwill with Julien that he lent him a wrist cannon for a small up-front deposit.

'Don't worry, miss, I promise to keep my aim adjacent to your home,' he thought, strapping the object to the outside of his right wrist.

Cracking open another pouch, he took a small wax ball and scraped it across a rough strip running down the side of his wrist cannon. As the ball began to fizz, he dropped it into his weapon and aimed.

Pop!

A sharp bang filled the air as the explosive hurtled toward the woman's home, finally crackling to the ground a few feet from her residence. Before it landed, Evan lay flat-bellied in the grass, ensuring his cloak hid him from any watchful eyes.

Two of the knights turned their horses and galloped for the woman's home. She clung to the railing, eyes crushed together in fear as they approached.

"Are you ok, madam?" one asked, dismounting and walking to the porch.

Her watery eyes met his, unsure how to process him approaching her in earnest. Looking past the one that greeted her, she saw the second had taken a defensive position with his shield in case more attacks followed.

"I...I, don..."

The knight lifted a hand firmly. "It's fine, madam; let's get inside before another barrage reaches your doorstep."

She instinctually turned to lead him inside, then stopped and threw her back against the door.

"Wait!" she cried, holding one arm in front while the other clung to the doorframe.

On the hill, Evan watched through his spyglass as she argued with the guardsmen, pointing to another home and pleading. Suddenly, he wasn't so sure the thief was inside.

'I don't imagine someone fighting this hard to protect an injured drifter.' he pondered, pulling his gaze from the spyglass to get a wider view.

Thirty yards ahead of the woman's home, two stubby-framed figures – hidden beneath black cloaks – entered an alley from a beaten-down brick building. He peered through his device again for a clearer view, noticing two pairs of pink three-fingered hands exchanging a satchel. The one with the satchel tucked it under his cloak before taking off on all fours. The other hurriedly waddled away in the opposite direction.

"Definitely Chyterian," Evan noted aloud, jumping to his feet and running for his horse.

After mounting his ride, he sparked and shoved another explosive down his wrist cannon, firing it towards the one furthest from him. He had to alert his employers of what he'd found. While the horseback guard galloped towards the crackling light, he raced along the cliff's edge after the second Chyterian.

'It must be the injured one,' Evan thought, noting how it had to maintain an upright run, *'Just a few paces more and I'll have him.'*

His current position on the downhill run put him a few feet above the closest rooftop. Looking over his shoulder, he saw the thief was several paces behind him.

'Perfect.' Evan told himself before dismounting and hopping to the roof below.

'Only five paces now…' he plotted, crouching on the edge, *'Now!'*

He shot his last explosive at the thief's feet, who curled his short, furry arms over his rodent-like face as a litany of tiny sparks crackled. Evan leaped from the ledge, feathered cloak flapping as he fell one story. He tucked his knees in time to roll perfectly, putting him within arm's reach of his target. Snatching the nearest arm, he slammed an elbow into the back of it, causing the Chyterian to fall forward, howling in pain.

'Must have grabbed the wounded arm,' Evan thought, sliding a knee onto the downed thief's spine.

"Where's your friend going?" he interrogated.

"We'll never hand it over," he cursed back, squirming desperately to escape.

"Fine, I'll just take you back. Now, give me your other arm," Evan demanded, pushing his elbow down harder.

"Gyaaaaaah!" the Chyterian shrieked, flailing his free arm to avoid Evan's capture.

SLAM!

Evan's eyes darted forward, searching for the noise.

SLAM!

Doors of the two nearest buildings shook.

CRASH!

They flung from their hinges; splintered wood scattered as several tainted bodies tumbled through the openings.

"What in Varkin's name?!" Evan yelled, jumping to his feet and drawing his sword.

His pursuer distracted; the Chyterian rolled onto his back and tossed red powder at Evan's eyes.

"Damn thief!" he bellowed, waving his free hand about, trying in vain to ward off the pepper mist burning him.

"You're the thief!" the Chyterian yelled in return, his voice coming from a few yards away, "I hope they eat your heart last so you suffer longer!"

Evan ran towards the voice, swinging his electrified sword to keep the undead at bay. A jarring pain hit his shoulder as one of the tainted slammed against him, toppling him sideways. Rolling to his hip, he pressed his fingers against one set of eyelids and pried them open, fighting his body's urge to keep them shut. Most of the zombies were to his right. Their faces twisting into gleeful toothy smiles as they trundled towards their next meal. He scrambled to his feet and darted left, leaving the alley toward and reaching the main road. Prying his eyelids open again, he scanned the area for signs of the thief but didn't spot him. After noticing a door ajar ten paces ahead, he sprinted for the opening and slammed it shut behind him. He pressed his back against it and slid to a seated position on the dusty wood floor.

The door thumped against his spine as the monsters clawed and shoved it. Hurriedly patting his belt, he found his small canteen of water. The shoves became slams as the tainted knew a few inches separated them from mouthfuls of flesh.

"C'mon, open!" Evan cursed, clumsily trying to unscrew the metal cap.

Another slam pushed him forward, allowing an arm to sneak through the gap.

"Shit!" Evan yelled, ducking a swat from the creature. Its skin was a mixture of black and blue flesh. Warts and divots covered the sickly limb.

He rolled onto his back and shoved his feet against the door, keeping it shut and limiting his exposure to the mangled arm searching for him. Gritting his teeth, he fought the pain searing his eyes and channeled his last ounce of focus to his fingers.

SLAM!

The jolt from the door caused him to fumble the canteen.

"Focus..." Evan said through gritted teeth. "Finally!" He yelled, ripping the cap free.

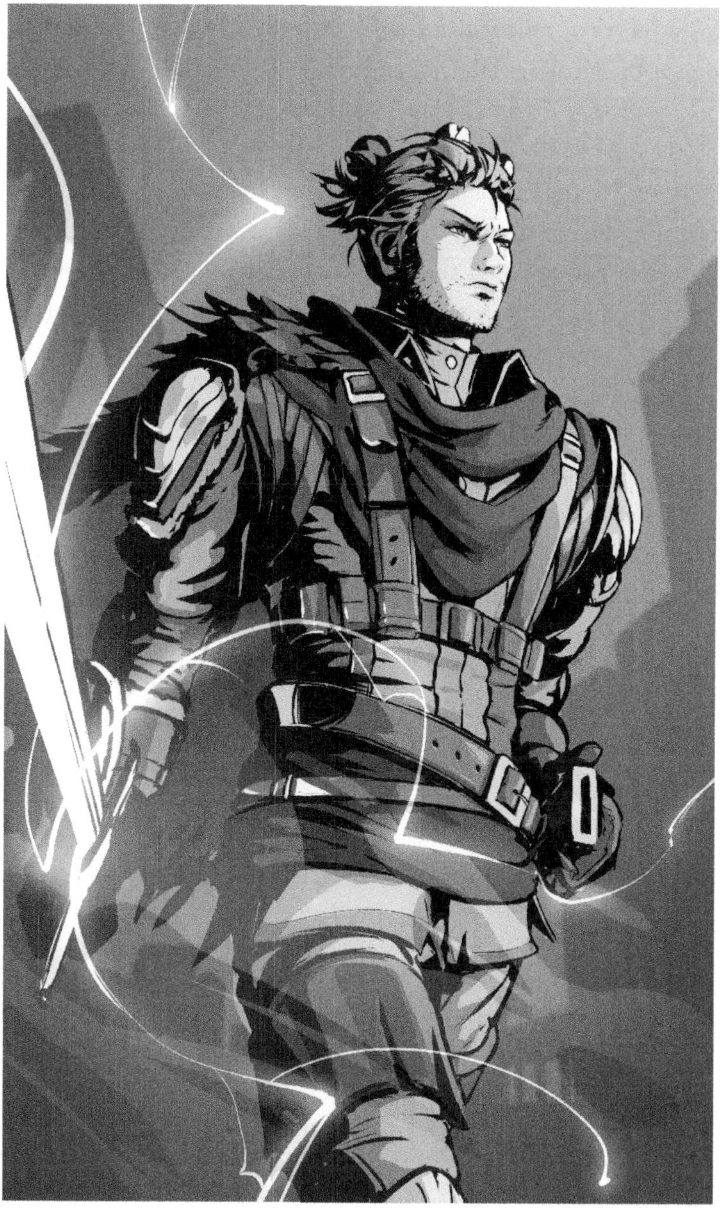

He yanked one set of eyelids open and drenched his pupil in water, then followed suit with the other. Relief washed over him as the burning finally dissipated.

"Now it's a fair fight, you bastards," Evan hissed, pushing off the door and rolling to his feet.

The pack of tainted tumbled forward on top of each other, clogging the doorframe. Evan took a deep, satisfying breath and collected his sword off the floor. Squeezing the hilt sent sparks flinging off its blade. He lifted it high overhead and slashed down, slicing a surge of emerald energy through the clump of monsters. Arms and legs writhed frantically as the lightning sword cleaved their skulls in two.

The few townspeople outside gawked at the display, unsure what to make of this cloaked figure stepping over a pile of half-chopped corpses. Turning his head towards one of the onlookers, he removed his hood.

"Which way did the Chyterian go?"

CHAPTER FIVE

FIRESIDE PLANS

O**RANGE FIRELIGHT** flickered in front of the slender Hiroyan wearing a dark green robe. Two of his guards – outfitted in copper-plated armor – approached him. One was tall and slender, his armor perfectly fitting his lengthy frame. The second was two feet shorter and barrel-chested.

The shorter one removed his helmet, sweat beading his brow. "We've finished it, Sire," he said, wiping his perspiration away.

"Good," their King replied, clasping his hands behind his back, "I should have known a village worshiping Alrin didn't have the stomach for exterminating them."

"The woman believed they'd eventually find magic to heal the living corpses," the tall guard added, "That's why she fought so hard to keep us out."

The King grunted. "And to think, we merely thought she was hiding the Chyterian."

He motioned to the guards, granting them leave, then turned towards the cowering creature behind him. Staring down, he noticed its thick, hooded cloak was slashed and tattered, exposing bits of fur matted in dark violet blood.

'If only he'd listen to reason,' he thought, sighing.

He signaled to the guardsman standing over the Chyterian, who unleashed another lash of his whip upon their prisoner. Instead of the loud cries it gave earlier, it just whimpered and croaked.

He motioned for one of the nearby servants and pointed at his feet. The man hurriedly removed his overcoat and placed it on the ground before the King. He nodded in thanks before kneeling on it in front of his prisoner. Grasping its chin, he lifted the tortured creature's furry face to meet his.

"I will not ask again, vermin. If you wish to see the light of day, tell me where your accomplice took the map?"

The Chyterian coughed. "If I tell you, who's to say I still wouldn't meet the same fate."

The King's eyes narrowed. "You desire assurances? Let me show a gesture of goodwill," he looked over to the servant, "bring him some water."

The servant returned with a waterskin and knelt next to the prisoner.

"I'll do it myself," the King said, taking the waterskin from him, "here, take a drink."

The Chyterian's black eyes blinked uneasily at the offer.

"It's not poison," the King responded, answering the silent question.

Swallowing down the lump of fear and pain filling his throat, the prisoner pulled himself to a seated position and drank greedily from the leather bag. After gulping its contents, he dropped it and panted heavily. Looking down at the waterskin, he swallowed again. Not to remove fear but to accept his fate. He knew any benevolence was pageantry. He looked his captor dead in the eyes but said nothing. Staring into those emerald pupils, he found no signs of compassion. Only greed and wrath lived within that soul.

Finally, he spoke. "You wish to know where my companion took the map? Maybe you should ask your brother."

The King's face twisted into an expression of pure hatred. "I don't know why he ever employed you wretched things for anything beyond cleaning manure from the stalls."

The Chyterian snorted a brief laugh. "Your answer explains why he never trusted you with the Rehnarian's greatest secret."

Sharp pain crossed the Chyterian's cheek as the King backhanded him.

"My brother was a vagrant who fled his duties to buy an abandoned castle. Pretending to rule a kingdom he never built," the King snapped, rising to his feet. He looked to another servant, bedecked in a red vest and dark trousers. "How long until sunrise?"

The servant removed a pocket watch from his vest and approached the firelight for a better view. He turned to his leader and rubbed his balding head. "Five hours, my King."

He looked to the guardsman standing over their captive. "Take him back to your tent and whip him once each hour until you see the sun."

He turned on his heel and strode back to the largest tent in the camp, followed by two green-robed men.

"Sire," Aethin said, hurriedly following him, "Maybe if we continued using a more benevolent strategy, we could gain enough favor to get an answer."

"He's right, Sire," Edgar continued, "You saw how he responded to you sharing our rations with him. That was the most he's said all evening."

King Sunasa shook his head as he parted the curtains, entering his tent. "You cannot reason with a lowly mongrel who's been given duty beyond his worth. Pain is the only way to humble such a thing to your will. You saw the light in his eyes when he spoke of my brother, Kaevir. That rodent looks to him like a savior," he stated, sitting on a leather padded chair, "So, in turn, I must show him I'm the demon. Then he'll know I must be answered to."

Edgar looked to Aethin uneasily at the response.

Sunasa growled, "You two never had the stomach for leadership, just like Kaevir. It's why Father chose me to rule."

Aethin stepped forward. "Brother..."

"Call me Sire," Sunasa interjected.

"Y...Yes, Sire," Aethin replied meekly, "If the prisoner dies, how do you intend to find the map?"

Sunasa observed him with a curled brow, sharing a look of pity that he even had to ask. "The townspeople said your hired sword chased after another Chyterian. I've sent a scouting party after them. Once they're captured, I'm sure we'll retrieve the map Kaevir hid."

"And what if they don't have it, Sire?" Edgar asked earnestly.

"Our father, the late King, entrusted me with the future of our people. You've both seen the desecrated state of our world. This is the only chance to find whatever magic the Rehnarian nobles used to become immortal. Because if another Kingdom uncovers it first, we – like every other nation – will become their slaves," Sunasa answered.

The two brothers nodded and took their leave. He watched them shuffle past the curtains and into the night. Turning his head, he stared at a map fastened to the wall. It showed the lands from his home city of Shima – the Hiroyan capital – to the edge of Lysgahr, which was the Rehnarian capital. Following the red dashed line, he surveyed the distance their campaign had taken them. He examined the next town over, studying its boundaries.

"Father, I will ensure that map is found, and I swear the Hiroyans will enjoy the spoils of that magic," he thought aloud, "And if our people cannot have that gift, then I will burn whoever finds it."

CHAPTER SIX

THE HUNT CONTINUES

Gripping his swords hilt, Evan lit his weapon with buzzing blue energy, giving light to the dark stairwell. Holding his sword aloft, he could see the remaining section was clear of any undead. Only a single door sat a few steps beyond the landing ahead.

Reaching for the handle, he took a deep breath to steady his nerves. Twisting it slowly, he readied his sword to defend himself from the unknown beyond the threshold. Shoving it open, he lept into the room, eyes darting furiously for signs of living corpses or hostile bandits.

He found nothing.

Relaxing his posture, he approached a window on the other side of the room. Taking a seat on a weathered daybed, he lifted his helmet free and placed it on a nearby stool. Staring at the helm, he observed all the scrapes and dents. Every one of them earned after the Cataclysm. It only took a month to have the same markings of a veteran gladiator.

'I might have more markings than the Champion,' Evan mused with a smile.

Staring out the window, nighttime fog lazily crawled over the town below. These conditions weren't ideal for Chyterians, who relied primarily on their keen sense of smell to know where an enemy lurked. He hoped it would force his target to hide again, giving him time to rest before he set out in the morning.

'I'll test my view from the top,' he thought, exiting the room and continuing up the central flight of stairs. Reaching the upmost floor of the bell tower, he readied his sword again, lighting it to ensure none of the undead monsters – who didn't show signs of heat – occupied the bell room. A calm breeze limped through the four arched openings, bringing a ripe odor to his nostrils. He whipped his head left and found a pair of glowing red eyes poking out from behind a brick pillar.

Pursing his lips, Evan took one step forward, lighting the space ahead. There was only one race whose eyes glowed at night.

"You can come out, Gremling," Evan stated assertively, "I'm not one of those flesh eaters, and I won't harm you. All I ask is to have my kindness returned."

The short figure crept from its hiding place and into the bright blue light. A green head with a single strip of auburn hair met Evan's gaze. The taut skin meant it was young. However, regardless of age, Evan knew better than to underestimate a

Gremling. They were the fiercest race in Yohme and rarely journeyed alone.

"I have a few rations to share with your brothers and sisters if they keep their weapons sheathed," Evan offered, knowing Gremlings were favorable to bartering. "If they don't, they'll be met with equal hostility," he continued, also understanding that they didn't accept deals proffered by weak hearts.

The Gremling's eyes narrowed. "I travel alone."

Evan's back stiffened, eyes darting around the room for others. "You don't need to lie. I'm not here to…"

"Oh, save your posturing for someone else," the Gremling interjected, turning away from him toward the stairs. "Now that the world's been poisoned, I don't have time for all the back and forth. The infected are growing in numbers. Slitting throats of the living only builds their ranks."

Dumbstruck by his bluntness, Evan's grip on weapon slipped, causing him to nearly drop it. Recovering, he swiftly rose it, using the light to find the Gremling, who stood at the arched threshold leading downstairs.

"Wait!" Evan called, "Have you seen a Chyterian in the city?"

The Gremling stopped, placing his hand on the brick wall.

'He's maybe four feet tall,' Evan thought, *'If he's actually being honest, how's he surviving on his own?'*

"What happens when you find him?" the Gremling replied.

Evan swallowed, taking a beat to decide his next words carefully. Reaching into his satchel, he retrieved a small ball of twigs encased in a crusted powder. He set it on the stone floor and ran his boot heel over it, scraping it along the ground. The small orb sparked before crackling into an ankle-height flame.

"The fire from this sparker will last 'til morning," he said to the Gremling, trying a friendly approach, "Stay here, away from the infected roaming the streets, and maybe I can convince you to help me."

The Gremling shrugged. "Alright, Kah'zyin, I'll take your offer," he replied nonchalantly, taking a seat near the flame.

Evan smiled and joined him. "I'm Evan," he greeted, extending his hand.

"Grymjer," the Gremling replied, reaching out and accepting his handshake. "Now, if I'm going to listen to you all night rather than sleep, I'm going to need some of those rations you mentioned," he continued, leaning back on his forearm.

Evan huffed a light chuckle, reaching into his satchel. "Are you a fan of dried pork?"

Grymjer's ears perked, his expression brightening for the first time.

"I'll take that as a yes," Evan said, smiling.

Grymjer happily took the salted jerky, snatching a hefty bite with his pointed teeth. Watching him eat, Evan observed several scars crisscrossing the pale green skin on his arms.

"Have you stayed here long?" Evan inquired.

Grymjer shook his head. "I'm here scavenging for trade items. Most of the jobs come from people outside that won't risk entering the city."

Evan relaxed, leaning against a pillar. "Is your tribe making the requests?"

Grymjer scowled, taking another bite of jerky rather than answering.

Evan nodded. *'Alright, clearly a sensitive subject. Never met a Gremling unwilling to speak about family before.'*

"I'm a Traveler like you, looking for a thief who stole a large number of jewels from my employer," Evan said, changing the subject.

"And he's a Chyterian," Grymjer replied.

"Yes," Evan answered, "He'd be easy to notice since his fur is dark as night with white patches near his face, hands, and feet."

Grymjer finished chewing his bite before answering. "So, you plan to kill him and get the jewels back."

Evan shook his head. "No. I just need the jewels, not his life. He was a servant of my employers before he fled. With the world torn apart, he took an opportunity to enrich himself."

"Who are your employers?" Grymjer inquired.

"We both know Travelers are better suited keeping that information to themselves," Evan answered.

Grymjer sneered. "Of course."

Evan leaned forward, handing another strip of dried meat to his fireside companion. "Well, do you have any leads?"

Grymjer folded his arms, raising his eyes to meet Evan's. "I know the best passage out of the city. It's likely the only one he's found, and I can take you there. But in return, I require your help as well."

Evan raised an eyebrow. "What type of help?"

"Normally, I'd have to wait until daybreak to leave. But after seeing that sword you have, I'm guessing you can chop through the zombies clogging the tunnel exit."

"Why not use one of the main gates?" Evan asked.

"The ones we need are barred shut," Grymjer replied, "The only one open is the northern gate, which is where I'm assuming you came through," he rose from his seat and walked towards the stairs, "Are you coming or not?"

Evan tilted his head and shrugged. "No time like the present."

"I think I'll join the undead if I have to smell this sewage much longer," Evan stated, doing his best to keep the tied kerchief above his nose.

"We've almost reached the end," Grymjer stated flatly, marching through the murky sludge water a few paces ahead.

"There," he whisper-shouted.

Evan stepped beside him, holding his sword aloft to see what lay ahead. He could hear sloshing, but the light from his sword didn't reach far enough to see what made the noise.

"There's only two staggering around," Grymjer said quietly, his Gremling eyes able to see in the pitch-black darkness. "Don't worry, I'll lead you," he finished, walking past Evan and unhooking a curved pickaxe from his belt loop.

"Wait," Evan interjected as his companion strode forward, unphased. "We don't want to attract more."

Grymjer waved him off. "There're no side paths, so it's only these two. Usually, there's a lot more at night since they return to the surface at daybreak."

Evan squinted. "I've never seen any follow a pattern that complex."

Grymjer shrugged. "They travel in herds. If enough of them do something, the rest follow."

Evan grabbed his shoulder. "You wait here; I need to hold up my end of the trade. They'll only take a minute at most."

Looking down at Grymjer, he noticed his expression turn dour. Evan felt an odd mix of pity and admiration seeing the young Gremling become perturbed at having to stand down from combat.

"I need you here," Evan said, "If one gets behind me, I'll require your night vision to direct me."

Advancing, he waved his glowing sword in a particular pattern, readying it to strike down the two undead. Closing in, Evan noticed they didn't have the hanging flesh he'd seen before, instead having a skeletal outside with fleshy organs underneath.

Swinging his weapon, he lopped off one zombie's arm, then cleaved the second and shoved his boot into its chest. It tumbled against the other, sending them splashing into the sewer water. Flipping his sword into a downward grip, Evan raised the glowing blade, readying it to plunge into their heads. He paused as the water hissed around them, turning into steam.

"Fall back!" Grymjer yelled, "They're boilers!"

Evan lept away, yet some of the white-hot smoke caught his cheek. He yelped in pain, staggering towards the wall and placing his gloved hand over the burnt skin. Looking to his right, he noticed the water turned to vapor after the two creatures were submerged.

"How do you kill them?!" Evan yelled.

He felt the young boy yanking his arm. "You can't, they'll burn mist for several hours."

Evan took his lead, following him a few feet away, then halted.

"What are you waiting for?" Grymjer asked heatedly.

Evan tugged his arm free and faced the boilers, raising his blade like a javelin. Squeezing the hilt, it filled with crackling blue energy. Grymjer stumbled back, tripping over a rock and falling on his side. He sat up quickly, watching bits of lightning streak off the sword and snap at the brick walls and ceiling. Evan grunted in pain, clenching the hilt as best he could against the sword's fierce convulsing.

'I won't risk letting them live,' Evan thought, charging as much energy as he could muster.

The two undead had crawled to their feet and stood just ten feet away. Twisting his torso, he threw his weapon at the pair. Streaks of blue magic shot from the sword as it plunged into the chest of one monster. A burst of energy caught the second zombie, sending it smashing against the wall in an explosion of bone and intestines. The impaled zombie shook rapidly as magical energy surged through its body. It, too, popped in a spray of bones that clattered off the walls and ceiling. Its work finished, the sword went dark and fell to the murky water.

Evan dropped to one knee, lungs gasping. After several heavy breaths, he felt something snatch his shoulder, but he didn't have the strength to fight back.

'Of course, there was one more hiding,' he cursed.

"That was awesome!" a familiar voice whooped triumphantly. "You even blew the iron bars free."

He felt a tiny hand pull under his armpit, urging him to rise. Faint torchlight lit the area around him. Soon, his weapon was presented before him.

"I got your sword," Grymjer stated confidently, "C'mon, I'll lead you to the surface, and we can set up camp."

Evan followed the pull of his new companion, trusting the young Gremling's guidance out of the obsidian darkness towards the fresh air above.

CHAPTER SEVEN

THE MAP

A YELLOW TOOTHY smile greeted Evan and Grymjer as they entered the shop.

"*This is the guy?*" Evan whispered to Grymjer.

His companion nodded. "*He's the most connected treasure hunter in this region.*"

This shopkeep wasn't the usual type. Rather than the slender or short ones Evan was accustomed to, this man was nearly eight feet tall and extremely muscular. His olive-green skin, pointed ears, and thick hair meant he was a Gremling. However, he'd never met ones this size before. The immense merchant leaned an armor-clad arm on the counter. Evan squinted to observe

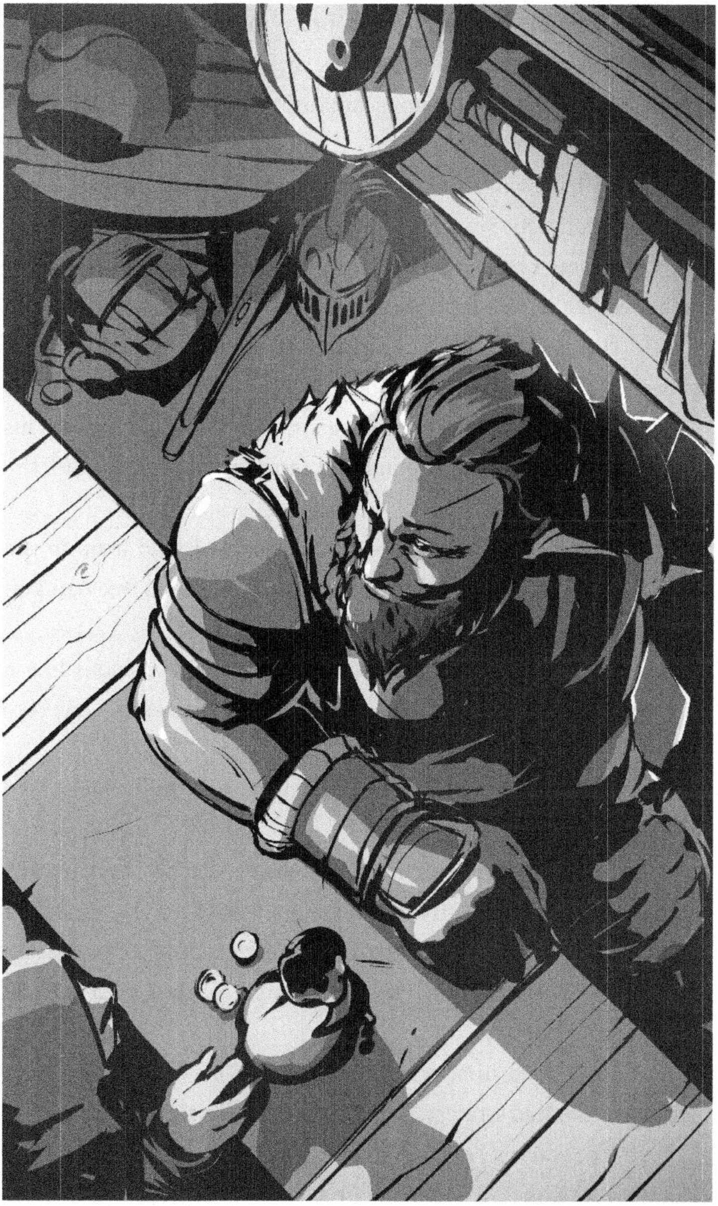

it better. Past his leather forearm brace ran a series of silver and black spiked plates reaching past his shoulder. The colors on the armor swirled in a continuous mixture, like running your hand through oily water.

"What brings you back, Grymjer!?" the shopkeep asked enthusiastically, his voice gritty and deep.

Grymjer motioned to Evan. "My friend here is looking for someone. We're hoping you can help, Myrkor?"

He stood upright, crossing his arms while raising an eyebrow. "That depends. He got any coin?"

"I'll do you one better," Evan interjected, reaching into his coat and placing a thin, cylindrical, corked waterskin onto the counter.

Myrkor carefully plucked the item and held it up to the dusty light cast from a dingy skylight. He rubbed his free hand on his chin while inspecting it.

"Based on the engravings in the leather, it looks like a Kah'zyin stamina potion." His eyes returned to Evan. "Your race easily has the best alchemists."

"NOT A CHANCE!" another voice called from the back of the shop.

A tall man approached the counter next to Myrkor. His short black hair was scruffy as if he'd just woken up. He scratched his messy hair with a hand wearing a fingerless, leather gauntlet.

"No one could top the alchemists I worked with back in Okita," he said firmly.

Evan eyed him, noticing the armor he wore appeared to be leather, but had strategically placed thin slits throughout.

"So, you're O'dachi?" Evan inquired.

"Damn proud of it," the man said confidently, flexing his arm. Black and red scales shot out of the slits in his armor, covering his appendage.

Evan smiled. He'd known a few O'dachi during his time as a palace guard. They were a very proud race occupying the northeastern mountains. They rarely backed away from a challenge and never hesitated to tell you as much. He'd always enjoyed a good laugh heckling the ones in his squad. He could tell from Myrkor's grin that he clearly enjoyed the same.

Evan pointed to the vial in Myrkor's hand. "What does your friend think? Is that potion a worthy trade?"

Myrkor turned to his companion. "Give it a look, Kellen."

Kellen held the vial up, observing it for himself.

"It's decent," he said nonchalantly, tossing it back to Myrkor. He walked towards a few work benches at the back of the shop. "Worth enough to tell 'em what they want to know."

"Hey!" Myrkor objected. "Don't give away my leverage in this negotiation. We don't even know who they're looking for?"

Evan approached a wood shelf mounted to the stone wall with steel bolts. "We're looking for a thief who stole some valuable jewels from my clients," he selected a red potion from the shelf and showed it to Myrkor. "Considering you're one of the few shops I've seen with healing potions; he's likely shopped here."

Myrkor's eyes narrowed. "I don't give away details of my customers to anyone that just tosses goods on my counter."

Kellen, currently working at a crafting table, turned his head towards the conversation. "Oh, come off the surly routine, Myrkor. Grymjer's running with him, so he'll tell the guy you're bluffing to get a better deal."

Myrkor slammed his hand on the counter. "Dammit, Kellen! Give me a good reason why I don't tie you up and toss you on the next caravan back to Okita!"

Grymjer approached the counter, hands on his hips. "He's right, Myrkor. Now, go ahead and tell us where the Chyterian went who bought one of your potions over there," he said, thumbing behind him.

"Why would you assume that?" Myrkor inquired, crossing his arms.

"There's a drop of blood on the ground you didn't clean up," Evan added, setting the potion back on the shelf. "I gave you something worth well more than what he bought, so I'd argue our negotiating is done. Tell us where he is, and we'll be on our way."

Myrkor huffed. "Well, you're no fun. Everyone being so blunt really killed the mood of this barter," he complained, grabbing a piece of parchment and quill from a desk. He placed it on the front counter and began to draw. "He wanted directions to the caves on our side of Lake Bailin. Unfortunately for you, there's three caves overlooking that lake and he could be in any one of them." He pointed the quill at Grymjer. "If you choose the wrong one before that potion kicks in, he'll be long gone."

Grymjer grabbed the freshly drawn directions off the counter and walked towards the door. "Thanks, Myrk," he said with a wave.

"I hate when he calls me that," Myrkor grumbled under his breath.

Rain and wind howled across the maroon evening sky, ripping through the tall fir trees and chilling the two weary hikers.

"The first cave was already a miss," Evan called out, huddling under his cloak. "Do you think he was being honest with us?"

"Myrkor wouldn't lie to me," Grymjer stated confidently. "Let's try this cave, and if he's not inside, we'll set camp there for the night. Even if he's healed, I doubt he'd make it far in this weather and we'll know exactly which cave he's in."

Evan sighed, biting his lip. It'd taken a quarter-day by carriage to reach the caves after leaving the shop. Thankfully, Grymjer's understanding of this area meant they found a stable quickly. Of course, given the Kingdom's current state, two armed coachmen had ridden in the carriage as well.

'Can't say I blame them,' Evan thought, recalling the daggers strapped to the hips and boots of the coachmen.

After reaching the trailhead, they had to trek the remainder on foot. Stomping uphill through the harsh conditions was more exhausting than usual. They hadn't slept the night before, choosing to push through instead, not wanting to miss their last chance to catch the Chyterian.

Chasing him had morphed into something much more than he'd initially assumed. He wasn't sure it was even worth the money anymore, but with how deep he'd gotten, there was no turning back. He'd invested too much time to walk away with only the downpayment, especially since he'd promised Grymjer a share of the purse for his help. He also wasn't sure how the Hiroyans would treat him if he decided to abandon their request.

'Their leader seems like the type who'd track me down and settle that score,' Evan thought. *'Considering he's willing to chase this servant across the entirety Yohme to recover some jewels.'*

"Stop!" Grymjer whisper-shouted, sticking his hand out.

Evan squinted, looking ahead past him. His eyes grew wide. A faint orange light flickered from the cave opening thirty paces ahead.

Grymjer turned and motioned for him to get closer. He took a knee and leaned in as they developed a plan.

"Let me go in first," Grymjer said. "If the person in there is the one you're looking for, I'll give you a sign."

Evan's eyes narrowed. "What's the sign?"

Grymjer waved him off. "Don't worry about that. You'll know when you hear it."

Evan took a deep breath, gesturing an open palm towards the cave. "I'll follow your lead."

Grymjer nodded and smiled before charging towards the cave. Evan followed, coming to a stop just outside the entrance. He pressed his back against the jagged stone in wait as his companion entered.

Each second that passed felt like an hour.

Finally, after a minute, he heard something.

Tilting his head, he placed an ear as close to the sound as possible. It wasn't chatter like he thought, instead the light patter of small, quick footsteps.

His heart thumped.

'The thief's trying to escape again.'

As the steps drew closer, he whipped around the corner, unsheathing his sword.

"It's me!" a small gravelly voice yelped.

He lowered his weapon but didn't sheath it.

Grymjer lowered his little green hands, no longer shielding himself. "It's him back there, but he doesn't have long to live, and I don't think he has what you're looking for."

Evan stormed past him, heading towards the small Cave's end. Rounding a corner, he found the Chyterian lying before a fire with his shoulders and head against the stone wall. The rat-like snout slowly turned to view him, beady black eyes locking with his own.

"You're the one the King hired?" he said, followed by a few coughs.

Evan squinted and stepped closer, noticing the creature was clutching his right arm. It was swollen with red vine-like tendrils climbing up from his fingers.

"Bit by one of the tainted..." Evan noted aloud, taking a cautious step back.

"It happened on his way here," Grymjer interjected. "He also told me the one who hired you isn't looking for jewels," he finished, holding out a scroll.

Evan returned an uneasy look at Grymjer, gently taking the scroll and opening it. A red dot pulsed at the top left. In the center was a series of lines inside a square.

"Is this a map?" Evan asked.

"Yes," the Chyterian answered, his voice raspy and half-dead. Sounding as if he'd gargled poison.

Evan quickly knelt across the fire from him. "Why would he need this?" he asked, pointing the scroll in his direction. "Why would he need to chase this treasure when he has plenty to collect from your stuffed pockets?"

"You believe that ruse?" the Chyterian replied before another fit of harsh, throaty coughs. "Your employer didn't send you to collect lost jewels; he sent you after the gift of Duraté the Abundant."

Evan's stare hardened. "You're claiming this leads to the Rehnarian's greatest treasure? The gift from their god?"

The Chyterian grunted, preserving speech for more important answers.

Evan gave Grymjer a suspicious look.

Grymjer pointed to the scroll. "This is what I came to tell you. It was the only thing in his satchel. He said the red dot represents whoever holds the map, and if you follow it through that maze, it gives you a path leading to the All Giving Fruit."

Evan stood up, holding a worried expression. "You mean to tell me; he's been carrying a direct path to what the Rehnarian rulers have eaten for centuries to acquire eternal life." He shook his head. "A lot has happened since the Cataclysm, but even this seems unbelievable." He walked over to Grymjer, handing him the scroll. "And why would a scroll of such importance not have any identifying markings? It doesn't tell you where that maze is located."

"It doesn't need to," the Chyterian interjected. "It was my master's. He knew which temple held the entrance."

"Who was your master?" Evan inquired.

The Chyterian chuckled. "By the shaved look of your horns, I'd assume you're Kah'zyin military?"

Evan held his tongue, trying his best to keep a still face with no tells.

The Chyterian continued. "He ruled the largest nation of your people. My master was Kaevir, the King of Herrgal."

Evan took a long, slow sigh. It was hard to believe any of this. "I think that monster's bite has turned your brain rotten," he stated, breaking the silence. "The jewels must be buried around here somewhere."

As he went to leave, Grymjer held up a hand. "You saw that map had a beacon. It's clearly been enhanced with magic to lead its user to a treasure of some sort. And we both know magic of that level isn't something a lowly servant has access to."

Evan pursed his lips. "Well, Chyterian, if you really worked for Kaevir and this is his precious item, why would he send you to hide it."

The Chyterian took a moment before speaking. "I only have so much left in me, and I don't think it will be enough time to convince you. All I ask is that you keep that map from King Sunasa. After the Cataclysm devasted Yohme, he saw it as an opening to obtain the All Giving Fruit and rule the entire continent."

Evan looked to the cave's ceiling, desperately trying to sort through everything he'd heard.

He lowered his eyes to meet Grymjer's. "There's only one way to know if this has a shred of merit. Stay here and watch him while I return to my employer."

CHAPTER EIGHT

THE RUSE

After half a day of travel, Evan located the Hiroyan camp. They'd moved around the walled city he and Grymjer escaped and set up one town south of Myrkor's shop. He stood atop the grassy hill, looking at the forested mountain range behind him. The mix of violet and lavender light casting through the clouds highlighted the beauty of Yohme. Returning his gaze to his feet, he surveyed two freshly slain zombies. Their rotting, gray flesh a reminder of the world he actually inhabited — one of chaos and crumbling remains.

Sheathing his sword, he continued down the beige dirt trail, eventually reaching the grouping of tents surrounded by soldiers wearing armor colored in deep green and slate black. The customary Hiroyan colors.

"You lost, boy?" one of the soldiers said as he approached.

Evan shook his head. "I'm looking for King Sunasa. We've struck a deal, and I've come to deliver."

The soldier eyed him suspiciously as another elbowed him. They spoke in hushed tones to one another. All Evan could make out was one mentioning his shaved horns.

'He must have said a Kah'zyin might be looking for him,' he thought.

"Wait here," one soldier said, breaking the silence and motioning for him to sit near a warm fire.

He obliged, taking rest on a bench made from a half-cut log as the second guard left. After several minutes, the guard returned with the Hiroyan leader.

"So, you've returned," Sunasa said, approaching the fire.

Evan stood calmly. "I brought the stolen jewels," he said, holding a small satchel aloft. "Unfortunately, the Chyterian was bit by one of the tainted in the city. I found him in the forest, turned into one of the undead."

The Hiroyan crossed his arms. "And you didn't bring his body back to prove this?"

Evan raised an eyebrow. "We know very little about this plague; I can't risk carrying a disease-ridden corpse for miles."

The Hiroyan nodded. "Fair point, having an outbreak in our camp could be fatal." He stuck out his hand. "Very well, hand over the purse, and I'll assure you get paid."

A guard approached Evan, collecting the bag and returning it to his leader. He maintained a still face and even breath as he eyed the tall, slender Hiroyan digging through the large pouch. He eventually handed the bag back to the soldier and nodded affirmingly.

Evan sighed in relief, extending a hand thankfully. "It was a pleasure assisting you."

He wasn't sure what felt better, knowing he'd receive good coin for completing this request or the fact that nothing the Chyterian said was real.

'Like I thought, another lying thief trying to clear his sullied name.'

Hands snatched both his arms and slammed him down on the bench. He yanked at the soldiers holding him but couldn't break free. Sharp stings of rough metal from their steel gauntlets pressed into his skin.

Sunasa stepped forward. "You think I'm naive?"

Evan's face turned to a fearful expression, unsure what to say.

Sunasa shook his head. "My men told me you asked to see King Sunasa; is that correct?"

Evan didn't answer, realization flooding over him.

"I never told you my title nor the title of my brothers. I'm not quite sure how to reconcile that along with that," Sunasa announced, pointing the guard holding the satchel.

Evan had given the soldier that name to test the Chyterian's words, which he feared were coming true.

"I only assumed that from your banners and army," Evan said. "I planned to ask for more coin if you were, in fact, the Hiroyan King." He hung his head. "I'm sorry to have insulted you..."

"Where's the map," Sunasa interrupted.

Evan returned a quizzical stare.

Sunasa chuckled. "Don't insult me with this act. Clearly, someone tipped you off." He strode around the fire and leaned close to him. "You throw some cobbled-together jewels in a bag and expect me to believe you?" He stood, offering a huffy, quick laugh. "I'll admit, at least you added some of Hiroyan origin. It shows you're craftier than most." He placed a hand on his shoulder. "Take him to the cages. He has until nightfall tomorrow to tell me where he's hidden the map." He leaned down, lips a few inches from his ear. "If you wish to keep those horns planted in your head, I suggest you tell me where it is. If you come clean by morning, I might even let you join us as a scout," Sunasa finished, then walked away, waving.

Evan felt pinching pain again as he was jerked upright, another guard snatching the sheath of his sword and cutting the strap off his back. The same soldier continued cutting at his attached supplies, taking everything but his clothes. He looked about nervously, taking in every bit of his surroundings, looking for an opening to escape. Thudding pain exploded in his stomach as a gloved fist smashed it. Another thud smacked the back of his head, turning his vision to black.

Blinking sluggishly, Evan slowly regained his senses. Placing a palm against his head, he braced his skull from the thumping pain radiating inside. He was surrounded by vertical red metal bars. Instinctively, he snatched one and shook it, testing its durability. It was sturdy, along with the rest of the cage, which had a solid metal top and bottom. By his estimation, it was at least four feet tall and about the same amount wide. He slumped his back against the bars. Noticing bright stars overhead, he hoped it was still the first night.

'I doubt they'd let me sleep through an entire day,' Evan thought, his mind wandering fearfully to what awaited him when Sunasa eventually returned.

Looking to his left, he noticed another cage occupied by something covered in dark fur matted in caked blood. His first instinct was to call out and see if they'd be willing to devise a plan with him. Then he thought better of it, noticing a guard sitting in front of a small fire twenty paces away. Giving the prisoner a second look, he couldn't tell exactly what color the fur was, but it definitely wasn't the one he'd met in the cave. He relaxed a bit, knowing they hadn't found their target yet.

'At least what they want is still hidden in the hills, which buys me some time,' he told himself.

Eyes darting around, he noticed no one had discovered he'd regained consciousness. Taking a long breath, he rested his head against the steel and closed his eyes.

'C'mon, Evan think, there's got to be something you can do to bust out of here.'

Clunk!

Evan's eyes shot open after hearing the sound of something plunging through metal. A glowing arrow had pierced the guard's head and was sticking out the back of his helmet. Glancing across the camp, he didn't see anyone. Not that he could see much beyond the dim firelight. A small glowing light bobbed towards him about three feet high. He scurried towards the front of his cage, desperately hoping he was right.

"*Evan,*" Grymjer whispered, now standing in front of his cage. "*I can let you out, but only if you agree to help me?*"

The request shocked him. Not the thought of helping Grymjer, whom he was extremely thankful to see, but that he would risk coming into this camp to free him just to gain a favor. Maybe it was why he was so beloved and well-connected, finding men at their worst and procuring obedience in exchange for something life-altering.

"Sure, whatever you need," Evan whispered back. *"Just get me out of this cage."*

Grymjer nodded, then turned towards the darkness behind him. A slender figure stepped into the lantern light, making themselves visible. A feminine, foxlike face with ears poking through a hooded cloak stood next to him.

'*He knows Rehnarians? And not just any Rehnarian. One wearing formal cleric robes?*' Evan thought, noticing her attire was colored in an ornate mixture of white, blue, and orange.

He eyed her as she raised an outstretched palm. Suddenly, something shot from her wrist, and he instinctively covered up.

ZAP!

He didn't feel anything.

Slowly lowering his arms, he noticed the lock had fallen to the ground, and the Rehnarian stood before him with a thin wooden object in her hand. It had a blue medallion embedded in the side and a smaller blue gem on its tip.

'*What kind of person has a wand hidden up their sleeve?*' Evan wondered. '*And how in the name of Varkin does Grymjer know them?!*'

The Rehnarian then walked over and shot the lock off the Chyterian's cage.

"C'mon, Evan. You have to help us carry him out," Grymjer told him, extending a hand.

Evan looked at the lump of fur occupying the other cage. "I don't think we can escape if I do that."

Grymjer gave the Rehnarian a worried look. She returned his gaze with narrow eyes, indicating that her help came with a price. Evan let out a heavy breath, rushing over to the curled-up creature before placing a hand on its side, seeing if any air still filled its lungs. After feeling movement, he nodded affirmingly to himself and grabbed its arm, lifting it over his shoulder. Grymjer joined in, helping him bring the prisoner out of the cage. Evan ducked down and scooped up the Chyterian's leg, hoisting him across his shoulders like a large sack of potatoes.

He pivoted to face the Rehnarian woman. "Lead the way."

She nodded, turning and marching in the opposite direction. Following her, he began to wonder where the rest of the watch had gone; surely, there was more than one soldier patrolling the camp. His answer came as he stepped over one lying on the dirt with an arrow through his eye. He shook his head, wondering if the story he'd heard back in that cave would be more believable than whatever explained the alliance between Grymjer and this magic-wielding archer. He decided to shelve his questions for tomorrow; all his focus had to be on the present if he wished to escape undetected.

As the sun rose, Sunasa was awoken by loud, furious chatter outside his tent. He ripped his blankets off and threw on a long tunic before marching outside.

"Sir!" one of his soldiers yelled, racing to him. "Several of our men our dead, and the prisoners are gone!"

His eyelids scrunched angrily as he glared at the section of the camp where the cages were. "What happened!?" he bellowed.

The soldier winced briefly but didn't show too much weakness for fear he'd be executed. His leader was hot-headed and vengeful on a good day. Hearing this news meant the nape of someone's neck was due to greet the sharp side of Sunasa's sword.

"All the guards watching the cages were slain by arrows. A few even had burn marks like they'd been struck by lightning," the soldier said quickly.

Sunasa bit his lip, contemplating how he'd handle this setback. There were several moves he could make, but it was crucial to choose the best one.

"We'll pack today and head for Lysgahr," he finally said.

The soldier nodded. "Are we planning to intercept him?"

Sunasa held a firm stare toward the hill in the distance. "If we find him on the way, I'll gut him myself. However, he clearly had help from a powerful magic-wielder. Which could mean a Rehnarian is helping him. If that's the case, we'll move to our second plan."

The soldier saluted. "I'll tell the scouts to go looking for the elixirs, Sir."

Sunasa waved him off, sending him on his task. He understood that he had to pivot and try another method at reaching the dungeon, which sat inside Lysgahr, the capital city of Rehnar territory. Since the map was gone, he'd have no leverage to get inside. Hiroyans and Rehnarians despised one another, and without that item to barter, he knew they'd turn him away at first sight. Changing tactics, his best men would search for potions he could use to disguise himself. Wearing the appearance of another race gave him a favorable chance to join another group already allowed inside. He'd heard rumors during their campaign that the

Rehnarian capitol was flowing with people searching the dungeon for The All Giving Fruit. However, he was also informed you were only allowed inside if a citizen of status sponsored you.

"If a Rehnarian freed them," he stated, rubbing his chin, "then I need to find somewhere we can hide near the city before word of my campaign reaches Lysgahr."

CHAPTER NINE

A NEW DEBT TO PAY

APPROACHING THE LAKE, Grymjer helped Evan lower the body to the rocky shore. The Rehnarian had ordered them to enact a burial for Elicio, the Chyterian, from the cave. The one they'd freed at the camp was his brother, Háscar. Evan felt fortunate but also guilty that Grymjer had ensured he was freed from capture. Not wanting his new companion to be put in that position.

"*She found me with him, and he was turning,*" Grymjer had told him earlier. "*Thankfully, I'd already hid the map. I told her she couldn't have it unless I talked to you first. Then we tracked you all the way back to that camp, and I couldn't believe how fast she found you. I knew Rehnarians are expert hunters, but it was something else to see it up close."*

At first, he thought the little Gremling had only helped him to avoid possible retribution from the Rehnarian. If that were the case, though, he wouldn't have immediately palled up to him upon their return to the cave. He could have left or, like most Evan met on the road, immediately raised his guard to avoid becoming attached. Considering his only real friends after the collapse were back in Herrgal, it didn't hurt to add another. At least if things went that route. Grymjer's show of loyalty and growing trust was definitely worth keeping, even if it only lasted until they parted ways after burying Elicio.

The fox-faced woman stepped forward, pulling a small object from her belt that looked like the hilt of a dagger. She motioned for Háscar to join. Wrapping his hands around hers, they knelt their heads in prayer over the fallen body. He stepped away as she raised the hilt high in one hand. Evan watched her squeeze until a yellow blade of energy emerged. She plunged it into the dead chest of Elicio, whose body burst in a puff of gold ash. She remained knelt over where his corpse had been, pushing the blade further into the stone as flakes of ash fell around her. A gold beam shot from the rocks and sprouted into a tree made of light with several branches.

Watching the act gave Evan a strong sense of comfort. In his previous work, he'd been on duty for formal processions, so taking part in this one rekindled a feeling of order he desperately missed. The current Yohme was overrun with decayed structures and a plague-stricken populace. This moment – no matter how short – showed the incredible magic of the once greatest nation in the connected continents.

"If you stare into the light too long, it will capture your spirit and hold you hostage," the Rehnarian said, placing a hand on his shoulder. "Seer Barthóhl delivered this magic to remember the dead. However, he also warned that if they aren't allowed to move on, they may return to claim someone still living.

Evan shook reflexively as his daydreams were interrupted. It was the most she'd said since he'd fled Sunasa's camp.

He nodded respectfully, turning to face her with his hand extended. "I never got the chance to know who I should be thanking for rescuing me."

She observed his hand for a moment, a utilitarian look of plainness on her brow. Eventually, she returned his gesture, shaking his hand with her fingered paw.

"I'm Elleya," she said before leaving to join Grymjer and Háscar, who were a few paces ahead. "What time should we ride to Lysgahr?" she asked them.

Háscar shook his head. "I won't be joining you, Elleya. I plan to return north to Herrgal. I need to inform King Kaevir's advisors about Sunasa's movements."

"You say that as if the King cannot accept the news himself?" she replied with a quizzical look.

Háscar sighed. "Master Kaevir's quarters crumbled in two when the comet hit. He's being treated but has not awoken since it happened."

Elleya's expression hardened, turning to Evan and Grymjer. "Can I count on you to help me protect Duraté's gift from Sunasa?"

Grymjer stood silent as Evan rubbed his chin. He wasn't sure how to answer. His conscious sought a return to civilization, and in a peculiar way, the idea of ensuring a clearly evil king didn't obtain the most powerful relic in Yohme scratched that itch.

However, he knew better than to blindly trust someone asking for his help. If he'd kept his guard more appropriately up, he wouldn't have been captured by Sunasa in the first place.

"If we're going to join you, we can't do it for free," he said, testing her.

"I can guarantee you more than coin," she replied. "Once we reach Lysgahr, I'll replace your equipment. When we secure the All-Giving Fruit, you'll receive riches well beyond what you can earn out here as a Traveler."

Evan huffed. "We know better than to accept a mission without securing something up front." He pointed to the carriage they'd taken. "On our way to Lysgahr, we'll stop and get me a sword and shield. It can be the rustiest one they have, but I can't travel that far without a weapon." He crossed his arms. "If we run into a pack of tainted, or worse, Sunasa's men, I'll be dead or shoved in another cage before the sun sets."

Elleya eyed Grymjer. "And what about you? Any upfront demands?"

"I haven't decided if I'll join," he said, patting Evan on the arm. "Sorry, friend, but I'm not sure I want to dive any deeper into this mess. I have it pretty good right now, at least as good as someone can after the world crumbles."

Evan looked at Grymjer thoughtfully, then back to Elleya. "You have until we reach the next settlement to convince us."

Evan relaxed against the wood wall of the carriage now that it had reached a smooth road. He'd braced himself for the last several hours as they'd bumped and bounced along open fields.

'We're only another hour or so from Myrkor's shop. She's persuaded me, but I'm not sure she'll convince him,' he thought, looking at Grymjer.

The green gremling raised an eyebrow. "So, you're a cleric for the Rehnarian church, yet you want us to help you find and store the All-Giving Fruit? Why won't the others in your order join you?"

Elleya held a firm stare. "King Kaevir was in alliance with my people. I was stationed at the Duraté church in his country. I don't have much sway with the clerics in back in my nation."

Grymjer huffed. "There has to be others that agree with you and would partner up?"

She shook her head. "The ones that survived have already formed parties and are actively exploring the dungeon. They wouldn't want to add someone unknown that doesn't instinctively have their same pack tactics."

Grymjer glanced at the fabric ceiling, gathering his thoughts.

"Look," Elleya continued. "Our order was created to ensure the prosperity of the nobility through Duraté's direct gift to them. When Kaevir aligned with us, we gave him a map through the initial maze. Then he could secure the gift if they were to fall." She leaned forward, glaring. "The entire council of seven, our godly rulers, were killed in the Cataclysm. Now, Kaevir is close to death. If Sunasa reaches it first, everyone will fall under his rule."

Grymjer shrugged. "Your rulers had the fruit, and all it did was keep them young. Just because he gets some extra time doesn't mean we're all doomed."

She sighed. "I know you don't believe me, but working with Kaevir, I understood, better than anyone, how cruel Sunasa is. He's not just looking to merely prolong death. He's wanted to rule Yohme since birth, and his vision for the continent is not one you want to live in."

Grymjer huffed. "It sounds to me that Kaevir just bad-mouthed his brother to you all this time, and you bought it like the last ounce of water in a drought."

Evan turned to Grymjer, raising an eyebrow. "Did you forget where I was a day ago?"

Grymjer glanced back at him. "If he's the first King in Yohme to kidnap someone, I'll jump from this vehicle head first into a rock."

Evan laughed. "I know what you mean, but look at this from my view. We have an opportunity to do something more than just survive."

"But what if we don't collect the fruit?" Grymjer replied. "I know it's not exactly a holiday festival living here, but I've made it work. I'm sure you'll do well on your own too. Especially without the serious risk involved chasing her around."

Elleya uncrossed her arms, placing one on her knee and gesturing the other to the young Gremling. "Aside from riches within the Rehnar vault, if we succeed, I've shown you both that I have enough coin to equip you with the best weaponry when we reach Lysgahr. Even if we fail, you'll walk away with wares well beyond what you'll find out there."

Grymjer lowered his gaze, rubbing his chin thoughtfully.

He raised his head. "Alright, I'll join you on this, but if I find out you're lying about anything, I get to walk away and keep the gear."

Elleya nodded. "You have the word of an Aurëlie cleric."

"That settles it just in time," Evan interjected, pointing out one of the small windows. "We've reached the city."

The carriage stopped outside one of the massive stone walls. Long green vines curled up while patches of shrubbery had grown across the top. Evan noticed a few soldiers on the upper walkway, their foxlike snouts poking through helmets as they peered down at them. Elleya held her wand aloft, casting a yellow ball of light that hovered over them. Evan noticed the soldiers suddenly left their perch.

"Follow me," Elleya said, following the ball of light as it traveled slowly toward the wall. Seconds later, it dissolved into it and created a translucent doorway, which the trio walked through. "We'll go to the square first. It's the best place to find the appropriate gear before we delve."

Snaking along a few weathered stone roads, they turned the corner around a turret and finally reached the square. Evan couldn't believe his eyes. Unlike the rest of Yohme, the Rehnar capitol was buzzing with people and commerce. Huts and blankets lined every available space, and most had someone perusing through them.

"How is this possible?" he asked aloud.

Grymjer eyed him with a confused expression as well.

"It looks great from this vantage point," Elleya replied, approaching one of the walkways lined by several shops. She looked at the two over her shoulder, noticing they were still frozen in awe. "Where we'll go after this is definitely not as appealing."

Evan tilted his head in acceptance before following her.

"Is this all because of the dungeon?" Grymjer asked.

She nodded. "You could say it's the silver lining. Once it was known that the council was gone, the clerics sealed the city and started planning what should be done with the dungeon housing the All-Giving Fruit. Some believed we should wait until a new council was declared. Others believed it should be eaten by whoever can reach it, and they would rule." She said, stopping at a booth to grab a glazed roll of bread, which she handed to Evan. "Everyone joined their chosen faction and now chases the gift of Duraté. The merchant activity here is a result of that constant pursuit." She placed a bronze coin on the counter, nodding in gratitude to the shopkeeper, then grabbed another roll that she gave to Grymjer.

"There wasn't a fight over who would get to step inside the dungeon?" Evan asked, taking a bite. His posture melted upon the sugary, warm bread hitting his tongue. He hadn't tasted food this good since the comet struck.

"It's against Aurëlie decree to war with one another in any Rehnarian city. Duraté is a god presenting abundance and growth. Striking someone down would be in direct defiance of her will," she answered. "However, once inside the dungeon, that decree is no longer held."

Grymjer gave a worried look to Evan, who shrugged in response.

"I knew we'd have to fight someone or something eventually," Evan said, taking another bite. "Despite all the holy preaching, I knew there'd be conflict at some point."

"It's not conflict," she said pointedly. "We're all given a chance to reach the gift, and whoever obtains it will represent the worthy cause."

"How can you be so sure?" Evan asked. "Having it brought out in the open will create more opportunities to take it."

She shook her head. "It will be brought to the vault, which only clerics can access. None would defy a religious decree."

Evan huffed. "I guess it's good you still have faith. Hopefully, the rest are as dedicated as you."

Grymjer bit his lip. "If every Aurelie cleric is hunting this thing already, how are we supposed to beat them to it?"

"We have the map, which takes us straight to the heart of the dungeon. No one has reached that far yet," she answered, waving them to follow her down an alley between a row of huts. "Once you get your equipment, we'll…"

Evan threw up a hand, interrupting her. "Actually, it's not going to be just us three. As capable as I believe we all are, we're going to need more members. I'd say at least five or six in our party would suffice."

Elleya's eyes narrowed, unsure how to answer his brazen request. "We're not letting strangers join us. We still need to coordinate our group tactics. Adding more would only complicate that."

Evan selected a sword off a wood counter covered in purple cloth and observed it. "That's why it's best we find people now. Then we can practice with them before any habits form."

He held the weapon up to the light, noticing it was comprised of two different metals. He lightly squeezed the hilt, and half of the blade glowed a deep crimson red. His hand felt something give back, urging him to press further. He relented, and the sword went back to purely metal. It was nice knowing the weapon could do more if pushed, but he'd wait until they were outside the cramped merchant square to experiment further.

"How do you suggest we determine who can join our party?" Elleya asked, crossing her arms.

Evan thumbed towards the weapon. "You can start by getting me this sword."

She rolled her eyes, retrieving a few gold coins and placing them on the counter. "And then what?"

Evan smiled. "You're a renowned cleric; clearly, if you spread the word, there's got to be like-minded people in this city that would join. I've even seen other races while we've been here."

"Alright," she replied, sighing. "I can leave written notes on the request boards around town. However, most who answer a call from an unknown party aren't clerics or experienced treasure hunters. As I said before, there's only a few of us who haven't joined a party at this point."

Evan turned, motioning towards the expanse of booths and huts behind them. "I'm sure there's got to be a few worthy people out there, ready to delve with us."

CHAPTER TEN

UNEXPECTED ALLIES

EVAN HELD HIS FACE in his palm. The straggly group of three that showed up for their open request was well below his worst fears. Two of the three were Rehnarian, but unlike the lush orange fur of the cleric already in their party, these two men had gray running throughout theirs. They'd set the tryout to occur on a grassy hill a quarter mile from Lysgahr. Watching the pair of elderly fox-faced people totter up, Evan prayed for more to come. The next one that came was an even worse fit.

"I heard you're looking for someone to delve through the dungeon with," the third arrival had stammered after hoofing his way ten paces uphill to the apex. *"My uncle came to Lysgahr for his trade shop…"* he leaned over, hands clasped on his knees to catch his breath. *"Joining a party would help me get more items to sell,"* he'd said.

Evan observed the portly young man who only reached his hip in height. He'd hoped that if they were to have a Koln join, it would be someone with magical skill like Gillium. Nothing about this person gave him that impression. The boy wore a tattered cloak and weathered clothing. He also didn't have any equipment on him that showed he'd be an asset, just a single waterskin on his hip. One that he drank greedily from after he finished huffing and puffing from the short uphill walk.

Evan looked at Grymjer, who had his face buried in his palm as well. Glancing at Elleya, she gave him a knowing stare of derision.

"Sorry, I guess you were right," Evan mused aloud, turning away from the ragtag group and shaking his head.

"Right about what?" a gruff voice bellowed behind him.

He spun his attention back, noticing two new attendees arrived.

"Myrkor?!" Evan remarked quizzically.

Myrkor shrugged. "I got word about you three traveling to Lysgahr. Heard you even had a Rehnar with you," he said, pointing to Elleya. "I thought maybe you were inside the city already, but Kellen spotted you on the hill."

"And it's a good thing I did," Kellen interjected, scratching his matted hair. "He made us trek out here and camp on word from some Hiroyan."

Evan swallowed, his posture growing tense. "What exactly did you tell this Hiroyan?"

Kellen shrugged, hand behind his head nonchalantly. "I told them we hadn't seen you since you stopped by for that potion. One of them asked if we'd seen a Gremling or Rehnarian traveling in the area. That's when Myrkor over here got the bold idea to find come here."

"And I was right," Myrkor said, pointing to the trio. "Not only are you with a cleric, but you're gathering troops," he shot a glance to one of the scrawny Rehnarians, tilting his head. "Although, I hope you've got more... *experienced* ones than this," he finished, choosing his words carefully.

Kellen looked to his friend, raising an eyebrow. "I doubt any of these schmucks could lift a sword."

Myrkor covered his eyes, shaking his head. "What have I told you about insulting people we're trying to make a deal with..."

Evan stepped forward. "What deal do you propose?"

"The big guy wants you to let us into the city so we can move our shop there," Kellen stated.

Myrkor nodded. "That's correct. One of our regular partners mentioned all the commerce going on in there. If you can get us in, we'll offer you some excellent items from our stash," he said, thumbing behind him.

Evan squinted to get a better look. In the distance, he noticed a caravan peeking out from behind a few trees.

"How do you know them," Elleya whispered to Evan.

Evan raised a hand cordially. "Give us a moment," he said before turning away from the two new arrivals.

He motioned for Elleya and Grymjer to join him. They obliged, circling him closely.

"Look," Evan started. "We *need* these two in our party. Grymjer trusts them, and considering they were able to bring their whole shop out here, adding them will give us more equipment too."

Elleya licked her lips nervously. "You still haven't explained how you know them."

"It doesn't matter; they wouldn't join us in the dungeon," Grymjer said, crossing his arms. "If Myrkor decides to go after the treasure, he'll do so with Kellen only. I haven't heard of him working with anyone else before."

Evan's eyes narrowed. "I assumed you only worked with him after the Cataclysm?"

Grymjer nodded. "As far as trading in person, yes, but his reputation was well known throughout all the Gremling tribes east of the capital, well before the fall."

Evan rubbed his chin. "Let me see what I can do..."

"How can we trust merchants? Let alone two, who, by all accounts, won't have an interest in securing the fruit?" Elleya asked.

Evan smiled, thumbing over his shoulder. "Transactional people like them are perfect. They'll only be focused on what they get from the deal and won't have motivations beyond that." He pointed to Elleya. "Before I make an offer, though, what does it take to get a shop in the city? Can we promise them a space?"

Elleya shrugged. "Once you're allowed inside, no one dictates who's allowed to trade. The eldest of our order and the nobility that remained deemed it best to let it grow organically."

Evan's brow furrowed. "Has word gotten out that anyone can have a spot once they're inside?"

"I don't believe so," Elleya answered.

Evan took a steady breath, contemplating what else he needed to know. "How can we get them in the city, and what are they allowed to bring?"

"Only clerics, like myself, or other governing officials can allow admittance. Also, anything brought in must be inspected," she replied.

"Does the inspection of a cleric count?" Evan asked.

She nodded. "You were both let in on my word without being questioned."

Evan held a finger to his chin, pondering the best course of action.

He turned back to Kellen and Myrkor. "We can offer you a place in the square, but we'll need something from you first."

Myrkor raised his chin, crossing his arms. "Alright, I'm listening."

"Have you heard why merchants are having great success there?" Evan asked.

Myrkor bit his cheek, holding a plain stare to mask his emotions.

Evan tilted his chin. "Considering how quiet that made you and that your friend over there didn't say anything, I'll assume you don't. Well, there's a relic my cleric friend here needs, and we're looking for people to help us find it. Everyone is doing business in service of that goal."

Myrkor grunted. "Somehow, the one cleric you work with is who everyone's helping?"

Evan motioned toward the wall. "Several groups are helping other clerics. However, the group that finds it first will be much richer. After hearing about your reputation from Grymjer, having you on our side means we'll have the best shot. After you help us secure it, we'll get you a space in the square and give you a third of any earnings we get for recovering it."

"We want half," Myrkor stated pointedly.

Evan blocked his mouth from view, speaking over his shoulder to the other two. "That's perfect. The four of us non-Rehnar get a fourth each, and you get the fruit." Evan said, nodding to Elleya.

She shrugged affirmingly. "It doesn't concern me how you plan to split your share."

Grymjer, hands on hips, gave Evan a confident smile. "I was worried we'd need to abandon the mission if we couldn't find anyone. Getting Myrkor and Kellen will be a massive boost to our chances at success."

"Alright," Evan said, leaving the group and approaching Myrkor with his hand extended. "Half it is. We'll help you gather your things and head inside."

Myrkor chuckled, returning his handshake with a beaming smile. "You've got yourself a deal."

CHAPTER ELEVEN

REAL INTENTIONS

Evan watched the large, lime-skinned man dig through a wooden chest.

"There it is!" Myrkor exclaimed, holding a blue satchel covered in gold swirling lines. "This…" he continued, showing it to Evan. "Is a Loquûl satchel I found in the Whispering Peaks. It has no limit to what it can hold."

Evan's eyes widened. "I guess you're carrying all our gear then."

Myrkor waved a finger. "It has no weight limit, but it can only carry what you can shove inside. I'm willing to carry potions, blankets, and the like. Stuff we won't need unless we're setting up camp or taking a rest. Anything you need quickly in a fight, like healing or magic enhancements, you'll want to keep yourself."

Evan nodded. "Sounds fair to me. I'm heading back to the square to snag better armor; anyone care to join?"

Looking about, he noticed Elleya, Grymjer, and Kellen shaking their heads.

"I'll come along," Myrkor said, raising a beefy hand.

Evan waved casually to the others as he and the hulking Gremling left as they continued organizing their wares. Elleya's status allowed them to bring Myrkor and Kellen's caravan inside the city, which they parked behind a small stone church near the square. Her connections as a cleric were quite valuable, since she was able to convince the priest to let them leave it on their grounds.

"So, what did you need to get?" Evan asked Myrkor as they snaked through a row of tents.

Myrkor grunted. "I'm not here for me; I'm here for you."

Evan's posture stiffened like a board. "Me?"

"Yes," Myrkor answered. "I don't think you understand what we'll be up against."

"I haven't told you where we're going," Evan answered cautiously.

Myrkor's eyes narrowed. "If a Rehnarian holy warrior decides to form a party, there's only one reason."

Evan shot him a hard glance, holding his tongue.

"You're after Duraté's All-Giving Fruit," Myrkor said. "I couldn't tip my hand earlier, or she may have rejected us. The Aurëlie order isn't kind to treasure hunters. They only want someone of Rehnarian descent obtaining that item."

Evan swallowed, unsure how to answer him.

"Look," Myrkor continued. "You don't have to worry; Kellen and I don't plan to take it for ourselves. I'm purely after it for the historical significance..."

Evan turned to face him; finger pointed at his chest. "So, you admit you plan to take it?"

Myrkor rolled his eyes, hands on his hips. "According to the legend, there's nothing to keep. You need to use it or retain it in the temple of Duraté. No one's taken it outside and lived."

Evan bit his lower lip. "She claims we'll be securing it safely until a new council of seven is formed."

Myrkor held a finger up. "But she never mentioned taking it out, correct? She wishes to hide it somewhere else. Somewhere that only she – or someone that knows the location – can reach."

Evan rubbed his chin, staring at his boots.

"Don't mistake my intentions, Evan," Myrkor said. "I've heard from my connections here that several parties have the same intention. I've been dying for any chance to delve into that dungeon. I want to find it before anyone else, because whoever does will be etched on the marble walls of Rehnarian holy temples for eternity. Unless another comet hits," Myrkor finished, laughing.

Evan sighed. "So, being famous to Grymjer isn't enough notoriety for you?"

Myrkor laughed again, this time a deep belly laugh that shook his entire torso.

"I don't care what the rest of them say about you, Evan; you're alright by me," Myrkor sarcastically said, slapping him on the shoulder.

"Wait, what?!" Evan replied quizzically.

Myrkor waved him off. "It's just an old Gremling joke."

Evan huffed. "All this planning torched my sense of humor. Getting back to what you mentioned earlier, that I'm *not ready*..."

Myrkor nodded. "You need much better equipment than what you have now if we're going to make it after the maze. That sword you showed me earlier isn't bad, but you'll want stronger armor and a small shield."

"A small shield?" Evan answered quizzically.

"Yes. You need something to block with that isn't too heavy. You'll also want chest armor and a helmet that covers your face. We don't know what enemies lie past the initial maze. Thankfully, no one's seemed to get past it yet, at least from what I've heard. So, there's still time to catch up..."

"How do you know all this?" Evan interrupted.

"Information is the most important tool an explorer has. I've been friends with a couple of the merchants who have shops here. Now, let's go see someone who has what you need," Myrkor answered.

"Why didn't you have one of them let you in?" Evan inquired.

"They were worried about competition," Myrkor answered flatly.

"Oh, you mean like the shop you're going to open here," Evan replied.

Myrkor shook his head. "No, they're worried I'll be competition to the other delvers who've already started searching. The merchants I know have been supplying a few of the best parties. If one of them found out they let me in; the party would spread the word to boycott them to any delvers they're friendly with. Honestly, I could care less about opening a shop in this place; once you're inside, anyone can set up here."

"You already knew that?" Evan asked with a smile. "And I thought you were just looking to make some coin. What else should I be aware of? It seems you know as much as Elleya."

"I only know what's been filtered out to me by shop-keeps who've stopped by looking for items they can't get inside Lysgahr. I'm sure that cleric knows much more than I do," Myrkor replied. "It's this one over here," he finished, waving Evan over to a large burgundy tent.

He followed the Gremling inside, ducking through the fabric entrance. His eyes grew wide upon seeing the selection on hand. The tent had to be imbibed with the same magic as Myrkor's bag since it was larger than it appeared outside. To his right were rows of cases lined with shelves housing greaves and boots. On the opposite side were two rows of stands holding breastplates. Turning his head to the back, a tall man smoked a pipe with two long horns growing from his head. Behind him was another set of shelves with helmets on them.

"Ah, Grymjer, you finally made it in, old man," the merchant said.

"No thanks to you, Elias," Myrkor retorted.

"I'm Kah'zyin," Elias replied. "You think the guards are going to let me bring some Gremling from the western mountain in here?"

"They let you bring in the potions I sold you?" Myrkor said with a wry smile.

Elias waved a hand, leaning back on his stool. "That's a completely false equivalency, and you know it." He leaned forward, puffing on his pipe. "Did you come find my tent just to chastise me, or were you looking for something?"

Myrkor gestured to Evan, who was still standing near the entrance. "My friend here needs some armor and a shield for the dungeon."

Evan pointed to the row of chest armor. "I was looking for something lightweight."

Elias nodded, walking around the counter to join them on the gold rug in the center of the store. "You'll want one of these two. The first," he grabbed the edge of the sleeve between his thumb and forefinger. "Is quite light and actually enhances any defensive spells you use."

Evan scratched his chin. "I'm not much for casting. I'll be wielding a sword."

"Ah," Elias replied, holding a finger aloft. "You'll actually want this one. It's a bit heavier than those two, but it does quite well at enhancing energy weapons."

Evan raised an eyebrow. "How did you…"

Elias waved him off casually, inspecting the shoulder plat on the armor he moved to. "I've seen plenty of blades shaped like that one in your sheath before. They always have split metal, which means one of the materials channel energy."

Evan tilted his head, impressed at his knowledge. He observed the leather armor, which was a mixture of crimson with black straps and buckles holding it together. As he continued inspecting it, Elias marched eagerly behind the counter.

"This is the helmet and greaves you'll need to pair with it," he said, placing them on the counter.

Evan turned away from the armor and approached the items. The helmet had a face covering but with slits across the section covering the mouth. A long feather sat on its top and cascaded to the back. Both it and the gloves had the same color pattern as the chest plate.

Evan set the helmet back on the counter. "Do you have a shield that pairs with these?"

Elias wagged a finger. "You don't need one with this set. Put them on, and I'll show you."

Evan shrugged, grabbing the chest piece first and pulling it on overhead before putting on the other two.

"Now," Elias said. "Quickly make a fist and pull yourself into a guard. Make sure you put your arm forward to block."

Evan did as he was instructed. Nothing happened.

Elias shook his head, coming around the counter to join him. "Your stance is all wrong," he said, grabbing Evan's limbs and pulling them in the right position. "Like this," he finished, demonstrating the move in front of him. He went back behind the counter. "Now, you try."

Evan took a deep breath, hoping that steadying himself would yield a better result. He did a quick pivot, flexing his arm and squeezing his fist into a guarded pose.

"Oh wow!" he exclaimed as a tall shield sprung from the armored forearm section of the glove. In a slight crouch, it covered him from his ankles to just above his head. It was translucent with a faint, red glow. When he tapped his finger on it, it felt like thick glass.

"Full sets like that one usually have an added ability," Elias said.

Evan stood straight, and the translucent red magical shield disappeared. He looked down at the glove in amazement. He'd been exposed to some very capable armor and weaponry during his time in the capital, but he hadn't seen one in person that created an additional effect when worn in a set.

"Where is this from?" Evan asked.

Elias smiled. "There's been some positives from the comet. It tainted those who wielded magic inside them but enhanced non-living items that use it."

Evan bit his lip, thinking back to the feathered cloak he had that Sunasa stole. It, too, seemed more capable than the magic he was used to. Before the fall, all the wielders had occupied the highest stations in society because their power could rarely be challenged. He realized that power would now shift to anyone capable of finding the best equipment.

"How much for the set?" Evan asked.

"It'll be one gem for each piece," Elias replied coolly.

Evan dug three round emerald crystals from inside a pouch on his hip and placed them on the counter. *'Thankfully, Elleya gave me a healthy stipend to spend here.'*

Elias pursed his lips. "You'll need four; you're buying two gloves, a helmet, and a breastplate."

Evan laughed. "You didn't specify each individual piece. I'll be generous though and throw in something extra," he finished, tossing three extra coins on the counter.

Myrkor chuckled, crossing his arms as he observed the negotiation.

"I don't think you understand, young one. Unlike most in the square, I don't barter," Elias said, huffing on his pipe. "Place the items on the counter, and you can leave."

Evan's posture stiffened. He'd bartered with every merchant in Lysgahr so far, and the abrupt dismissal took him by surprise.

Myrkor slapped Evan on the back, retrieving another gem from his pouch and placing it on the counter. "He's new around here, friend. Cut the kid some slack, and I'll cover his difference," he pointed to the additional coins. "You can keep those as a token of our gratitude."

Elias rubbed his chin for a moment. "I accept your apology," he said, plucking the money from the counter and placing it in a pouch behind the counter.

Evan nodded to Elias, his face a mixture of perturbed and thankful emotions. He followed Myrkor's lead as they left the shop together.

Myrkor leaned close to Evan once they were several paces from the entrance. "He's half O'dachi, so his pride is quite strong," he said, looking skyward. "After the fall, he claimed there wasn't enough time left in this world to waste on banter over goods," he shrugged. "I disagree, but he's not the only one that feels that way. Kellen's taken a similar stance."

Evan tilted his head in acceptance. "I'll take a grumpy O'dachi merchant if it means having armor with inherent spells."

Myrkor laughed. "I'm sure it seems novel now, but from what I've heard, there's plenty more we'll find inside the dungeon."

CHAPTER TWELVE

ENTER THE DUNGEON

A SENSE OF GRANDEUR washed over Evan as he stood before the temple. Despite its battered state, the building retained its beauty. Long columns at least fifty feet high lined either side of the entrance, which had a whisp of gold mist billowing out.

"Of all the things destroyed in this room…" Elleya said, placing her hand on a fallen column that was cracked in half.

Evan held his tongue, watching her trace over one of the words written around the side. He knew her religious convictions viewed any injury to this holy place as a moment to mourn. His eyes left her position, tracing along the massive antechamber to a series of paintings along the wall.

'That's what Myrkor's after. Can't say I blame the guy,' he thought, noticing one of the scenes depicting a Rehnarian in a cloak holding a golden pear. *'Alehskahr, The First, finder of the All-Giving Fruit,'* he said to himself, reading the description beneath it. He eyed a few more, noticing some were damaged from large cracks in the walls.

"This is very interesting," Elleya called to the group.

She stood in front of the entrance, which, upon closer look, had a translucent black mist hanging inside the entrance like a curtain. Beyond it, you could see a long hallway made of large gray bricks.

"You shouldn't be able to see through this," she continued, sticking her arm through it. After a moment, she pulled it back slowly. "I didn't want to believe them, but it's true."

Grymjer pointed to the entrance. "You act as if you haven't been here before…"

Elleya faced him, a calm expression on her brow. "I've been to the temple of Duraté many times before the Cataclysm. However, after the fall, no one was allowed inside the antechamber unless they had a party to delve for the gift."

Kellen stepped forward; arms crossed. "Should we be worried?"

Elleya shook her head. "No. It seems now that magic has become tainted; you can freely come and go. Before, once you entered, you couldn't leave."

"I'd say that's a good thing," Myrkor added. "Gives us an opportunity to come back and resupply if we need."

"We're not here to dig for items to sell," Elleya sternly replied. "I know you're planning to establish a shop. But we're not doing that until we've finished our mission."

Evan bit his lower lip, bracing for further argument. He hadn't spoken to her or Grymjer about what Myrkor had told him, thinking it might cause dissension if the others weren't sure of his true intentions. Speaking with him in the square, seeing his eyes light up, he knew Myrkor was being honest. But trying to relay that secondhand wouldn't hold the same weight.

"I understand we're pressed for time, but if we need to resupply, then this is a real advantage," Myrkor responded casually.

She sighed. "You're correct. However, as I told everyone on our way here, we can find items inside the dungeon. Since they'll be at the later stages, they'll be better than what's available outside."

"Well," Kellen said, approaching the mist cloaked entryway. "No time like the present."

Elleya smiled in agreeance with the proud O'dachi, following him inside. The other three joined soon after. Upon entering, torches along the walls gushed flames that fell in fiery clumps to the stone floor, exploding in puffs of smoke. Evan watched Elleya, noticing her perplexed expression showed she didn't trust the fire's behavior.

Reaching into her satchel, she retrieved the map and opened it. Holding it up for everyone to see, she showed them the red dot glowing right at the entrance. A line slowly appeared, weaving its way through the maze.

"We follow this, which leads us to the entrance of the trials," she instructed. "There's going to be monsters throughout our walk to the end, so would you guide us," she continued, handing it to Grymjer. She then extended the wand from under her sleeve. "Some of them can only be killed by Rehnarian magic."

"I'm happy to be the guide," he answered, taking the scroll. "I happen to enjoy cartography, so I'm going to take notes during our travels."

SQUISH!

They each took a reflexive step back at the sound.

"Let's quit talking and get to work," Kellen stated, his massive sword had slashed through a zombie's green skull ten paces away.

Evan couldn't believe how quick he was. He looked around at the others, wondering if they'd seen him move. He saw a wide smile on Myrkor's face.

"Time to move," the large Gremling said with a laugh.

After only being in the opening maze for an hour, they were close to the end. It was quite a blessing to have this map in their possession. Evan smiled, knowing that Sunasa and his men would have to trek through blindly if they ever made it inside Lysgahr.

'And if there's one thing Rehnarians hate, it's Hiroyans,' Evan thought with a chuckle. *'Good luck getting past the wall, you kidnapping snake.'*

The two races had many conflicts dating back to well before he was born. Even though he grew up in a time of peace between their nations, he knew the sting of old wars still lingered amongst the Rehnar and Hiroyan people.

"One more left, then we take the second right," Grymjer announced.

After the first turn, the narrow hallway expanded as they stepped forward.

"It's fine," Ellya called out. "The maze creates illusions to scare off delvers from reaching the exit."

This area was lit with metal sconces housing blue flames. Unlike some of the earlier sections, this space only had a few on either wall, making for a much dimmer view. Peering ahead, Evan noticed a pack of people stalking forward. He drew his sword as one of their hands raised.

"Wait!" a voice among them bellowed. "Help us escape!"

The group of three staggered towards a lit sconce. He could see they wore heavy metal armor from head to toe.

"Our supplies have run out, and we don't know where to turn," one of them explained. His raspy voice sounded hollow and dry.

"Figure it out y..." Kellen started. He was cut off by Myrkor, who placed a firm hand on his shoulder.

Elleya looked at the large Gremling; it was the first time he'd interrupted his friend before. Myrkor dug in his satchel and took a waterskin, which he tossed to her.

"Thank you for your share of abundance," she said in a prayerful tone.

Holding her wand above the waterskin, it sent a cloud of silver dust over it. The item expanded in size as she held her head and prayed under her breath. The three men took it from her eagerly and ripped it open, drinking greedily.

Suddenly, the end of the hallway raced toward them, coming to an abrupt stop that shook the room. The three men disappeared, and a wooden door shimmered to life inset in the wall ahead.

"You said this place would bring illusions to make us divert. It also wants to make ones that test our loyalty to the creed of Duraté," Myrkor said, giving a knowing glance to Elleya.

She shot a thankful smile back.

Opening the door led to the final right turn Grymjer had mentioned before. After taking it, they reached a smaller antechamber that was decorated in a similar style to the one at the entrance. On the opposite end was a large marble arch around a black misty entrance. This one was much taller than the first they'd entered. Elleya crouched down, walking carefully across the room on all fours, scanning the floor.

"You see any traps," Grymjer called out.

"No," she replied, reaching the other side. She held her wand before the entryway, a humming light emitting from her wand as she traced a pattern over it.

All light left the room. Then, one large red flame burst from a massive brazier bolted to the stone above the door, some twenty feet up.

"YOU HAVE REACHED THE TRIALS," a loud feminine voice bellowed.

"NOW, YOUR FIRST TEST TO PROVE YOU'RE WORTHY OF MY GIFT."

Sections of the wall lifted in vertical rectangles around them. The group instinctively formed a circle facing out to the newly created entrances. High-pitched screeches, like wounded animals, echoed from the openings. A few tainted undead corpses crawled out. Quickly surveying the area, Evan noticed more than ten entered from the three openings he faced. He assumed the other side – covered by Kellen and Elleya behind him – faced similar numbers. Grymjer stood to his left, holding a small crossbow. To his right, Myrkor reached into his satchel, digging for a few moments before pulling a hammer out with a three-foot handle. Behind him, Kellen flinched his body, covering himself in his race's natural scale armor. He twisted his large sword about in a circular pattern, warming himself up for the incoming fight.

Elleya leveled the first shot with her bow, catching one of the ghoulish creatures between the eyes. It melted into a pile of oily goo. The other zombies screeched, clamoring forward as more funneled out from the openings.

"There's more of them?" Evan yelled, thrusting his sword through one's head as it charged him.

He squinted as the part of the explosion of goo splashed onto his helmet.

'Good thing this has a face covering,' he thought, hacking into another one.

A few more staggered forwards, each meeting a similar fate from Evan's blade. He went to yank his sword back from one stabbed on the ground, but it wouldn't budge.

"Dammit," he yelled, tugging on his weapon. "I think it's stuck in one of them!"

His eyes grew wide with shock as the pile of ebony slime around his weapon began to harden. Five more poured into the room, all of them lumbering toward him. The first three snatched his arms. The only thing that saved him was the last two falling into the first, knocking all of them to the ground. He felt the stench of rotten fruit as one opened its mouth to bite him.

'I hope this works,' he thought, twisting his body in the best imitation of Elias' instructions, despite being stuck on his back.

The shield popped out from his forearm, slashing through a few limbs as it emerged. It was the only thing between him and becoming dinner for the ravenous undead. The zombie that tried to bite him earlier continued chomping its mouth against the energy shield.

"I need a hand!" Evan yelped through exhausted lungs.

The pressure against his body by the crushing pile of monsters made it nearly impossible to speak.

THWIP!

An arrow whipped through the skull of the one chomping at him.

"Hang in there, Evan," Grymjer yelled.

A second later, a massive green hand snatched the tattered armor of the next zombie. It was yanked to its feet and met with a hammer to the side of its skull. The hammer's head had expanded fivefold and was covered in a glowing blue energy. The force of the magically enhanced blow sent the creature flying into a wall, splattering to bits.

Finally free, Evan scrambled back to his feet. He ducked as another swung for him. He made the shield again, catching it under the chin and knocking it a foot off the ground. A gold arrow zipped through its skull. He turned his head and saluted Elleya, who nodded in kind. She turned and zapped another charging zombie with her wand.

He noticed there weren't as many on their side since Kellen's flurry of quick attacks was flaying them as fast as they entered. Returning his attention to his side, there were only three crawling over the pile of wet undead bodies.

"I haven't seen any more come from our side," Grymjer stated, pulling a dagger from his boot and stabbing one of the crawlers in the head.

Myrkor snatched one on the back and lifted it again. "You want one more, partner," he called to Kellen.

A second later, the O'dachi leaped into the air, sword pulled back and held with one hand. Midair, he shoved the blade through the monster's body and slammed it to the ground. His scale-covered fist shoved down, crushing its head.

Evan marched to the last one, spinning his blade in both hands to a downward grip and squeezing the hilt. It glowed red and hummed as it filled with power. He stabbed it down, and the body beneath him burned. Yanking back the weapon, he slackened his grip, and the flame extinguished.

"Glad I got the chance to test this out," he said, sheathing his sword at his waist. He looked to the rest of his party, each of them wearing a satisfied look. "I think we make a pretty good team."

"I have to agree," Elleya said, returning her bow behind her back. "Each of these trials is meant to test the party in a specific way. No two stages of this dungeon will be the same."

"Will we see more of this type of monster?" Grymjer asked.

"Yes, but this particular challenge won't happen twice," she answered.

Grymjer sighed in relief.

"That map was a real leg up," Myrkor said. "According to what we've heard from the other parties and merchants in the square, we've made it farther than anyone else."

"YOU HAVE SHOWN YOU CAN WORK AS ONE," the goddess' voice interrupted. **"YOU MAY ENTER THE NEXT STAGE."**

The black mist reappeared in the tall exit, this time with bits of gold-dusted smoke like the first entrance.

"YOU ARE THE SECOND GROUP TO COMPLETE THIS TRIAL."

CHAPTER THIRTEEN

THE NEXT TRIAL

GRYMJER SHOT A worried glance at the group. They each had similar expressions, except Kellen.

"Good," he said. "I was worried this was going to be too easy."

Elleya crossed her arms. "The map only gets us to this point, so it was never going to be easy."

Kellen shrugged.

"I assumed we'd have an advantage since we hadn't heard of anyone else getting this far," she continued.

Evan rubbed his chin. "Even if one group is farther than us, we're still well ahead of the majority exploring this stage."

"You're right," she answered. "But we don't know how many more trials they've beaten. We need to hurry. I had hoped we'd be the first."

Myrkor stepped over one of the melting corpses. "I wanted to ask you this earlier, but I wasn't sure you'd know, Elleya, but why are we only the second ones?"

She faced him, confused.

He continued. "I know the council died in one of the collapsed castles, but there had to be members of your order who still knew how to complete the dungeon. I know the trials change every time, but the maze has always been first."

Elleya tilted her chin up, understanding him. "Yes, there are still some experienced clerics. But this maze is completely different in layout from before. That map we used is the only record that actually works, because it finds the end once the user enters. There were some magically enhanced like ours in the city, but they were destroyed when the nobility's castles fell. Any copies kept outside royalty were handwritten and wouldn't adapt to the changes."

"Alright," he said, approaching the stone archway cloaked in black mist. "Grymjer, you got all the notes you need before we move on?"

He smiled, holding up a tiny, leatherbound notebook that he stuffed into a hip pouch. "Ready when you are."

They all looked about; each giving an affirming glance before heading to the doorway and stepping through the darkness. Unlike the lifeless stone hallways from before, they were met with what appeared to be the inside of a wealthy manor. The ceilings were at least twenty feet high and decorated with thick wood trim that cascaded down sections of the wall. At their feet was a veined marble floor with a lush polish that sparkled from large candlelit chandeliers hanging overhead.

Instinctually, they grouped together and moved as one. While this stage appeared beautiful, they knew eventually their surroundings would devolve into something terrible. After slinking around multiple halls and passing through several rooms, they were met with nothing.

"This might be another maze," Myrkor suggested, stretching his back. After walking the entire time in a defensive hunch, his back popped loudly when he arched, sounding like a cow bone being snapped.

"It's possible but very unlikely," Elleya answered, taking a moment to stretch as well.

The current place they stood in resembled a dining room with a large table in the middle. The center of the table had a large lit candle. Each of the rooms before had similar decor.

He scratched his chin, observing a painting on the wall. "Evan, Kellen," Myrkor said. "Any chance you can go to the last room we were in and tell me what's on the paintings? I think it's the same as these."

They nodded and left through the double doors behind them, weaving around the corner to the last room.

"HEY!" cried Evan as a similar set of double doors shut behind them, one room over.

"Shit!" Myrkor blurted, hearing the loud bang of them slamming.

He rushed to the door of their room, yanking on the handle. When it wouldn't budge, he removed the hammer from his pack and swung. His weapon clanged off a translucent barrier, emitting sparks into the air.

"I can't get in!" he called to them.

"We'll find a way out," Evan yelled back. "Just don't go farther ahead. We need to avoid being separated."

"What's on the paintings?" Myrkor asked.

Kellen walked over to one. It depicted a man standing on a game board made of red and white squares. "It's a game of Tactician."

"Mine is a man running along a road, and the path is crumbling behind him," Evan added.

Before they could look at the final two paintings in the room, the ones they'd described melted off the wall.

"They're changing," Evan announced to Myrkor outside.

The piles of liquid reformed into knights without helmets. Instead of eyes, they had lumps of crystal. Evan unsheathed his sword and sliced it across its face. It howled and fell to one knee, clutching at the shattered crystal eyes. Evan squeezed his sword's hilt, and it burst into flame. Swiping down, his blade cut halfway through its head. He kept pressing, shoving the fire down as it melted through the armored body.

Behind him, Kellen rammed his weapon through a similar creature. It fell to the floor, and he slammed his boot on its chest, yanking his sword free. He swung again for its neck, severing the head free. Its arms collapsed listlessly onto the floor, and the doors opened behind them.

Myrkor rubbed his chin, looking to the floor thoughtfully. "Were those hard to kill?" he asked, jutting his chin towards the room.

"No, not really," Evan replied.

"Good," Myrkor said. "I need you to check the other rooms we've been through and tell me what those paintings look like as well."

"I'll join them," Elleya added. "I have something I want to see myself."

Myrkor looked to Grymjer on his right, who was feverishly taking notes. "You're way ahead of me, pal," he said, chuckling.

As they walked back, the doors of the room they'd be in slammed shut and disappeared. Only a cherry wood wall, like the rest of the halls, remained. They all looked at one another, seeing if anyone had a thought to share.

"Alright," Elleya said. "Let's go test your theory."

After entering the fourth and final room they'd previously been in, the three of them walked out, only one crystal knight corpse lying on the floor behind them.

"My assumption was correct," Elleya said. "Only the paintings you describe become those crystal-eyed knights."

Myrkor's eyes narrowed. "Each room we re-entered has disappeared after we've described the paintings. But what's the connection," he wondered aloud, touching a finger to his jaw in contemplation.

Grymjer raised his notebook. "From what I've gathered, each of them has the same four pieces of art. The man running on the trail, the game of Tactician, a hand covering a mouth, and a letter being burned."

"Crystal-eyed knight is a term I've heard experienced Tactician players use before," Myrkor added. "The ones I've played with called someone that when they were too eager. The joke is that their eyes light up like jewels when they think they've won, but in actuality, they've tipped their hand and inevitably lose."

"We clearly need to know what the paintings are but get punished when we speak them," Elleya said.

"The letter!" Grymjer shouted. "Follow me," he instructed, waving for the group to follow.

They ran through the exquisite mansion until a hallway with rooms on either side appeared. They walked into the first one, and Myrkor extended a hand to Grymjer.

"Can you write down the paintings and give me the pages?" Myrkor asked.

After collecting them, he folded them up and placed them over the fire. A blue smoke burned, and the wall at the end of the room shot upward, revealing a passage.

He looked back to the group, smiling. "It's nice not all of them end with slicing up melting undead ghouls."

Evan laughed, patting him on the shoulder as he followed him through the opening. After they all entered, the wall slammed down. A single light shone down on the room's center, revealing the floor was the same red and white squares from the game in the painting. Looking up, Evan noticed a balcony section around the room.

"DISPLAY YOUR WITS AS A TEAM. CHOOSE THE BEST AMONG YOUR PARTY TO LEAD YOU THROUGH THIS GAME."

A sheet of parchment appeared in each of their hands, along with a quill.

"Who should we…" Evan started.

"We shouldn't make the decision out loud," Elleya interrupted, holding her hand up. "I think we'll be punished – like we were in the rooms – if we speak."

"Alright then," he answered. "Testing our ability to work together when we can't communicate," he finished, nodding at Myrkor before looking at Elleya.

She nodded back. Grymjer and Kellen understood the silent gesture as well. They each wrote a name on their sheet, and it vanished upon the final stroke of ink. A new page appeared.

"NOW, WHO IS THE WORST AMONG YOU TO LEAD YOUR PARTY THROUGH THIS GAME?"

Evan looked to the group and shrugged, not sure who to pick. After they finished writing, that page vanished as well.

"MYRKOR, YOU ARE CHOSEN AS THE BEST TO LEAD, STEP FORWARD."

He raised his eyebrows at the group, smiling appreciatively.

"YOU WILL NOT LEAD YOUR PARTY. YOU CAN ONLY BE AS STRONG AS THE WEAKEST AMONG YOU. KELLEN, YOU HAVE BEEN VOTED AS THE LEAST CAPABLE TO LEAD."

"Hey! Really, guys!" Kellen interjected.

"THIS TRIAL IS YOURS TO FAIL."

Gold mist swirled around his body until he vanished. He appeared on the balcony with a loud pop. The rest of the group had mist swirl around their body next, until they reappeared on the last line of squares on the board. Evan tried to turn, but his body wouldn't budge. He tried to speak, but his mouth wouldn't open.

A crystal-eyed knight appeared on a square at the opposite end of the board from him. Across from the other three were different creatures. One was a human form in robes with a lizard head carrying a spear. The second looked like a tree with arms carrying an axe, and the last was a regal-looking wolf wearing a crown and robes resting on its haunches.

"Hey, Myrkor, how do you play this game?" Kellen called down, leaning on the balcony rail.

He didn't answer.

"Damn, they can't talk," Kellen cursed under his breath.

Everyone in the party stood still, unmoving. Kellen felt something pinch his palm and quickly yanked it back. The tiles on the rail were moving to his position, forming themselves into a two-by-two-foot square. Red mist swirled and created small glowing replicas of his companions. On the opposite end of the marble tablet were the enemies made of white mist.

"Ok, Kellen, you can figure this out..." he thought aloud, scratching his head.

He placed his fingers on Myrkor's piece, and a few words hovered over his head.

Defensive Stance
Offensive Strike
Counter Attack

He touched the other pieces, and the same words appeared over them. Taking a moment, he rubbed his chin, wondering what move he should make first.

'It's only seen us fight inside this place,' he thought. *'I think I can use that to my advantage.'*

Looking at the board, there were five tiles between his team and the enemy's pieces. They were laid out in three rows; the row in the center had three, and the two in front of each line of pieces had two.

He took Elleya's piece and chose *Defensive Stance* by touching the word with his other hand. Then he tried placing it on the third row. The board buzzed and glowed red, sending the piece back.

'Hmmph, they can only go so far,' he thought, taking her piece again and placing it in the middle of the second row. It hummed with a gold light and stood firm.

He lifted his eyes and watched as the enemy sent the Lizard piece to her square. The tile was big enough for both of them to stand on. The two stood still, not moving.

'I guess the actions happen after the movements.'

He grabbed Myrkor and put him in the staggered square behind Elleya to her right and chose *Counter Attack*. The tree piece moved forward one square. He put Evan in the other square, staggered behind Elleya to her left, and selected *Counter Attack* as well. The Crystal Knight went to the same square Evan was on.

'Interesting choice. I think they're hoping to surround her.'

He left Grymjer in place and chose *Offensive Strike*. The Wolf was placed immediately to Elleya's right. He took a deep breath, staring intently at his actual friends on the board below.

The lizard struck first, stabbing its spear at Elleya. She quickly made a shield of energy with her wand, deflecting the blow. The Tree swung for her as well, hitting her in the side and knocking her to the ground. Her piece disappeared from the board.

'Damn! They can only take one hit on defense!?'

Myrkor dug in his pack and lobbed a bomb, which lit the tree creature ablaze.

Kellen smiled. *'One for one.'*

The Crystal Knight and Evan's pieces swung their swords, which clanged off each other.

'Must have chosen the same thing as me,' he thought.

Grymjer's piece knocked an arrow into his crossbow and shot the Lizard in the stomach. It fell to one knee but didn't disappear. The wolf stood still, unmoving.

'Must have chosen defense for that one.'

All the remaining pieces glowed gold. He grabbed Evan's piece, which now had the *Counter Attack* option missing.

'Alright,' he told himself. *'I can use each action once. And clearly, something about Grymjer's attack didn't kill that other piece, but that damage has to count for something.'*

He left Evan in place and chose the defensive option. The Lizard moved one square back to the last row, so he put Grymjer in the second-row middle with a counter move. The wolf went to Grymjer's space, and he moved Myrkor forward to the Lizard and chose offense. He held his breath. Hoping he'd made the right assumptions.

The crystal knight's sword clanged off Evan's shield. Myrkor took out his hammer and raised it, a massive sphere of energy emerging around it. He slammed it down on the lizard, who wasn't able to stop the blow. It squished him into a pile of emerald blood, then disappeared.

The wolf leaped onto Myrkor's back, sinking its teeth into his neck. Kellen's stomach dropped as his piece disappeared from the board.

"You're gonna pay for that one!" he yelled, jabbing a finger in the wolf's direction.

It turned its head and smiled up at him, blood running down its teeth. He flinched at the taunt, not expecting the opposing pieces to do something outside the rules he'd noticed so far.

He glowered back. "You're not going to like what happens to you," he muttered, taking Evan's piece.

He halted. Noticing he only had an offensive move with him and a defensive move with Grymjer. He took a moment to think, trying to recall what the remaining pieces had done before.

A rising lump of fear climbed up his throat, realizing he was trapped.

'If I move Evan after either piece, he'll get countered or blocked. And Grymjer only has defense, so he can't do anything this round,' he stood still, pondering his options for what felt like an eternity. *'Either the pieces get their actions back, or the one with the least pieces loses. No matter what happens, I'm screwed. I can't believe I got suckered into this. Leaving no one with a counterattack.'*

He paused, an idea leaping to the front of his mind.

"The game has to account for this," he said. "I hope I'm right…"

He took Grymjer and selected his last available option, *Defensive Stance,* then placed him in front of the wolf. He pulled Evan back one space, and the knight stood its ground. He wanted to turn away, knowing everything he chose in the round was a complete gamble. While he wasn't someone who played Tactician, he'd heard enough about it to know that it was spoken of as simple to learn and hard to master. His O'dachi upbringing taught him to stand his ground, to stare defiantly at the one trying to kill his friends. The inside of his stomach, twisted in knots, begged him to look away and hope it all worked out.

'Die on your feet, never on your knees,' he told himself, face becoming a scowl of fierce determination.

Evan felt his arm jerk against his will, reaching into a pouch on his hip and snatching a metal sphere. He lobbed it at the knight, who raised its sword, knocking the bomb down. It exploded on the square between them. The blast sent the knight back one square, but after a moment, it took its place on the same tile again.

'What the hell is he thinking up there!' Evan yelled in his mind.

He still couldn't speak, but if he could, he'd tell Kellen to make completely different moves. All the ones so far resulted in them losing more of their party. He watched as the wolf beast growled and lifted a large paw overhead. He braced himself to watch another friend die while he was stuck like a statue. The pain of each loss stung like the tip of a knife pressing into your ribs. Having to stand in place like an impotent fool felt even worse. Like the remaining length of the blade being shoved past your ribs and through your innards.

'Why the hell did I let Grymjer get caught up in this,' he cursed.

The paw came down for Grymjer's head.

He ducked the blow, then shoved his boot knife into the wolf's neck. It disappeared.

"YES!" he shouted internally.

He wanted to raise his fist high, to cheer, to curse the enemy. But the game wasn't over. He stood in place, waiting for Kellen's decision. He hoped it would be as lucky as the last one.

Kellen pumped his fist as the wolf vanished. *'Wait 'till Myrkor sees what I figured out. Or better yet, I'll play dumb when he plays me. Then catch him with this tactic.'*

His assumption that defense would defeat counter attack had been correct. He believed the game could never end if it were simply taking turns slamming swords against shields. He touched Grymjer's piece and noticed all the options had returned.

"Now you're cornered," he chided with a smirk.

He placed both pieces to attack the final knight. He leaned one arm on the banister, watching it block Grymjer's boot knife before Evan lit his sword ablaze and levied a melting slice through its middle. He was startled as the gold mist swirled around him once more before reappearing next to the other two survivors in his party.

"You did it!" Grymjer yelled, running up and punching Kellen in the side.

Kellen shrugged, a casual grin on his face. "I just did what I thought Myrkor would do."

Evan looked away, hands on his hips. "Where's the other two?"

Grymjer licked his lips nervously, eyes darting around for a sign their friends would be returned. Each passing second felt like an eternity. Eventually, the doors they'd entered swung open behind them while a set of stairs unfolded from the balcony.

"YOU HAVE SHOWN EVEN THE LEAST AMONG YOU IS WORTHY OF LEADING. YOU MAY CONTINUE."

Ignoring the voice, they looked at one another, unsure how to process their incorrect assumption about the trial. They'd foolishly thought that if they won, it would return what it had taken.

CHAPTER FOURTEEN

FRIEND OR FOE

SILENTLY, THEY LEFT the room through the entrance they'd taken. Evan slumped onto a tufted chair, unsure what to do.

"You're still alive!" a gruff voice bellowed.

He turned to see Myrkor wearing a wide-brim smile. "We were dropped here after getting knocked out of the game, which seemed odd since I assumed we'd be killed if you didn't win."

Elleya stood next to him with her arms crossed, the edge of her mouth in a downward grin.

"Any chance you'd like to thank me for the big win back there," Kellen joked, nodding his chin up to her.

She rolled her eyes, arms still folded. "Of course I'm glad the party remained intact, but don't expect me to shout for joy when you got me whacked by that giant tree during the first round."

Kellen threw up his hands. "I had to use you as bait, or else I wouldn't have been able to take them out."

Her eyes narrowed. "I was bait?"

"Now, now, you two," Grymjer interrupted, walking over to Elleya and patting her on the arm. "No need to fill the room with all this love."

"Pretty dumb joke, kid," Kellen huffed, walking over to a chair next to Evan. He unsheathed his sword, then raised a palm to Myrkor.

Myrkor grunted and shoved a hand in his satchel, retrieving a whetstone and tossing it to him. Kellen plopped onto the chair and began sharpening his blade.

Evan laughed, shaking his head. "I was debating if I was going to have to leave or keep pressing on. Thankfully, I can put that decision to rest."

Grymjer raised an eyebrow quizzically. "You were still thinking of moving forward after that? Even if we were down to three?" He looked away, scanning the walls. "This place does weird things to people."

"It's commendable," Elleya said, walking to Evan and placing a hand on his shoulder.

"Thanks," he replied. "Should we get going?"

Myrkor held up a hand. "Actually, I think we should look around here first. The dungeon is known to have an incredible cache of items, yet we've found nothing of worth so far."

Elleya whipped her head around.

"Hear me out," he continued, holding both hands up defensively. "I know what the end goal is, but these challenges will only get more difficult. When you guys walked out, all the doors that vanished in the hallways reappeared and sprang open. There's got to be something worthwhile in one of them, and I'm not talking about jewels or trinkets. There might be items we can actually use."

"You're right, Myrkor. It's worth a look," Elleya replied.

Grymjer nudged Myrkor on the arm, and the two wandered off down a hallway.

Kellen eyed them as they left. "I'll stay here and watch the entrance to the next stage. There's still another party out there."

Evan eyed Elleya. It was something he'd forgotten in all the effort to survive the last trial. Observing her furrowed brow, it seemed she'd forgotten too.

"Parties aren't always hostile to one another," Elleya replied.

Kellen huffed. "That was before the fall. I'm not trusting anyone out here that isn't in our group."

"Very well," she said, motioning to Evan. "Let's see what's down the other section."

They briskly strode down the hallway, a sense of ease and simplicity about their search. Having beaten the trial and the rooms reappearing meant the traps and monsters were no longer a threat. Passing one room, something caught the corner of Evan's eye. He went inside, looking to confirm what he'd noticed. The room looked different than before. Instead of resembling a dining hall, it had a fireplace roaring and four chairs around a short table. In its center was a set of five vials hovering an inch above the wood.

"Elleya, I think we've found our first reward," he announced, walking over and plucking one.

It had an aged label with elegant cursive writing on it.

— Enjoy the abundance of invigorated spirit. —

"Any idea what this does?" Evan asked, handing her the vial.

She looked it over. "Your stamina won't wither for several hours," she answered. "I'd definitely save it for when we come across another hoard of monsters."

"Noted," Evan replied, grabbing the four remaining vials and placing them in a pouch on his belt.

She walked over to one of the paintings, stuffing the vial into her own pouch. After running her finger along the frame's edge, a loud click could be heard. A section of the wall opposite her slid open. Inside the four-by-four area was a large wooden chest.

"This has got to be better than the vials," Evan said, smiling.

She approached the chest cautiously, removing a tiny knife from her belt. The blade was short and curved, with a circular finger hole on the handle. She flipped it in her hand to a downward grip, then knelt by its side and pried at the edge.

"Shouldn't it open for us?" Evan asked.

She looked at him. "Some of them don't hold gifts."

"Oh," Evan replied. "Good to know not everything is safe once we beat the trial."

AAAAAAHHHHHHHH!!!!!

"Was that Grymjer?!" Evan asked, his posture jolting upright.

He ran down the hall his friend had gone, turning the corner as another scream rang out.

"What in Varkin's name is that?!" Evan shouted.

A wooden chest was opened, but it wasn't mere boards and bolts. Tiny arms and legs had sprouted from it. Glowing beady red eyes were nestled on top of the chest, and it was chasing the little Gremling around the room, gnashing a full set of jagged teeth. Myrkor was running after it, trying to strike the vicious thing with his magic-enhanced hammer.

Evan wielded his shield and charged in, slamming the creature from the side, causing it to topple end over end across the floor. It bounced against the stone tile surrounding the fireplace. Stuck on its side, it kicked and flailed, skinny limbs unable to pull itself upright. Myrkor swung for it, smacking the creature into the roaring fire. It squealed as the crackling flames engulfed its wood body.

"That's why we pry at the edges first," Elleya said, strolling into the room.

"Would've been helpful to tell us that ahead of time," Myrkor retorted.

She crossed her arms, shrugging. "Duraté's edict states you learn best by experience."

Grymjer snatched a nearby chair, climbing to his feet. "I think verbal instruction is good enough for things that could eat me," he said after a heavy sigh, dusting himself off.

"There's far too many monsters I'm aware of for me to name them all, and divulge their weaknesses," she argued.

Evan shot her a glance, brows raised in a mix of expectation and disappointment.

She sighed. "Duraté's edict also says that I'll grow in abundance from sharing my knowledge," she gestured towards the paintings. "You were right to inspect objects that gave us clues earlier. I'm guessing you opened the wall, Myrkor?"

He nodded, crossing his arms as a confident smile grew.

"As you noticed," she continued. "While it was hostile, it wasn't as formidable as the knights. There are tricks and traps that can trigger when exploring post-victory, but to my knowledge, that critter is the worst of them."

"Should I be worried about these?" Evan asked, holding up a corked vial.

"No," she replied. "Anything meant to hinder our delve will show itself immediately."

"What ya got there?" Grymjer asked, striding forward and eyeing it, hands on his hips.

"You can have it," Evan answered. "There was one for each of us. Elleya said they'll keep us from becoming fatigued for a certain amount of time."

"Hand me two, and I'll hold Kellen's," Myrkor said. "He has me carry most of his items so it doesn't weigh him down. By the way, how many rooms did you walk through? We still have a few more on our side."

"Only one left for us; I wouldn't mind inspecting them all as a group," Evan replied.

After several minutes of prowling the two nearby rooms, they'd found one healing potion for each member. Walking back, they made their way to the one Evan and Elleya had left behind. It had the décor of a study, with bookshelves lining the walls to the ceiling and two high-back chairs. This time, they weren't greeted by a table in the center with hovering potions.

Evan noticed something different about this place.

"It's the only room without art on the walls," Evan announced. "Any ideas where we should look first?"

Myrkor rubbed his chin, standing at the entrance. The other two approached the shelves and selected books.

"The only thing that stands out," Myrkor said. "Is that the fireplace is the only wall without books on it."

Evan approached it. The fire was dim but holding a consistent blaze. On the mantle was a candelabra that he picked up carefully. It held five candles, but none were lit, so he took each one and used the fire to light them. After setting the last one back in its place, he waited, holding it up and walking around the room. Nothing happened.

Evan shrugged. "That was a dead end," he said, returning it to the mantle.

"Wait!" Myrkor shouted.

Evan startled and leaped back from the mantle, ready for something to attack him. He slowly raised his eyes from behind his arm. As the fire danced on the candles, it showed a few words on the marble tile behind them.

I CAUSE DEATH, YET MAKE YOUR DAY

I AM THE BEGINNING AND THE END

I CAN BE SEEN, BUT NEVER PURCHASED

"What could that be?" Grymjer asked, scratching his head.

"Whatever the answer is, I'm guessing that's the book we need," Evan replied.

"Beginning and end? You can't buy it..." Myrkor pondered aloud, staring at the ceiling with crossed arms.

Elleya and Evan continued browsing the shelves, calling out titles to Myrkor in hopes it might spring the correct answer in his mind.

"Hold on," Myrkor said, holding up a hand. "What was that last book?"

Evan took the last one he'd read aloud. "Bailen's Decree Through the Church of Delos."

Elleya growled as he read the title.

"Not a fan of their religion, I take it," Evan surmised, wearing a half-smile.

"Bailen is the god of time!" Myrkor announced. "The answer is time!"

Evan's brow rose, realizing he was correct. He opened the book, flipping the pages in an attempt to find the next clue. "I actually saw this one in a few other places before we started calling out their names."

"You won't find the answer in there," Myrkor said, snatching the book from Evan.

"Hey!" he reflexively yelled back.

Myrkor raised a hand. "I was worried you'd read some of it aloud," he continued, closing the book. He held it up towards Elleya. "Duraté and Bailen aren't on the best terms, are they?"

She took a step from the book, reflexively distancing herself from it. "The Delos order worships a god that betrayed this world and the growth Duraté brought."

"See," Myrkor said, looking at Evan with a wide smile. "It's the holy text of this god's sworn enemy. I assumed if you read any of it, you'd trigger a trap."

"Why would there be multiple copies of it here?" Grymjer asked.

"To destroy it," Myrkor said, tossing the book into the fire.

The letters behind the fire disappeared in a puff of smoke, extinguishing the flames on the candles and in the fireplace. The section of marble wall began to turn, a crackly creak of grinding stone ringing throughout as it did. Walking slowly toward the room, Evan noticed a single hanging light over a wooden stool. This hidden area had books lining its walls as well. Peeking his head in, he looked around but saw nothing. He sighed in relief as he entered.

WHOOSH

Something fell swiftly and snatched him, ramming his back against the wood floor.

"Dammit!" Evan howled, stinging pain shooting up his neck.

He grabbed at whatever held him down, noticing it seemed to have furry arms.

"Wait!" a raspy male voice hissed.

He felt the slick touch of sharpened metal against his throat.

"Who are you people?" the assailant asked.

His companions had run towards Evan to help him, but stopped upon seeing the dagger at his throat.

"Are you here to delve for the gift?" the assailant continued.

"We're not monsters looking for your hide. You can release him," Elleya said.

A pair of glowing yellow eyes rose to survey them. The once pinched lids opened wide as the figure realized who was speaking to him. "Elleya, is that you?"

CHAPTER FIFTEEN

BARTHÉLEMY

THE FURRY FIGURE LEAPED off of Evan, who pulled himself to a seated position.

"You know him?" Evan asked, thumbing over his shoulder.

Elleya strode one pace forward, squinting in the faintly lit room to better observe who stood before her. The man was clearly Rehnarian, but his fur was a mix of deep brown that could be confused with black. He wore a similar garb to her, with a hooded top that had short, loose sleeves. However, he wore dark blue pants with strips of armor instead of the long-slit tunic she had. He stepped forward, illuminated by a nearby metal sconce, and lifted his hood.

Her stomach sank; she hadn't seen this man in years. So long, in fact, that she couldn't be sure of the exact count. His posture and face wore a different personality than the plucky and jovial classmate she once knew from the clerical academy. A scar ran across his face from his right eye down over his snout to the opposite cheek. His gold eyes no longer held the hopeful spirit of his former years. They'd fossilized into a calloused, dimmer shade of amber.

"I'm surprised to see you down here," he said, breaking the long silence.

She swallowed down the lump in her throat. "Are you here alone, Barthélemy?"

He grunted a noise between a laugh and annoyance. "I had one, but they left. After the last trial was complete, they fled," he sneered, walking over to one of the walls and leaning against it. "Deep down, I knew they didn't have the stomach to survive here, like you," he finished, nodding his nose up to her.

She scowled, arms crossed. "I'm guessing a trap caught you in there after you won?" she asked, unwilling to acknowledge his last comment.

He shook his head, reaching behind his back and pulling a pouch around his waist. Digging through it, he retrieved an apple and took a bite. She watched as he chewed, knowing his pause was an intentional means of poking her.

Finally, after a few more bites, he answered. "We lost. And after that, they decided to head back. I wanted to see if anything useful was around here," he thumbed to the room he'd been inside. "I got trapped in there until you opened the door."

"You said you lost?" Evan asked. "But your whole party was able to leave?"

He raised an eyebrow, taking a beat to decide whether he'd answer the Kah'zyin. "Duraté tests her believers in many ways. It turns out whoever's chosen to lead is the only one facing death," he gave a brief sigh of frustration. "The dungeon picked the little guy in our group to go up there. I knew he should've stayed back from the beginning, but he was the nephew of two brothers in our party. They stood firm that he needed to come, that he could handle it," he shook his head. "I was the only one in our party who'd experienced the trials. The rest of them were all knights guarding the palace before the fall."

"How old was he?" Grymjer asked, a nervous tone underlining the question.

Barthélemy huffed. "He was fifteen," he answered, taking another bite of his apple. "He was a squire, a pretty good one, honestly. Had he been older, he'd probably be a better fighter than his uncles," he kicked himself off the shelf, standing upright and stretching. "But it doesn't matter now; what's done is done."

Evan looked to Myrkor and Grymjer, who returned similar expressions. Each of them unsure how to ingest the idea that this Rehnar Cleric was unfazed at the idea of someone in his party, let alone a teenager, dying.

"What did it do to him?" Myrkor asked, a suspicious stare crossing his brow. "You said he died, but when we were in there, I didn't see any enemies on the balcony?"

The scarred Rehnarian casually glanced at him, yellow eyes sizing up the large Gremling. "Each member who was defeated got sent outside. Once the last one appeared, the doors opened. And since you seem to really want to know, he was completely mutilated," he answered, stepping up to Myrkor. He rose his head to stare him directly in the eyes, a few feet above. "Each limb severed from his body, splayed out while his blood pooled beneath him and shaped in the crest of growth," he paused, letting the words fully sink in. "If you plan to push on to the next stage, you should know the consequences," he looked to Elleya. "And if you decide to follow her, make sure she stays put and doesn't run off."

"We completed the trial, unlike you, Barthélemy!" she snapped, eyes filled with rage, unable to hold her tongue any longer. "After the fall, a small part of me hoped to find you," she turned on her heel. "Now, I wish you were still trapped in that room," she finished, storming off.

A slim smile grew across his mouth as he watched her leave. A large green hand snatched his collar and lifted him off his feet. He flipped his curved dagger and quickly put it before Myrkor's throat. The two held their sinister stares. Neither willing to speak or retreat. Myrkor's other hand held his hammer, and Barthélemy's knife was within slitting distance of Myrkor's skin.

"Hey! Hey!" Grymjer shouted, running to them with his hands raised. "Let's maybe start fresh here, ok?" he said quickly, trying his best to diffuse the tension. "I'm sure we can get him and Elleya on the same page."

Barthélemy lowered his knife. "There was a time I'd trust her with everything I owned. But that time is well over."

Myrkor slowly lowered him to his feet. Evan noticed the perturbed glare he gave Barthélemy meant he only released him because Grymjer asked. The whole scene had oddly created better camaraderie, knowing how loyal Myrkor was to each of them.

"Next time, keep that smirk off your face, runt," Myrkor growled, shoving his hammer back in his satchel.

Barthélemy eyed him. "I have no quarrel with you or anyone else in this party, but you need to know the real motivations of the people you place your trust in."

Grymjer stepped forward, extending a hand.

Barthélemy's back stiffened, unsure what to make of the sudden friendly gesture. "You wish to introduce yourself?"

Grymjer nodded. "I'm Grymjer, he's Evan, and your new best friend behind me is Myrkor."

Barthélemy laughed, then sighed. "I appreciate your attempt at levity, but I'm returning to the surface. You can ask Elleya why I won't join you."

Grymjer held his arms out. "After everything that's happened to Yohme, old grudges aren't worth keeping. Whatever score you have to settle with her, is it really worth it? Even at the cost of finding the gift?" he stepped forward, raising a finger at him. "We're the only two groups to beat the first trial. I'm sure we'd reach the final stage with ease having you in our party. And I assume you have the same thoughts on what to do with once it's recovered," he pointed up to the ceiling. "I know with the factions breaking out among the Aurelie clerics, it won't be easy to find others to join. And since you had a party of non-clerics before, I bet you'll be forced to cobble together a worse group than the last."

Barthélemy ran a finger along his chin, pondering his words. He pointed a finger at Grymjer. "You should be a merchant up there," he answered, a plain tone returning quickly after his moment of laughter earlier. "You clearly know how to bargain. However, I'm afraid I could never trust her," he turned back to Myrkor. "You clearly seem capable of delving to the farthest stages, but understand that even with the state the surface is in, it's safer up there than down here," with that, he strode from the room, leaving the three of them to contemplate what they'd just witnessed.

"Damn," Grymjer said, hands on his hips, staring at the floor. "He could really help us survive down here."

"He's not worth it," Myrkor interjected, glaring at the doorway. "Anyone who takes pleasure in seeing pain on their friend's faces isn't someone we want, no matter how skilled."

Evan patted him on the shoulder. "I have to say, it was pretty cool seeing you lift that guy with one hand. I'm sure Elleya will appreciate you defending her honor," he finished with a laugh.

Myrkor tilted his head. "Something about that devilish smile made me want to slap it off his face with my hammer," he shook his head and shrugged. "But Grymjer here saved us from wasting time and energy fighting the living."

"Let's go find Elleya, I'm curious to know more about him," Grymjer added. "If we run into him again, he may be even more hostile."

Evan rubbed his chin, mind reminiscing about conflicts within his own squads as a palace guard. "While I agree with you, I think it's best if we leave that wound alone for a bit."

Grymjer took a deep breath but said nothing. Silently acknowledging Evan was correct. The three of them walked into the hallway, back to Kellen's position, watching the door. He'd finished sharpening his large blade and was holding it up to inspect it against the light. Elleya now sat on the bench he'd once occupied, using the same whetstone to sharpen a few arrowheads.

"Heard you got some decent potions," Kellen said, whipping the sword in a circular practice slash. He then shoved it into the sheath behind his back. "You ready to hit the next stage."

"Are you ready, Elleya?" Evan asked, a soft expression on his face.

She sat stoically for a moment, then tossed the arrow she'd sharpened into her quiver. She stood, slinging the quiver onto her back. "I take it Barthélemy isn't going to join us?"

"Would you want him to?" Myrkor replied quizzically.

"I'm not sure," she replied. "He seems to have changed since we last spoke, but when he looked up and saw it was me…"

The group watched her eyes turn reflective as they started to water.

She shivered, shaking her thoughts free, returning to her usual steeled resolve. "It's not going to happen, so there's no need to waste my breath debating what could be. We should get going."

Kellen shrugged, following her into the room and up the stairs. Myrkor, Grymjer and Evan eyed each other knowingly, then followed them to the balcony.

CHAPTER SIXTEEN

SEPERATE WAYS

THROUGH THE MIST in the arched wood frame, they could see a stone path lined with hedges. They'd stood on the balcony, observing the door to the next stage. Unlike the ones before, what lay beyond changed after a few seconds. One moment, it was a dock resting over a river. Another minute later, it was a different scene.

"Any idea what's next?" Evan asked Elleya.

"Let's enter at once so we don't get split up," she answered.

"I don't think it's wide enough," Myrkor objected.

Looking back, Evan sized him up. Returning his eyes to the doorway, he was right.

"It's cycling through the same set of places," Grymjer said, hand on his chin as he watched the mist.

"Alright," Kellen said. "Let's all just pick the same spot."

"I'd suggest the dock," Grymjer replied. "I think it's the best of the five."

"What else has it shown?" Elleya asked.

Grymjer held up a hand, counting each one out on a finger. "There's the hedge maze we first saw, an overgrown orchard, a bridge in front of a castle, a garden filled with statues, and the dock."

"What's your reason for the dock?" Evan asked.

"It's the only one that doesn't have a menacing presence. The rest of them appear like they were grown in a graveyard," Grymjer answered.

Ellya leaned close, watching the scenes as they disappeared from one to the next. "I don't see any patterns or ties to Duraté. And you're right that the dock seems the calmest."

Myrkor crossed his arms. "Do you think that's a trick to make us choose it?"

"I don't believe so," Elleya answered. "We wouldn't have been able to see through before the fall, so having the places change was the original test. Cleric packs would have gone in and been separated without knowing beforehand."

Kellen waved. "See you at the dock," he said, stepping through.

Grymjer and Elleya both stepped forward at the same time, then stopped. He waved politely to let her through first.

"Wait..." she said, holding a hand against the glowing black fog. "It's gone!"

"What's gone?" Evan asked, looking over her shoulder.

"Only four remain," she replied, her tone sinking.

"Let's go in together; we can both fit," Grymjer said, waving her to follow. "We can't leave him in there alone."

She gave him a knowing glance, and then they both stepped through the mist. Grymjer was allowed passage, but Elleya was spat back onto the floor. She scrambled to her feet and leaped into the fog without a second thought.

"Five places for five party members," Evan said coldly. He slapped Myrkor on the arm. "I'll find you on the other side," he finished, running ahead.

Myrkor slowly approached the fog, seeing the only remaining option was the bridge leading to a castle wall. "Let's see what you got, Duraté," he mused aloud, stepping through the threshold.

Grymjer grunted, head ringing as he pulled himself up from the stone slab. His vision shook a second longer before two became one, allowing him to see ahead. Staggered stone squares were inset throughout the ground; on either side of him was a tall green hedge. It was the only bit of color around, as everything else was a murky shade of black or gray.

He turned his hips and seated himself on a patch of soft black grass between the stones. Far in the distance was a single tower reaching well towards the sky. A single beam of soft light dropped down and kissed its roof, which was flat and lined with juts of stone.

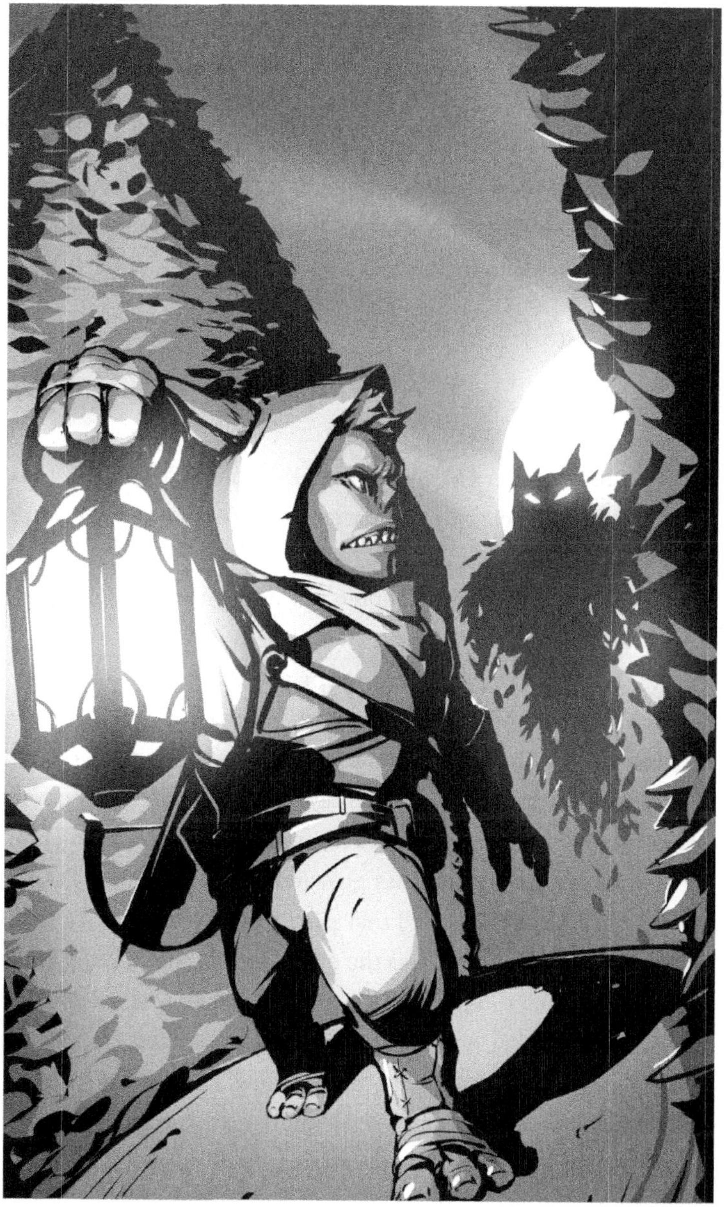

Understanding the goal given, he got to his feet and paced forward. There was no deviation or choice to his path yet, only straight ahead. He unclipped the small lantern on his belt and held it up, looking for any sign of danger.

After several yards of straight path, he was met with a fork in the road; seeing nothing hinting at the proper choice, he took the left turn and continued ahead.

Looking over either shoulder, Kellen didn't see any of his party members. The magical misty entrance disappeared, and after waiting several minutes, it didn't return.

"Pssh," he scoffed. "Should've known it would split us up at some point."

Looking to his feet, he stood on a soft dirt beach just before the dock. He heard the soothing sounds of the river's calm current underneath it. The shore on the opposite side of the river was twenty paces away with an immense stone wall built to keep him inside. It ran from the ground and through the clouds. Behind him was a wall of earth with vines growing down the side. Taking another step back, he noticed that past the cliff was a ray of light descending from above. It was the only source of light in the area.

He grunted, knowing it was a sign, then walked toward the vines. Grasping one, he yanked himself up and started his climb. Reaching halfway, something stabbed his palm; he yanked his hand back before the spikes could puncture his skin. Suddenly, he felt the sting again and let go, sliding down the steep grade to the beach.

He dusted himself off and walked to the dock. "Guess this is the way I have to go," he stated, looking down at the running water. It was only a few feet deep, with a smattering of rocks covering the surface underneath. Laying down, he dipped a finger and noticed it had no temperature. He sat on his knees, unsure how to accept it.

'At least it's not freezing cold,' he thought, standing once more.

He tensed his body, which covered itself in scaley armor except for his head. He preferred to have the helmet section of his scales off for this trek. While it didn't hinder him much, it slimmed his peripheral vision, making it tougher to see anything ambushing him. He hopped off the dock, landing with a small splash in the knee-height river. Looking to both sides, he decided to follow the current, which curved to his left.

After several yards of trudging along, he heard a rustle ahead. On the shore was a row of bushes one yard off the river. Slowly reaching behind his back, he carefully started drawing his sword. An arrow smacked his armored hand, and the sword fell back in its sheath. He ducked and ran through the water. Had he not possessed the speed of an O'dachi, his head would've received an arrow through it. Rounding back, he rushed the shrubs, ready to assault whatever had taken aim at him. His boots left light tracks as his speed increased on better footing. Noticing a tipped-over tree, he stepped on it and jumped skyward, yanking his sword free and slashing down. As he landed, the sword sliced through something that splintered into several pieces.

Eyes darting about, he didn't see anyone. He looked at the object he'd sliced, picking a wood piece off the ground. It resembled a crossbow with shielding, but it had been placed on a stand. Not seeing any other ballista or the person who'd used it

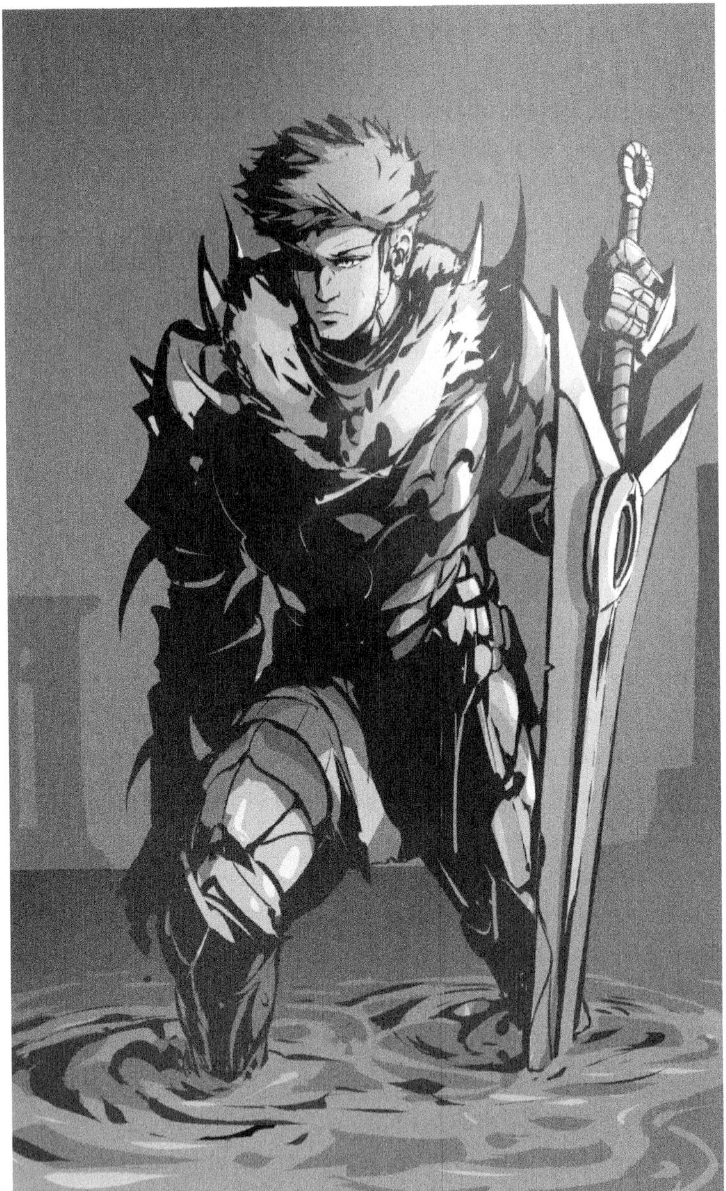

against him, he walked back to the river. This inlet was surrounded by the same vines and steep cliffside as before. He wasn't foolish enough to waste effort trying to shortcut his way up.

Stepping into the stone-floored water, he traveled ahead until he reached a new section of shore. An arrow whizzed by, which he slapped down with a backhand. Several more launched from ballistas hidden behind rows of green shrubs. He dipped his head, lunging away to avoid them. River water splashed around his feet as he darted for the shore. Once his foot hit the sand, he pushed off, but his body didn't budge. He fell to the dirt, which was sucking his foot deeper.

"What the hell!" he yelled, digging at the dark sand with his hand.

One of the ballistas turned on its axis, squaring up its next shot. He raised his scaled forearm, blocking the arrow at the last moment. More followed, causing him to tuck behind both arms. His heart raced as his foot sank deeper once he stopped digging.

A pause between fire gave him a few seconds to do something, anything, from being trapped. Throwing himself on his stomach, he crawled with both arms, hoping it would pull him free. He heard clicking as another volley was being loaded to fire. Clumps of inky sand flew through the air as he clawed his way to a nearby bush. Knowing he couldn't stay still for long, he shoved off the ground, rolling away from another fresh batch of sharp arrowheads. He stood, unsheathing his sword as he faced the ballistas.

Three small creatures wearing metal helmets let go of the handles to their weapons and faced him. They were only three feet tall with blue skin that hung from their body like oversized clothing. They snatched daggers from their hips and clanged them together, shrieking a battle cry. In one quick dash, Kellen sliced through their necks. The trio of heads all hit the ground in unison, thumping against the dirt like a dropped shoe. He sent his sword through the machines next, ensuring they couldn't be used against him.

Unlike the other land sections he passed, this one had a set of wide stairs. He took them carefully, unsure what awaited him at the top. Reaching the last stair, he was met by a wide road of bright yellow earth that snaked through a village. Eyeing the huts something was eerily familiar about them. Running his hand over the exterior of the nearest one, he noticed it was comprised of the same reddish-brown tiles of his own home. He'd grown up in a poor, nameless village several towns away from Okita. It was common for O'dachi to have remote villages along the main roads leading to the larger cities. Unlike some of the other nations in Yohme, where small villages had to move to avoid issues with the seasons or elements, his people stayed and cultivated a place for generations, refusing to yield to the environment. It didn't come without costs, as disease or starvation could wipe entire families from existence. Yet their stubborn spirit meant holding ground until the last man.

'I couldn't stay in that tiny place,' he reassured himself.

He'd been the only one who'd left without his family's permission. While his place of birth wasn't riddled with famine or malady, he yearned for the chance to join the military under their nation's king, Noshi.

Striding ahead, he ran his fingers along another tiled wall, the balance of rough and refined texture reminding him of what he'd left behind. His eyes drifted to the ground, which had the same perfectly raked road of gold soil. His shoulders tensed; his spine tingled in suspicion. It was too perfect. Whoever, or more importantly whatever, had created this scene for him knew exactly where he'd come from. There was no other possible conclusion. Kneeling, he took a pinch of earth between his fingers and rubbed it together. If this was an illusion, it was an exquisite one.

"This dungeon hasn't earned the right to mock me," he muttered under his breath.

With proud heritage running through him, he refused to be enamored with this illusion. He ripped his sword from its sheath and dashed ahead, slashing down the nearest wall. His movement had him skid to a stop just past the tiled hut, which tipped over, cascading into rubble. Dragging his sword by his side, he cut through the opposite home. As it toppled, he dragged his sword through the supporting walls of a few more.

"You dare destroy our homes and leave, coward!" a deep voice growled.

Glancing over his shoulder, he saw nothing. Attention returning ahead, he noticed a lone figure at the end of the road.

"What image did you plan to throw at me now," Kellen jeered, looking up to the sky.

The figure strode toward him. "I knew you'd lost your way, but this is beyond what I expected to see when you returned."

The glowing beam above the tower was miles away and didn't provide enough light to see who had been sent for him. He stayed in place near one of the few hanging lanterns. It would be foolish to rush into a fight with an unknown opponent.

'My dad was always such a stubborn ass,' he thought, smiling. *'But he was the best elder in our tiny little town. It wouldn't have survived so long without someone like him.'*

Kellen propped his large blade on his shoulder, chin held confidently. "You supposed to be the false ghost of my father?"

The figure grunted, stepping out of the shadow and into the light of a lamppost.

"You come back for the first time in years, and all I get is desecration and disrespect?" the figure angrily hissed.

Evan was startled, unsure how this place knew.

"Elgynn?!" he wondered aloud.

It was the spitting image of the man who'd taught him everything he knew with a sword. He'd been his greatest teacher in combat, even more than the military.

Elgynn swished a thin, curved sword half his height in an elegant pattern, displaying his capability with the weapon. He'd already cast his dark-red scales and stood just twenty paces from his pupil. The only place he hadn't enclosed himself in living armor was his head, a habit he'd passed on to Kellen. His long black braid wafted in the wind behind him. Glancing around, Kellen noticed the weather was getting harsher. A stiff breeze kicked dirt around them and brought a cold chill with it.

"I gave you the skills to keep our lineage safe," Elgynn continued, flipping his sword in a downward grip and slamming it a few inches into the dirt.

Despite the callouses he'd developed around his heart, the words still stung. Without Elgynn's knowledge, he couldn't fight with the speed and fury he currently possessed. After showing skill with a blade, Elgynn had taught him everything. Then he left his teacher behind without warning.

"It's not your place to order me around," Kellen said coolly. "First off, you're not even the real…"

"My soul is trapped here because you deserted us," Elgynn interjected, pointing a finger from a clenched fist.

"This place is meant to test us; and that's all you are, a test," Kellen retorted.

Elgynn lowered his arm slowly, bowing his head. "When the comet hit, I was sentenced to death. Or so I thought…" he looked up, eyes glowing bright with retribution. "I appeared here, in our village, and by the time I regained my senses, you arrived. I see now that Tenebri brought me back from the grave to rectify the worst mistake of my life," he yanked his sword from the dirt, swishing it overhead in one hand before pulling it down to a fighting stance. "Letting you leave."

Kellen grabbed his sword's hilt in both hands, drawing his weapon in front of him. He staggered his feet, ready to attack or counter. "Keeping me here wasn't up to you. It was my choice to make."

"You believe my knowledge was yours to steal?" Elgynn replied in a low, hostile tone.

"You gave it to me, and it's kept me alive even after society crumbled," Kellen answered.

Elgynn nodded. "I see. You're still among the living. Tenebri must be behind this meeting."

"This is Duraté's dungeon," Kellen interrupted. "You can crow about decisions from the god of knowledge all you want; it doesn't fool me."

Elgynn's eyelids tightened, face contorting into a mixture of contempt and acceptance. "Face me here and see for yourself if I'm merely a hallucination."

Kellen kicked off the ground, dust spinning behind him. His hefty bone blade clanged into Elgynn's thin sword, which he held in a horizontal block. The two stood, shoving against the other, seeing who would yield. After no reprieve was given, they hopped back, each establishing a new position.

Elgynn raced in, swishing and slapping a flurry of swings at Kellen. He deflected each one but was pushed back further with every block. Looking behind, he saw a wall closing in and leaped to his side. Elgynn's sword stabbed through a tiled hut. Kellen dove in, sword positioned overhead, and stabbed down at his distracted opponent. Elgynn threw his arms together and caught the sword between his scaled forearms in a cross-block. He kicked Elgynn in the stomach, sending him rolling back. Diving in, he readied his sword overhead in two hands, looking to slash down through his torso. Elgynn twisted and rolled on his side as Kellen's blade slammed into the dirt. He kicked the sword, sending it spinning away. Kellen kneed Elgynn's chest, which was met with a loud groan. He reached back, snatched his master's sword from the wall, and yanked it free.

Turning back to him, he swung down, looking to strike his unarmored neck. Elgynn tucked his chin and dodged the blow. He tried scrambling to his feet, but Kellen continued his attack, sending slash after slash and each time looking for the vulnerable spaces where his scales weren't. One strike for the neck, one under his arms after he tucked his face behind them. But Elgynn outmaneuvered each one.

'He fights just like him,' Kellen thought. *'I've got to do something he won't expect.'*

Kellen changed his stance, going for a stab instead of a swing. Elgynn pivoted and punched the side of the weapon after it came down, knocking it free. Kellen leaped back, knowing he needed a moment to reassess his strategy. He watched Elgynn carefully as he stood, neither willing to blink.

"I thought the military might make you better, but it's only taught you poor tactics," Elgynn stated, rolling his neck and arms. "To think, I sat all those years on that boulder with you. Looking over the farms and imagining how you'd take my place," he shook his head. "A pity you'll die here. At least it means both our souls will be free."

Kellen smiled, scratching the back of his head. "You shouldn't have brought that up," he said, a slight chuckle of overconfidence in his tone.

Elgynn glared, crouching and pulling his arms back, fist ready. "Now, you mock my teaching?!"

He lunged for Kellen, throwing a wide punch for his jaw. Kellen dipped and threw up a hand, deflecting it. The two exchanged fists, each blocking and ducking them perfectly. Their speed and precision gave them the appearance of an inky blur, two crimson brushes splashing paint across a canvas.

A fierce barrage of straight punches eventually caught Kellen. The halt of his sharp movements sent him rocketing back, ripping dirt and grass from the ground in his wake. His lungs heaved, but no air came. Mouth gaping, he held his chest as it thumped in bold pain. Elgynn stalked toward him, collecting his sword off the ground. Kellen flinched, covering his head in scales. They came to a point near his mouth, looking like a dragon's snout.

Elgynn paused. "You dare betray this fight by hiding your face? That tradition is only shown to enemies outside our race."

Kellen continued his retreat, slowly crawling away on one hip. Each pull taking a monumental heave of effort. It was the most common end to an O'dachi fight. Whoever took the first hit at their intense speed – even covered in armor – never survived the next one. Elgynn loomed over him now, sword held high and pointed down towards his chest. A direct stab with that weapon would slice between his scales, piercing his heart and leaving him for dead.

"Y…y…you really shouldn't have said that…" Kellen finally gasped between bouts of heavy breaths to refill his lungs.

"I have no more answers to give you; quit stalling and take your death in pride. At least hold to that tradi…"

"We sat on a log, not a stone…" Kellen blurted out. "You aren't him, so I won't show you my face in death."

Elgynn's eyes grew as wide as the mouth of a cave, grip on his sword softening. "You lie…"

SHUNK!

Kellen's heavy blade plunged into Elgynn's unprotected neck. He staggered back, blue, murky blood plummeting from his throat. Falling to one knee, he threw up an arm in a vain attempt to beg for Kellen's help.

Still recovering, Kellen stabbed his sword into the ground, using it to pull himself to his knees. He leaned against it, chest calming from its heaving to a slower, steadier rhythm.

"I'll give you credit," Kellen mocked, looking to the sky. "You really had me until that slip of the tongue."

As he swallowed, his throat burned, causing him to squint against the harsh pain. He told himself the tears welling in his eyes were from the injury to his lungs and not spilling up from his heart.

CHAPTER SEVENTEEN

MAZE OF THE MOON

After the fifth dead end, Grymjer wasn't sure if solving the maze was the actual goal. He scratched behind his ear, looking at the hazy orange light in the distance from the beam. It softly bathed the landscape in an eerie hue that made everything seem like it was on the verge of necrosis.

He ran his hand on a nearby hedge, inspecting it. It didn't have needles or anything that appeared capable of harming his skin. He clipped his lantern back on his belt and pulled a pair of rough leather gloves from a pocket on his outer thigh, then slid them on tight. He grabbed a section of thick roots behind the leaves and shoved his foot against the side. Pushing his bare foot against it, it felt capable of holding his weight. He jerked himself forward, grasping another bunch with his free hand then continued the sequence until he'd climbed to the top.

Carefully reaching his feet, he took a few practice steps, ensuring it could hold him. After some hard stomps and a few hops, he discovered it could bear his weight.

"If this damn dungeon wants to play tricks on me, I'm not above using a few myself," he said with a smirk.

Looking ahead, there was a layer of thick fog floating above the section closest to the tower.

"That's my clue," he noted aloud, crunching along the top of the hedge.

He followed each section until it allowed him to turn; a few times, he had to leap from one part to the next. Despite the shortcut he'd found, the end was far from his position. After a few minutes marching towards it, he looked over his shoulder, noticing the area he'd been wandering in for at least an hour was only a quarter of the entire maze. He huffed in approval of his decision and forged on, making his way towards the tower.

He paused, believing he'd heard the sound of rustling leaves behind him. He perked an ear, silently waiting, but after not hearing another disturbance, he continued. Met by another gap in his path, he took a step back, judging the distance. It appeared the same width as the last one he cleared, so he took two long strides before leaping across, landing on the massive greenery with a loud crackle as a few thin branches snapped under his knees. He heard the rustling again, but this time he saw something to accompany the sound. Green leaves swirled up from the hedge, forming an object inches away. The foliage whirled in a circular orb, eventually floating down gently in one big lump with four legs.

The green leaves continued swirling above the makeshift limbs, forming the body and head of a wolf.

"Of course, it made something to eat me," he cursed.

It tilted its mouth to the clouds above, howling. His ears perked as more rustling sounds from every direction followed. Reaching behind his back, he snatched his crossbow, which had a bolt ready, and fired it at the closest one. It landed right between its eyes, making the beast's body puff apart in a whirling oval of fronds. Charging forward, he heard snapping and barking as he ran straight through it. He glanced back, watching the cloud return itself to its canine shape.

He raced on, jumping gaps when needed, not embellishing a moment to see if he'd put any distance between himself and the creatures. Gritting his teeth, he pushed on despite the sharp stabs in his shins after landing leaps and the fiery ache with each breath. Deep in the pit of his stomach, he knew it would catch him, but he'd press on until he used every scrap of strength he had.

From the corner of his eye, he saw something bounding from his right, hurdling in the air from a section one yard away. Dropping to his belly, it sailed overhead, splashing against the stone and grass in a puff. He didn't wait to see if it would reform, knowing the answer. His eyes grew bright with hope as he saw what lay ahead.

"Only two sections to clear!" he yelled gleefully.

Bounding over the first gap, once his feet touched the turf, he tucked and rolled. His momentum put him back on his toes without breaking his stride as he raced down the straight section.

'Last one,' he reassured himself, seeing a break in the hedge wall ahead.

At his current pace, it was only ten seconds from his grasp. Rustling echoed to his right, and he slowed a bit, knocking another arrow to defend himself. His ears stiffened as the sounds of scrapes and flurries of wind drew closer. A hedge-wolf lunged for him, making him stop his run and turn to shoot it. The leaves puffed apart and flew past him, no longer in the shape of a menacing fanged beast.

Pivoting back, he started again but was too late, as another one dove in his direction. It smacked his side, sending him tumbling off his perched position to the ground below. Sticking out his arm and leg just in time, he was able to roll through, taking some steam off the pain of falling ten feet to the ground. Eyes darting ahead, he could see the glowing exit just over ten feet away. Scrambling upright, he pushed on, ignoring the searing pain stabbing his ribs.

Ten feet.

'C'mon, you can make it.'

Seven feet.

Tingling fear ran under his skin, hearing the predators gnashing at his heels.

Five feet.

He reached out, hand extended to the warming glow of safety.

Three feet.

"I can't die here!" he yelped as the pinch of a sharp bite snapped his heel.

He fell, smacking against the ground face first.

One foot.

He clawed at the stone slabs with gloved fingers, using every bit of energy left to finally reach the end.

Four Feet.

Stretching his arm, he watched as victory was yanked away. Feeling it pull him by his ankle, he twisted onto his back and kicked at the makeshift mouth. The leaves broke apart and reformed while he scooted away on his hip. He brought his crossbow out and fired, buying him a few extra moments to spend. A wave of green cascaded over him, knocking the crossbow free. It skipped across the path, landing into a bush. He looked in horror as it gobbled his weapon, ingesting it inside the large greenery. Unwilling to wait any longer, he clambered on all fours towards the glowing light.

One foot.

He could feel the comfort of its presence. Somehow, there was a genuine surge of warmth, like crawling under your favorite blanket.

There.

Standing slowly, he inhaled and looked behind, seeing the three leaf-wolves lurking. Despite being made of foliage instead of flesh, their faces gave an expression of hunger and anger. He laughed and took a step forward as hope returned to his soul.

CLANG!

His face was met with a set of thin black bars.

"What in Varkin's name is this!?" he yelled, shaking the gate. "I guess it's the same trick as last time," he mused aloud, placing his foot against it as he grabbed it.

Pulling himself up, he climbed a few steps before he saw it. Looking skyward, he realized there was something more he was meant to do. The gate had grown as he had climbed and was spread across the entirety of the maze. Exhausted, he pitifully slid down the iron bars. Throwing his back against the bars, he slumped to a seat on the floor. The wolves held their position, unable to touch him. Looking to his feet, he noticed the light coming through the gates cast a small semi-circle around him.

"I'm guessing I can't wait you out," he assumed aloud, ripping a branch from the hedge in frustration.

He threw it at the monster, which puffed apart and reformed into its leering stance. Sighing, he dug in the hip satchel on his left, which hung on his belt next to his lantern. In his hand, he had two sparkers and three potions from the previous stage, two for healing and one for stamina. The sparkers were great distraction tools and might hurt a weaker monster, but they weren't even close to his crossbow.

"I get the one place where my weapon is completely useless," he grumbled.

Rolling the sparkers in his hand, he wondered what he could possibly do to escape. Clearly, the gate wouldn't let him through until he either did something else in the maze or dealt with the monsters. Regardless of which option was true, both required dealing with the leaf-wolves. Being trapped in this tiny circle of light as predators stalked around him left him feeling impotent.

"What place do I have in this party?" he asked himself, unsure what he'd brought to the table.

The thought had been tickling the back of his mind since they reached the second stage. He hadn't been much help with the puzzles, and he certainly didn't kill as many monsters as the others. On the surface, his connections and charm brought value. Down here, those traits were inert.

"Is this the dungeon's way of removing the weakest from the team?" he wondered, looking at the hazy sky.

BOOM!

An explosion echoed across the island as smoke cascaded overhead. Quickly climbing to his feet, he noticed black air drifting high overhead, far to his left, well away from the maze.

"I hope it's a monster caught in that explosion and not one of us," he said, mind racing through what could have set it off. Taking a deep breath, he exhaled all the self-doubt weighing down his lungs.

"This isn't the time to feel sorry for yourself," he stated firmly. "If one of us was hurt in that explosion, you've got to help."

His eyes gazed up at the smoke as it grew thicker, he could see the top of a small castle structure peeking out. Its bricks appeared to be tumbling off in sections.

"Hang in there," he said. "I'm going to bust out of here and find whoever's stuck there."

Turning back to the wolves, he flicked his thumb across the top strip on the sparker ball and hucked it at one of them. It popped in a burst of bright dots, which crackled and then caught fire. Half of its leaves burned, and the other half rushed along the air to combine with one of the other remaining two. He held up his second one, glaring at his adversary. The leaf-wolf lowered, then puffed apart, forming a larger one with the second beast. It stood on all fours, close to three times his height. He swallowed back his fear, knowing he had to make his next choice free from any distractions. He flicked his last sparker and threw it high overhead. The creature watched it sail past, landing at the top of a hedge. It burst in a ball of light and flame, catching the large bush on fire. The fire continued quickly, snatching every connected piece of greenery in its fiery gust.

The leaf-wolf hopped closer to Grymjer with its back turned as it had nowhere else to go. He dumped everything from his satchel in the circle of light, leaving him with an empty bag. Racing ahead, he caught the beast off guard as his pack gathered up a chunk of its foliage. It recreated the limbs it lost and chased after him as he tossed the greenery he'd caught into the fire.

He was a few steps from the flames and could feel it lunge for him. Turning at the last minute, he covered his face, keeping it from taking his head. It snatched his forearm, sinking sharp green leaves into his skin. Before it could open its jaws for a second bite, he gritted his teeth and jumped back into the fire, dragging it with him. It howled in agony as its body was covered in flame.

Grymjer rolled out of the fiery hedge, his green skin turning a bright apple red from the burns. His clothes still ablaze and smoke filling his lungs, he staggered toward the light of safety as best he could. Each second, his heart thumped so loudly he thought it might burst out of his chest.

Fatigue and scorching skin made him fall to his knees, inches from the light. The fire had grown from the back of his shirt and pants to engulf his entire body. He limply fell to his knees in the semi-circle, and the flames disappeared, but his searing flesh didn't heal. His arm shook like a flag in the wind as he reached for the healing potion. The pain on his skin radiated across every inch of his body as he lifted the glass vial, but he fought on.

"We can't lose another," he told himself, popping the cork free with his thumb.

He rose it to his lips, thrilled for the sweet kiss of returning to good health. It tumbled from his hand and shattered on the stone. Trembling from head to toe, he felt his eyelids start to shut, his mental fortitude unable to overcome the charred state of his body. He collapsed on the surface, his head only a finger length from his second healing potion.

The young Gremling gasped, stretching an arm overhead and snatching the final vial. Rolling onto his back, he knew it wouldn't fall from his hand or miss his lips since he was already lying on the ground. He drank its contents greedily, knowing it would suck the pain from his person. White smoke hissed as his burnt flesh morphed back to a lively, bright green. Tilting his head back, he saw the gates swing open.

Laughing, he sat upright with a heavy sigh. His mind hadn't caught up to his skin and he still felt a few aches. Phantom pains were a common side effect of using a healing item so close to perishing. But none of that mattered; it was all temporary, and he couldn't hold back the nervous laughter as he was extremely grateful to be alive. The maze still burned, but any harmful smoke wafted away from the light. Gathering the items he'd dumped out, he went to put them in his pockets, then paused. The pockets hadn't survived the fire, nor had his shirt or leather armor. There wasn't anything nearby to carry them in, so he continued holding them in his arms as he crossed through the bright threshold.

A snap sounded behind him as he passed. Whipping his head back, the maze had reappeared in a picturesque state. Looking exactly as he'd found it. Eyes darting around, he noticed that the strip of land he stood on circled the tower and connected to the other areas they'd entered. Each one had a gate that clearly couldn't open unless the trial was won. His heart leaped for joy as he realized the one next to his exit was open as well. Turning his head to the tower, he noticed a door had appeared.

"I wonder who made it through first?" he asked aloud, pushing open the wood door with one hand as he held his collection of items with the other.

CHAPTER EIGHTEEN

RECOVERY

A GLOW OF SOFT CANDLELIGHT met Grymjer as he stepped inside. A long circular hallway ran to his left, which greeted him with a set of stairs when he reached the end. Continuing on the only available path, he took the stairs until they opened to a wider hallway. To his left was an opening overlooking the island. Approaching it, he looked onto the land below, hoping he'd get a better view of the explosion. A square-shaped castle was toppled in two. While he couldn't tell exactly how tall it was, by his estimation, the top half of the building had crumbled. Gray bricks spilled out on the courtyard between it and the tower. He looked to his feet, taking a deep breath, knowing he had no control of the outcome. All he could do was pray to Fira – the god of persuasion and hope – that she would be able to assist whoever was down there.

"Put in a good word to Duraté for us, will you?" Grymjer prayed, hands gripping the stone as he squinted intently for any sign of life in the rubble.

"I'm not sure Fira hears your prayers, but I can give Duraté your words," a gruff voice called in the distance.

Grymjer whipped his head around. At the end of the room was a robed figure behind a table.

"Come visit and replace your stolen wares," the voice continued, sounding like it came from a throat massaged with light-grit sandpaper.

He carefully approached the long table made of a semi-clear, solid material. Waves of blue and gold washed about inside the translucent surface.

"How did you make it this far from the square by yourself?" Grymjer asked, running a hand on the table.

"HA! I'm no merchant from the square," the voice laughed. He placed two bony hands on the table. "I'm an emissary for our god of abundance. Since you've reached this trial, she wishes to offer you a gift."

Raising his hands, he slowly panned them over the table. As he did, several items rose from the blue waves before the surface became solid again, like a shell washing on shore.

Grymjer eyed the pile of objects lying before him. Two stacks of clothes rested to his right, with a pair of boots next to each set. On his left were a crossbow and a single fingerless glove, accompanied by two bags.

"I take it I have to choose between these?" Grymjer asked rhetorically, picking up the crossbow and testing its weight.

"You can have it all if you wish," the robed man said. "Except..." he leaned closer to him, face finally visible from a cast of candlelight. His features were skeletal to the point that Grymjer wasn't sure if he had skin or yellowing bones. His eyes were beady and small, which appeared to have tiny dancing flames for pupils. "You can only take one of these," he finished, placing a bony finger on one of the bags.

Each one looked to be the size of a watermelon and had a strap running diagonally across.

"Care to explain what they do?" Grymjer asked, casually pointing a single finger with his palm up.

He wasn't sure of this creature's nature and wanted to present the friendliest demeanor possible. Especially when pressing it for information. He knew there was loot in the dungeon, and recovering it over the years was a major reason the Rehnarians maintained great power in Yohme. However, he'd always heard it had to be found rather than given.

'Likely a rumor started by them,' Grymjer thought. *'No need to share any benefits of this place with your enemies.'*

"Is there one, in particular, you're curious about?" the robed skeleton asked.

Grymjer scratched his chin. "I'm most curious about the clothes since the ones I'm wearing are pretty useless now."

"HA!" the skeleton laughed. "And to think I assumed that was your chosen clothing," he answered, shaking a slim finger at him. "I was impressed you'd made it this far with such humble gear," he slapped a hand on a pile of neatly folded fabric. "This one is much better at dealing with piercing damage: arrows, swords, daggers. Anything sharp and pointy," he stated before moving his hand to the other pile.

He paused, tilting his head up as the flames gushed beyond his small eyes. Grymjer waited and watched, squinting to better see what the eye flames were doing. He thought he could see something happening in them. Like a scene was playing for the robed creature.

"Ahhhhh!" it exclaimed, head lowering to meet Grymjer's perplexed stare. "It seems you played with fire. And quite well, I might add," it said, placing a finger on top of the boot. "This gear will keep you safe from it, even magic enhanced burns."

Grymjer's eyes grew wide. It was much better than the leather armor he'd gotten in the square. That set was decent at dealing with glancing sword strikes, as it was coated in a special lather. He'd been very appreciative to have it when they'd fought the zombies in the first trial, as it had saved him from their sharp nails. They'd swiped at him but never broken through or even cut the material. The properties this set offered were far beyond the benefit of his current clothes.

Taking the shirt from the counter, he noticed it was covered in a crisscross of bright brown and ocean-blue straps studded on the ends with brass buttons. The sleeves ran all the way to the wrist, clearly to keep every bit of skin safe from burning. He set it down and lifted the pants, noticing it was covered in the same material and pattern.

Something struck him, and he pointed to the armor-deflecting set. "Would someone be able to cut this up and use it with something else? Or would it lose its properties?"

"Hmmm," the robed skeleton laughed, bringing a finger to his chin. The flames erupted from his eyes again before returning to the conversation. "Whatever pieces remain, no matter their condition, would retain the ability to deflect edged weapons."

Grymjer smiled. "Alright, what do each of these weapons do?" he asked, pointing to the sets on his left.

"The one you held is a crossbow that you can load with several bolts held in a single tall case," it said, then hovered a finger over the glove. "This will allow you to throw fire spells."

Grymjer took a deep breath, letting it out slowly in puffs of eager laughter. "And I get both?"

"Yes. But…" it raised a finger, robes falling from wrist length to his elbow, revealing a yellow bony arm. "You can only take one supply matching it. The one for the crossbow has the cases and bolts you need. In fact, you can reach in and take them in perpetuity. However, if you chose the bag for the glove," he placed his finger on the buttoned-down opening. "You will get a few fire spells with varying effects."

Grymjer let out a long, low whistle, rubbing his chin. "So, I can have infinite bolts or several spells," he looked up from the table. "Does the glove come with a spell to start?"

The robed skeleton's jaw curved into a harsh smile at the question, appreciating his thoughtfulness. "It lets you hold a small flame in your hand, which you can't throw."

"But it can handle any spells I find in here or learn on the surface?" Grymjer asked.

It nodded affirmingly.

He ingested the answer, picking up the crossbow again, tilting it upside down to see if it came with any ammunition.

"And if I skip the bag for this, I take it I'll have to make my own cartridges and arrows?" Grymjer assumed aloud.

It nodded again.

He tilted his head, brows raising as he placed the weapon back on the table. Putting his hands on his hips, he took a few minutes to weigh his options.

"After what I did out there, I think this one's much better," he said, snagging the bag with the fire spells and setting it by his feet.

Opening it, he stared inside, noticing a few different colored flames dancing about. They appeared like a bundled multi-color campfire. Digging his hand around, he noticed it had room for other items.

"Will this only hold spells, or can I put other things in here?"

"You can fit a few items, but it's not made to carry everything. You will feel the weight of whatever you place inside," it answered.

"Will the spells burn what I put in here?" Grymjer asked.

"Not if you add them to the glove first," he replied with a smile.

Pulling on the glove, he noticed it was dotted with several of the same brass studs as the armor. Shoving his hand in the sack, he felt a surge of energy overtake him. Several images raced across his mind's eye, showing him what he could do with each spell.

He saw himself grasping his wrist with his free hand while the glove belched out a wave of green ooze. The sticky substance melted one of the crystal-eyed knights they'd fought earlier.

His mind then flashed to him creating a scythe of the same substance before slicing through a batch of ghouls.

Vision racing again, he witnessed himself curl a ball of black flame in his hand, which he threw at an armored zombie. It hit a wooden floor with a thud, but as it succumbed to the flame, the ground beneath it didn't catch fire.

Whisked to a new scene, his glove shot spurts of the same black flame, arching overhead and raining over more of the undead. They were within arm's reach, and his armor acted as an umbrella, creating a translucent shield that made the flaming orbs slide off while every enemy around him burned.

He shot back to the present, lungs sucking all the wind they could. Blinking fiercely, he grabbed the table to steady himself.

"Your choice has been made," the skeleton said, flames dancing from its eyes as it evaporated in a puff of lavender smoke.

Grymjer noticed the table was still there, but it was a plain beige marble rather than the blue and gold waves. Taking another steadying breath, he looked in his bag again. The flames were gone, and in their place was a set of four cards. Picking one up, it showed a picture of the glove making the spell. On the back were a set of words. He understood it was an incantation to attach the spell to another magical item should he lose the glove.

Dropping it back in the bag, he grabbed the other set of clothes and stuffed them inside, which took up a quarter of its space. Looking at the boots, he grabbed them but didn't put them in the satchel.

'Maybe someone can make use of them before we leave,' he thought.

Strapping the crossbow to his back, he looked around for anything else. After finding nothing of note, he strode ahead and pushed through a door at the opposite hall.

"ELLEYA!" Grymjer yelped, excitement filling his heart.

Her head whipped in his direction. "Grymjer! You've made it!"

She got up from her seated position in the rectangular room as he jogged over to her, arms extended. She clasped one of his firmly, choosing to shake it rather than hug.

"Forgot you weren't exactly the hugging type," he said with a half-smile, scratching behind his ear.

"I'm very thankful you've made it through," she replied softly, placing a hand on his shoulder. "We're the only two so far."

He ran a tongue to his cheek, unsure what to make of that. On one hand, he was proud. On the other, he was worried it meant they might be the only ones who survived.

He swallowed, deciding to change the subject. "Did you meet that weird guy with the table?"

She blinked, nodding confidently. "I did," she replied, shooting her wand from under her arm. It looked the same, but the sapphire inset on its handle and tip glowed brighter than before. "I got a few new spells and a new tunic."

He eyed her clothing, seeing it now had several glittery gold squares dotted throughout. "Did you know someone handed out gear after the trials?"

"Yes," she replied calmly. "But it's not very often that Duraté sends an emissary to assist a party. Preferring things be earned through discovery instead."

He rubbed his chin, the other hand on his hip, trying to decide if his next question should be direct or dance around his thoughts a bit.

"I'll show you something I learned," he finally said, walking over to the circle of five lush cushions on the floor.

She'd been sitting on one when he arrived, and at its center was a metal cylinder with wood inside but no fire. He lit his gloved palm and reached for a stick, lighting it before putting it back in the metal container. The rest of the wood bundle lit, creating a decent fire for the two to sit beside.

"That's extremely rare!" Elleya noted in surprise. "Usually, you're only given something to enhance what you already own."

"Well, Duraté liked my ingenuity and decided I deserved this. She also gave me new armor since my old stuff burned," he trailed off, then perked his head back up. "Was that explosion from your trial?"

"No, it was another one. I'm not sure who was trapped there. It happened after I'd reached the tower," she answered.

He swallowed, knowing he had to press her about something that hadn't sat right with him since he'd heard it. "I have to ask…" he took a deep breath, rubbing his neck anxiously.

"It's about Barthélemy, isn't it," she interrupted.

"Yes and no," he answered, taking a moment to curate his next question carefully. "The deeper we go into this dungeon, the more I see things that don't add up. I get rewards and traps we've never expected, and while you're familiar with the dungeon as a cleric, it seems like you don't have as strong a grasp as I'd expect for someone who's been with the Aurëlie church this long."

The corners of her mouth pulled in, eyes narrowing at his feigned accusations of her capability.

When she didn't answer, he continued. "When we ran into him after the second trial, he mentioned you ran away from something. Tell me, were you a deserter from the trials? And are you doing this because finding the gift will restore your reputation? Is the entire thing about Sunasa a façade? Is he just another greedy leader looking for treasure, and you concocted this grand story to lure us down here to help clear your name?"

She turned away, arms crossed, as she walked over to a stone wall lined with a shelf of trinkets.

After what felt like an eternity, she looked over her shoulder at him. "I did not enter the trials; as I said before, I took my calling in a church partnering with King Kaevir. While there, I learned from him and his officials that he'd been working with us for generations. He was the only one outside the council allowed to enter and take a bite of the fruit."

Grymjer held his tongue, leaning forward on his cushion as he listened eagerly.

"Sunasa is his brother, as well as King Noshi of the O'dachi people. Those three claim to be descendants of Bailen and another god's combined bloodline. Who the other is, history doesn't disclose. As I'm sure you're aware, Bailen and Duraté were known to despise one another. These deep-seated teachings have been passed down from Sunasa's father to him as he inherited his kingdom. Kaevir didn't believe in continuing the constant war with the Rehnarians and reached out to us," she told him.

Grymjer could tell she was being truthful, seeing the emotions in her eyes as she recalled her people's history. He continued listening as she told him more.

"After several years negotiating, they allowed him to purchase Herrgal, which sat between Sunasa and his prize, claiming the dungeon for himself," she paused, studying Grymjer's expression to see if it was worth continuing her story. Did he even care about any of this? Would he believe her or assume it was just a pile of lies?

"So, that's why they call him the vagrant king," Grymjer replied. "I didn't know he purchased that land; I'd heard he'd taken it from his brother."

Elleya shook her head. "That's a myth Sunasa has spread. The area had been fought over between the Hiroyans and Rehnar. We'd occupied the section that was sold to Kaevir."

"Do you know the price?" Grymjer asked.

"He was instructed to defend us from Sunasa should he advance again. Thankfully, the wars halted since their father was still alive and wouldn't let his sons go to war," she answered.

Grymjer shook his head. "How are they each a different race then? Wouldn't Kaevir and Noshi be Hiroyans? I know they've all lived well beyond my time in this place, but it doesn't make sense."

"It does when you know that Sunasa's father is the god, Bailen," she replied. "And he's never held a formal queen in his court. Those three each have a different mother."

"Wait," Grymjer said, putting everything together between her words and what he'd heard growing up. "You're saying Sunasa's dad is actually a fallen god? I thought the only way one could stay here is in a palace of their making, like the dungeon?"

"No, they can join the mortal realm, but at a cost. They lose much of their spiritual power and aren't able to shape the world the same way unless…"

"They build their temple in the mortal realm," Grymjer interjected thoughtfully, finishing her thought. "Is that why she never left this dungeon?"

"Yes," she answered. "And it's why she hands our leaders the gift of extended life and our holy warriors magic of her own design. The bad blood between those two gods extends to a time beyond the creation of Yohme and the other connected continents. Duraté created us and the dungeon. Bailen tried three times to create a society, which is where the Kah'zyin, O'dachi, and Hiroyans come from."

"So, the Hiroyans were his favorite, I take it?" he asked.

"They were the newest and sapped the last of his spiritual strength. If he survived the comet, he likely used whatever power he had left to build some kind of temple and save himself."

Grymjer shifted on his cushion, placing a hand on his chin as he pondered her words. "I appreciate the history lesson, as it does provide deeper meaning with your hatred of Sunasa, but to be honest," he paused, looking up at her. "It doesn't answer why Barthélemy called you a coward."

Turning on her heel, she strode to a cushion opposite him and took a seat. "I'm only hear out of my duty to the council of seven and Duraté herself," she snapped, glaring at him through the dancing flames of the fire burning between them.

"I know Myrkor and Kellen have different reasons for being here, and regardless of what your answer is, they'll probably push on," Grymjer retorted, face hardening. "But Evan and I joined you because it was the right thing to do. I saw what he'd done to that Chyterian and how he'd kidnapped Evan. If that's how he treats people he needs, I can easily assume what he'll do to everyone else."

Her head tilted, extending a palm in his direction. "It sounds like you believe me?"

"I believe you about Sunasa and his war against your people; what you've said there rings true. Yohme was stable when you and the Hiroyans were peaceful," he pointed a finger at her. "But if everything else you've said is a lie about why there are no other parties to join, then I'm leaving. I'd happily pool my resources with several groups who share the same ideals."

She sighed. "I've already explained…"

"Then tell me why Barthélemy said you fled. Is the only reason we're with you, instead of another party, because you need help getting to the gift without other clerics and reclaim your sullied reputation?!" he bit his lip as he finished, lowering his finger. He knew it was harsh to lay into her, but if they were going to continue working together, he had to know the truth.

She glanced away, eyes watery. "I have not lied to you," she answered in a hushed and defensive tone.

Grymjer swallowed, leaning on one hip in silence. He was tired and had nothing left to say.

Finally, she spoke. "Barthélemy was my oldest friend. His grievance comes from a choice I made. One that has nothing to do with my mission."

He sat upright, staring intently.

She locked eyes with him. "If you wish to know our past, I'll share it with you."

YEARS AGO

ELLEYA, AURELIA & BARTHÉLEMY

Walking down the academy halls, Elleya held the textbook tight to her chest. It was a habit she only showed when she was anxious. Her friend, Aurelia, accompanied her on their walk from the final class that day. She wore the same white and blue academy robes that split at the legs and flowed down to her calf. Unlike Elleya's red fur lined with dark brown, she had bright brown fur with white highlights.

The two had become inseparable during their years in school, along with their other closest friend, Barthélemy. The three of them planned to sign on for placement together, accompanying the council members in the trials.

"What's bothering you?" Aurelia asked.

"Nothing..." Elleya said, giving her friend a quick glance. Unwilling to share her true thoughts.

Her friend looked her up and down, clearly noticing Elleya's posture meant there was something more going on. She sighed, deciding not to press her friend further, moving the conversation forward instead.

"Are you coming to study cantrips with me?" Aurelia asked, bobbing her head towards the open library door.

Elleya shook her head. "I have something I need to do before we head to placement tomorrow."

"Alright," Aurelia replied, placing a hand on her shoulder. "I'll leave you alone tonight, but if you're moping around like this tomorrow, I want answers."

Elleya laughed. "I'm not moping; I'm just nervous for graduation." She faced her friend. "You know I can't keep anything from you. I'll share everything after the ceremony."

Aurelia smiled and gave her a friendly squeeze on the arm before heading into the library. As she watched her leave, a tiny bit of envy stung her. Aurelia was the prized student among her cleric class and didn't seem to have any fear of their eventual duty guarding the highest-ranking Rehnarians inside the dungeon. It was the only spot in the order that you could choose and wouldn't be denied. The dangerous work required massive numbers to ensure that the council made it safely to the end.

Aurelia's parents were Archdeacons overseeing an entire brigade of clerics that worked with Geneviè, the second eldest of the seven council members. She never wavered from following in her parents' footsteps, and her confidence in that decision spread to Elleya and Barthélemy, who planned to join her.

She clutched the book tighter as she took a turn down another stone-arched hallway. Her anxiousness grew rapidly as she drew closer to Barthélemy's last class. She wished, no, *needed* to catch him before he made it back to his quarters. She couldn't have the other boys he stayed with overhearing her confession.

When had it happened? When had her friendship with him grown into something more. She blinked rapidly, shaking her thoughts free from uncovering that truth. It didn't matter when it happened, only that it did. And she couldn't go into battle down the depths of that dungeon without him knowing. Her mind twisted from fear to glee, then another about-face into worry.

'I've sensed his nervousness around me, too,' she thought, assuring herself. *'And he always seems to touch my hand when he teases me.'*

Her eyes caught a hanging sign pointing to a short walkway lined with wood doors on both sides. There he was, standing with his boot against a wall, chatting with another boy from his class. His fur was an even darker shade of brown than Aurelia's, the only light bits being inside his tall ears and a tuft of white at the base of his neck. She waved to him, still clutching the book with the other hand. He caught her from the corner of his eye, then patted the other boy on the shoulder before leaving him to join her.

"Elleya!" he said enthusiastically, with a twinge of anxious laughter. "I'm so glad you're here."

He said a few more words, eyes looking to the side as he scratched behind his ear.

'He always does that when he's excited about telling me something,' Elleya thought.

"I have..." they both blurted simultaneously.

"You go first," Elleya said, running a finger along the hair behind her ear.

Barthélemy swallowed a lump of wariness away and steadied his posture. "Ok," he said, holding his hands up for a moment. "Here goes."

Elleya's heart thumped so loud she was worried he could hear it. She took a deep breath in a futile attempt to relax herself.

"You know how I've been weird around you lately," he continued, scratching behind his ear again. "It's because... well, I'm not sure how to share this since you've been my friend longer than anyone here."

Without thinking, she held her breath, unable to make any motion or movement. Her body still as a signpost.

"I'm seeing someone," he finished.

Her heart sank through her stomach.

"I know you're really protective of me and don't want me putting my feelings somewhere stupid before we graduate," he continued. The initial shakiness of revealing this to her had been broken. Everything he said after was in a joyous octave. "I know we all planned to stick together after graduation. And I think you'll be happy to know that hasn't changed."

"Wh-what do you mean?" Elleya stammered out, barely able to form syllables.

"That's the funny thing," he said. "It's someone you know. Someone you can trust with our plans."

"Who is it?" she asked, face turned slightly as her brow furrowed from the mix of pain and uneasiness.

Part of her wanted to know. The other half of her didn't want to hear it. She'd come all this way, planning every word she meant to spill, only to be struck down. However, she couldn't leave now. Who'd captured the heart of the one boy she'd been longing to confess her love to.

"It's Aurelia," he finally said with a broad smile.

Her heart flipped in her stomach as it tried to launch from her throat and onto the floor. She said nothing, using every inch of her mind to control her body from reacting.

"I know this has got to be surprising," he said, gathering one of her hands in his. As he held it, she couldn't stop her mind from darting back to all the other times he'd done this. Touched her in some way that made her feel seen. Seen in only a way love could. At least, she thought it was signs of love. In truth, it was another friendly gesture, one she'd been too foolish not to see as something more. "She told me I had to tell you before placement," he went on. "She thought it was best that we all went there without any secrets."

Her mouth remained shut, unable to respond with anything beyond an affirming "Uh-huh."

He patted her on the shoulder. "Let's go see Aurelia, she's been waiting in the library for us."

Elleya swallowed, shaking her head. "Why didn't she tell me?"

"Oh," Barthélemy replied, noticing her downbeat demeanor. "I thought it would look cowardly of me to have her do it. After all, I'm the one who asked her out. If I'm too scared to tell my best friend the truth, how can I expect you to fight alongside me in the dungeon."

She looked up at him despite everything inside her wanting to curl up in a ball and weep. "I don't really know what to say…"

"I know it's gotta be weird," he interrupted. "But come join us tonight."

Her posture stiffened as every muscle fought to keep herself standing. "I'm really tired, but I'll see you before the ceremony," she finally answered. "I'll meet you in the dining hall for morning tea."

"Great!" he replied. "My parents would love to see you again."

Barthélemy rounded the corner, Aurelia by his side. He found it peculiar that Elleya hadn't joined them after the morning events ended.

"You just have to give her time," Aurelia said, continuing their conversation. "I know it's weird for her to see us together."

Barthélemy sighed. "But she was acting awkward the whole day. My dad was upset that she barely spoke to him. I don't like the idea of her avoiding us."

"You know she's shyer we are," Elleya replied. "Anytime I watched her deal with something, she always took a day to herself before she got over it."

"You're right," he said, shrugging off his doubt. "I hope it happens soon, though, because we need her for our formation to work in battle. Our names aren't joining the maimed and dead ones etched on the columns."

Aurelia laughed. "It'll be fine. Now let's get signed up and go find her after."

Entering the large room, they approached one of the tall desks lining the back wall.

"What may I help you with?" the woman behind the counter said cordially. She was older, with a pair of glasses resting on the edge of her snout.

"We're here to sign up for placement as council guard," Aurelie said. "We wish to be put in the same collection as Elleya Béraul."

The woman tapped the edge of her glasses as she looked to the ceiling in contemplation. "Is there more than one Elleya in your grade?"

"Only a few in the younger years," Barthélemy answered, placing his dark-furred hand on the counter.

"Hmmm," the woman replied. "Well, the only Ellya that I've seen today came here a few hours ago requesting placement in the parliament sector."

The two looked at one another, confused.

"Is there any chance you can see if it's the last name I mentioned?" Aurelie asked.

The woman nodded, taking a moment to dig through a stack of papers on her desk.

"I hate to be the one to surprise you, but it's the same Elleya. Maybe someone filled out the form wrong?" she answered.

They looked at one another again.

"Let's go check on her. I don't think she's left her room," Aurelia said.

The two of them walked off at a brisk pace. Their apprehension only grew with every corner rounded, every hallway cleared, and every step taken closer to her room. Finally, they reached Aurelia's quarters. She held a hand up to Barthélemy as she went inside to inform the other girls that a boy was entering. A second later, she came out, tears streaming down her face, a single beige envelope in her hand.

"She left!" Aurelia shrieked. "This was on her bed."

Barthélemy took the envelope gently and opened it.

Aurelia and Barthélemy,

I didn't want to leave this way, but I couldn't stay any longer. Writing this down allows me to finally confess that I've loved you for some time, Barthélemy. I planned to share this with you after class two days ago. Sadly, your heart belongs to Aurelia. I wanted to follow our plan, to keep our incredible friendship as it was, but my pain would only weaken our chances of survival in the trials. I asked to be sent to one of the embassy temples in a neighboring country. Their schedules allow for frequent travel, so I'll visit once the sting of heartbreak has subsided, which I know it will. This isn't the right way to leave, but it's the only way I can process this. I know you two will be outstanding as guards for the council, and they'll be lucky to have you watching over them.

I'll visit soon,
Elleya

Finished reading it aloud, his eyes met Aurelia's, he noticed a few tears still running along the white fur highlighting her nose.

"How can she do this? Who could replace her in our team?" he muttered angrily.

Aurelia took a deep breath, leaning her head on his shoulder. "I wish I'd known; I could've done something, talked her out of this. Or at least said goodbye."

He swallowed the lump in his throat, dropping the note and hugging her back. "We can still find her before she leaves the city. We'll convince her to join us."

A thick fog rolled over the tower, and a thin Rehnar man wearing a short-pointed crown looked out from an opening at the top. The structure stood a few stories tall, and his position allowed him to oversee the group of clerics protecting him. They'd placed themselves in formation, surrounding the building.

"We will survive this and reach the next stage," he bellowed down to them. "Duraté spoke to me in this room, and we must protect this tower from destruction." He raised an open hand over them. "This abundance we receive!"

"THIS ABUNDANCE SHALL THRIVE!" the clerics shouted back in unison.

Barthélemy held a firm posture as he stood shoulder-to-shoulder with the other clerics. Despite the harsh stare he wore, his constitution inside was anything but. This was the fourth stage they'd faced and the constant linger of unknown threats at every turn was wearing him thin. He glanced to his right, catching Aurelia standing beside him. Her presence motivated him more than protecting the noble inside the tower. On her right was another cleric who had joined their pack, named Aloïs. He wasn't in the same realm of talent as Elleya. He'd fallen short on every stage so far, causing them to cover his mistakes.

'Thankfully, we're closer to the end than the start,' he told himself, noting that, at most, there were three stages after this one. *'Or just two if we're lucky.'*

Loud screeching echoed over the trees that encircled their position. The dungeon stages could take any form, and the one they happened to arrive in was a forest with a tower at its center.

After reaching it, they'd been warned of an incoming hoard of monsters. The exact scale and type of this wave were unknown. However, it was the last thing they needed to accomplish before they could set up camp and rest.

"I see one!" Aurelia called out.

Barthélemy squinted, looking for it. The creature crept through the trees alone. It was covered in blue and black feathers with a dark beak. Its arms and legs were human-like, but it had webbed talons for hands and feet. It held a spear with a single red feather hanging below the blade at its tip.

SCRAAWWW! the bird shouted.

Many of the Rehnar covered their ears from the piercing cry. The forest rumbled as a stampede of monsters charged them.

"Hold your positions; don't let them break your ranks!" another cleric yelled.

"Send a volley. Aim for their legs!" Aurelia called to her pack.

Barthélemy brought his bow forward and slung arrows at the creatures. Aloïs followed suit, but most of his arrows missed, skipping off the ground with only a few meeting their mark. Despite the issues with Aloïs' aim, the strategy worked, as many of the monsters toppled over, tripping the row behind them. Several had their necks or limbs snapped during the trampling, eliminating them from battle. From the corner of his eye, he saw Aurelia knocking several back with a blast of wind cast from her staff.

"Both of you press forward with shields on my signal. We have to break their ranks," she yelled to them over the screeching of dying beasts.

"NOW!" she commanded, waving her staff to cast a bolt of blue lightning through an oncoming herd.

Barthélemy brought the bow behind him; it affixed itself to a glowing circle on one of the straps around his armor. He snatched a rectangular piece of armor from his hip and slammed it against a socket on his forearm bracers. Metal shot from the top and bottom, creating a rectangular shield nearly as tall as him.

Now in position, he had to move quickly; their trio needed to advance behind the toppled birds so they could switch to an offensive movement. If they missed their chance, they'd be pushed back to the tower.

"Aloïs, you have to move!" Aurelia yelled. "I can finish off the ones at your back."

'Shit!' Barthélemy cursed under his breath, *'He's doing it again!'*

But he couldn't turn to look. He was already too far forward in his march. Glancing to his side, he noticed the other packs had pressed forward properly. Finally, he heard footsteps.

'Thank God he's finally here,' he huffed.

"Adjoining packs, fold in! Barthélemy, on your left!"

It was Aurelia calling out to him. He sidestepped and twisted, hoping to pull his shield up in time, but he was too late; he could feel the creature closing in. A spear stabbed through the extended arm of Aurelia as she shoved him aside. The bird monster continued its attack, shoving her to the ground. The creature rammed the spear down further, severing her arm from the elbow down. It left the spear stabbed in the dirt and reached a talon for her throat.

Barthélemy charged in, slamming the creature with his shield. Aloïs lunged forward and shoved a boot dagger between its eyes. He looked up at Barthélemy, then back to the front lines.

Barthélemy also turned his attention to the others, noticing they'd formed the line ahead of them so they could keep Aurelia safe.

"We need healers!" Barthélemy shouted.

He knelt next to her and yanked his own boot knife free, cutting a section of his shirt to wrap around her bleeding arm. Two Rehnarian men in white robes rushed to join him, running their hands over her, imbibing healing magic. The wound sealed, and they each took a side, lifting her off the ground before taking her back to the tower.

"I…I'm sorry…" Aloïs stammered through tears.

Barthélemy stomped over, snatching him by the collar. "Get back in the fight, you filthy wretch!"

He pushed him on, collecting the shield off the ground and shoving it into his arms.

"GO!" he yelled.

Aloïs stumbled forward, joining a group of men with a small gap between them. Barthélemy walked to his shield, snatching it off the ground. He took a step to join the others, then shook his head, clanging the shield against the metal socket on his belt, collapsing it back into armor. He walked over to her staff, staring for a moment at the blood splattered across the wood handle. The blue jagged jewel inset at its tip still glowed. He snatched it off the ground before marching back to the position his lover held moments ago.

"Make a funnel in five seconds!" he yelled. "I'm in position!"

A few of the clerics looked over their shoulders, seeing the young, dark-furred Rehnarian holding the staff overhead like a sword. They nodded to one another after seeing him take a readying stance, then opened their shoulder-to-shoulder formation. Their change allowed only one of the creatures in at a time. The rest of them were left clawing and stabbing at the shielded clerics.

Barthélemy lunged, jutting the staff forward. It shot a pointed bolt of light at the creature, blowing its head clean off its body. He continued assaulting each one that came after in a similar, brutal fashion—taking their lives as savagely as they'd tried to take Aurelia's. He kept the feverish pace, slaying beast after beast, until a loud horn sounded from above. He turned to the tower.

"Duraté has spoken! We've won!" the councilman bellowed.

The other clerics cheered.

Barthélemy turned from the group and raced back to the tower, hoping Aurelia was still alive.

"Did she die that night?" Grymjer asked, leaning forward as he waited anxiously for the end of her story.

"Thankfully, no," Elleya said, watching at the fire. "She lost her arm and, worse, the ability to defend our leaders in the trials."

Grymjer swallowed, unsure how to digest the way she'd ordered their priority. "Have you seen her since?" he asked.

Her eyes stayed on the fire, expression colder than before. "Yes. I came to the commencement after their group completed their delve. She told me what happened, but there was a distance in her eyes when we spoke. Before, she'd confided everything to me, but seeing her then..." she paused, crossing her arms. "She only shared the events without adding any of her true feelings. Barthélemy... well, he wouldn't speak to me. I heard he blamed me, saying if I'd been there, it wouldn't have happened." She ran a finger along the fur behind her ear absentmindedly. "That was the last time I saw either of them until we ran into Barthélemy after the second trial."

Grymjer leaned closer. "Do you think Aurelia's in the city? Maybe back in the square?"

She shrugged, arms still folded over her stomach. "Honestly, I'm not sure if she survived the comet. Last I heard, she was stationed to work in a temple near the Griln caves just outside Koln territory."

Grymjer bit his lip, eyes on the fire as well. "I hope she's still out there."

"It would take more than a comet to keep the Aurelia I know down," she replied with a sad smile.

"Do you think if Bar..."

"Please," Elleya interrupted, raising a hand. "I don't have anything more to say."

He looked to the fire, allowing the conversation to breathe. "If it helps, this seat won't be empty.

She shot a glance, eyes half-squinting in a mix of anxiousness and appreciation.

He continued. "Deep down, I've been looking for a reason to leave ever since you cornered me in that cave with an arrow pointed between my eyes."

She laughed, shaking her head. "I can understand your position."

He half-smiled, showing empathy for her. "I think I found enough pieces of your story that seemed suspicious that I created conclusions that weren't there. However," he got up from his seat, stretching. "I only ask that once we find the gift, we're going after Aurelia."

She looked up at him. "Why would you offer that?"

Placing his hands on his hips, he took a deep breath. "The way I see it, and it's one thing Evan and I understood, is that many of us lost our previous lives to the Cataclysm. Towns, kingdoms, governments, all wiped out in a flash," he said, snapping his fingers. "So, when an opportunity comes to reclaim some of that lost life in this desolate place, you better take it."

She tilted her head affirmingly. "I wasn't so sure when this all started, but I believe Duraté has brought us together."

He walked around the fire, wrapping an arm over her shoulder in a tight hug. "We'll make it out of this place with the gift. And you'll be the one to deliver it."

She laughed heartily at his sweet attempt to inspire her, letting her emotions fall from her mouth for the first time since they reached the tower. The entire time she'd sat with him recalling the tale, she'd told it stoically. Never allowing her face to soften from its stone-like presence. Calmness finally seeped in and eased her spirit. Looking up, she eyed the short Gremling, unable to hold back her beaming smile as she enjoyed the warmth of both the fire and his friendship.

CHAPTER NINETEEN

SEATS TO FILL

A **FORCEFUL BANG** rang across the sky. Evan looked towards the sound, noticing in the distance that the upper level of a castle was toppling over.

"I can't keep this up," he told himself, dodging a swipe from a large stone palm.

Four statues, at least three times his height, had come alive and attacked him for the last several minutes. He thought he'd found the exit, seeing a glowing entrance leading to the tower. However, upon reaching it, he'd been met with a black gate that sealed shut. He'd turned to see the eyes of the four statues glow with the same bright light before they commenced their assault.

"There's got to be a way to finish these damn things off!" he yelled, slashing his flaming sword through an arm.

As it hit the ground, another one grew in its place before he sliced off the other. They'd been at this dance since the fight started. Evan chopping limbs, and the effigies reforming them. He'd managed to avoid most of the heavy strikes, but one had caught him earlier, opening a large gash on his thigh that may have reached his artery. Using his military training, he'd jammed his elbow above it where his vein was to slow the bleeding, then guzzled a healing potion. It was the last one he had on him, as he'd stored the others with Myrkor.

Without any vials of life-saving liquid, he was more judicious with his counters and strikes. Dipping his head, he leaned under a swinging fist. Pivoting, he followed the arm with a backhand swing, cleaving it off. Before he could advance, he felt something slam into his kidneys, sending him skidding along the ground face-first. Lifting his chin, he saw one stomp towards him; hands clasped into one large mallet-like fist. It hammered them down, and he barely rolled away. The force of the blow caused it to fall onto its stomach. He watched as it pulled its arms close to push itself upright.

Then he saw it.

A gleaming medallion was stuck in its back. When he'd reached the gate, there had been a set of openings to its left, which he knew were meant for these. Leaping, he landed on its back and plunged his sword into its shoulder, carving an arm free. Out of the corner of his eye, he saw two of the four advance on him, readying the same hammer strikes. He side-stepped the move, and they both smashed through the one on the ground.

"Got ya!" he yelled, diving for the medallion.

He snatched it perfectly, somersaulting through and running to the gate. Slamming the piece in one of the open slots, it glowed, and the statue puffed into particles.

"One down," he said, turning on his heel and whipping his sword into position as he marched forward.

The two who'd smashed the finished one rose, while the third lumbered past them, taking harsh stomping strides. Evan jumped in the air; sword held in both hands at a low ready. His chin held high to bait the figure.

His feint worked.

Tucking his chin at the last possible second, it had missed him as he pulled his sword in a vertical slash across its torso.

"I knew it'd be in the same place," he thought aloud, seeing his strike knocked the treasure free.

His instinct was to reach out and snatch it, but he knew better. Landing on bent knee, he strategically left his head down, issuing another trick. The other two statues went to slam him again, but he was too quick, darting away as they ran into each other. Leaping on the closest one's back, he dislodged the medallion with the tip of his sword, then hopped to the other one and did the same.

Just like he'd predicted, the third one had chased after the jewel, wanting to protect its only vulnerability. He raced for the wall and shoved both in place on the slots just below the first. He turned his head back, smiling as the two evaporated into the hazy-colored air.

The last one grabbed its gem and looked at the short-horned Kah'zyin who stood before him. The way he stood with his sword covered in flames showed he was now the hunter. He took the last one down with ease, quickly finding an opening to lop its arms off and take the medallion back. He strode over to the wall and placed the final jewel.

As the statue died and the gates opened, he ran through them, eager to see how he could help. The explosion was one section to his right, and he hoped being on the winning side of the gates meant he could unlock them and go help.

He was wrong.

Facing the gate, he noticed it had the same glow as his before he walked through. To his left he saw another gate had the same bars on its exit. The other two right of his own were open.

"I'm not leaving until I know for sure," he told himself, sitting and facing the two glowing gates.

After what felt like eons, the one with the explosion swung open, and a large figure staggered out.

"MYRKOR!" Evan cheered, running to greet him.

The immense Gremling fell to both knees and then slumped onto his face. Evan realized he was littered with burns and wounds. A few on his back were very deep, and thick red blood was seeping out.

"Dammit!" Evan cursed, kneeling quickly beside him and searching for his satchel.

It was gone.

Patting his legs and what sections of upper clothing he had left, feeling for a sign that he had a healing potion.

He found none.

Evan yelled, slamming his fist onto his thigh. Suddenly, the final gate opened, and another of their party walked through. As he stepped out of the light, he noticed shaggy hair and a large sword carried on his shoulder.

"Kellen, come quick!" he called, waving him over.

Kellen saw who was lying in front of him and rushed to his side. "You got any healing potions?"

Evan shook his head. "I used them to survive my trial."

"Myrkor has all mine, so there's only one option here," Kellen replied, snagging one of the large arms and pulling it over his shoulder. "Help me get him inside."

Without hesitation, Evan snatched the other arm and helped him drag Myrkor to a door in the tower.

"Wait," Evan said. "It only lets one of us in each entrance here; I'm sure these exits work the same."

Kellen dashed away, bolting through the door of his trial. After hearing a knock on the other side of Myrkor's, Evan grabbed his dangling arm.

"I'm not taking any chances to get tricked by this place," he said, using it to shove it open.

He assumed whoever touched it was the one who had to enter. Whether he was correct or not wasn't something worth leaving up to chance. Kellen reached through and took his free arm, draping it over himself and pulling his friend inside. Evan ran to his door and rushed inside to help Kellen carry the mammoth of a man.

"The only thing I see is these stairs," Kellen announced, walking forward.

It took them a hefty heave of strength to make it up each step, as Myrkor was still unconscious and completely dead weight.

"Last one," Evan said through clenched teeth.

"Damn, it's another landing!" Kellen grumbled. "Let's lie him here, and I'll go see if one of the others can spare a potion."

"A potion is what you seek?" a gravelly voice cackled.

They turned their heads to see a robed skeleton behind a table covered in piles of gear. Without a moment to think, Kellen was in front of the trader's table.

"I'll take one," he said, hand extended to accept the offer.

"You must relinquish Duraté's chosen gift to receive another," the trader replied, waving a bony hand over a pile of neatly folded clothes.

"Yea, do it," Kellen snapped, hand still out.

"You don't want to hear what you're losi…"

"Just give me the damn potion!" Kellen interrupted.

The skeleton trader waved a hand over the gear, and it was gone. In its place was a pointy bottle with a glass stopper on top. Returning to his friend's side, he yanked the topper free as Evan opened Myrkor's jaw. Pouring the contents down his throat, they both held quick, anxiousness breaths, hoping they weren't too late. Every second was a singe of pain in their stomachs, each one a sign their friend was gone.

"C'mon, you big bastard!" Kellen said, slamming a fist on his chest.

He slammed it again and again, hoping to stir something in the ogre-sized man. Hitting it once more, their eyes grew wide as their friend began to sputter a few coughs. As the wounds closed, his lungs filled with air, followed by rhythmic breaths.

"Wha…Where am I?" Myrkor stammered before blinking slowly.

"You made it through the trial big guy," Evan said, grabbing Myrkor's shoulder in a hearty squeeze.

The green Gremling sat on one hip, rubbing the back of his head. "Are we the only ones?"

Evan shook his head. "I don't think so, their doors looked like mine after I went through. Although…"

"It could mean they died, and it reset," Myrkor said, finishing Evan's thought.

Kellen stood, extending his hand to Myrkor. "Let's go check."

Myrkor snatched his hand, a thankful smile growing across his face.

"The other two in your party are safe," the trader said cooly.

The trio snapped their heads to the robed figure.

"The O'dachi gave up his abundance for the potion, but you two still have gifts from Duraté. I suggest you don't discard them like he did."

Myrkor shot a glance to Kellen. "What's he getting at?"

Evan slapped Myrkor on the shoulder. "You were on death's door when we found you, and none of us had potions. So, when we got here this kind, creepy fellow gave Kellen one to use. However, he had to give up whatever items he was supposed to get."

"Let me exchange mine for something you want, then," Myrkor stated. "It's only fair."

"I like what I've got," Kellen replied, arms folded. "I don't plan on changing my gear for whatever this place cooks up."

The trader pointed a finger at his waist. "It seems you did take one of her creations."

The other two looked at him, noticing a long, thin blade sheathed on the opposite hip from them. Looking him over, Evan also noticed there was a pattern on his face. It was a series of slashes and lines that looked to be painted on his face.

"What did you fi…"

"Don't ask," Kellen said, cutting him off.

"Well, you want to look first," Myrkor said, gesturing Evan onward.

"Sure, why not," he answered, shrugging.

Viewing the items on the table, he noticed a set of daggers in a belt and a short sword with long, jagged spines opposite its sharpened side. Like a row of shark teeth. Next to the weapons were a set of folded clothes, boots, and an oval-shaped shield.

"Can I only choose one?" he asked.

The trader placed his hands on the two weapons. "You may take everything else, but only one of these."

Evan picked up the set of holstered daggers. "Is there something special about these, or are they just additional gear."

"Those are meant to be thrown, and whenever you do, another one takes its place in the holster," the trader replied.

"Infinite throwing knives!?" Evan said, taking one from its small sheath for a closer look. He set them down and picked up the solitary sword. "However, I do prefer a weapon I can wield with two hands. What's this one capable of?"

"It can raise those you kill to help… for a brief period of time," the trader answered.

Evan put it down quickly, almost disgusted at the thought of having recently killed creatures loping around him. He'd seen enough of the undead after the comet and had no interest in leading them.

"Why would I receive this?" he asked, confused at the massive difference between the items.

The trader's beady eyes looked to the ceiling as small flames burned upward. After a moment, he turned his attention to Evan. "Duraté believes the necro-dagger suits you better since you've shown the qualities to lead this party."

He started, wondering how she'd reached that conclusion. He never believed himself as the leader. He assumed Elleya filled that role, as the entire mission revolved around her goals. However, reflecting on the entirety of their journey, he had been influential on the party's creation. Had he not stayed, Grymjer would surely have followed him and the only reason they'd added Myrkor and Kellen was thanks to another decision he'd made. Still, the notion of becoming the party leader didn't make the idea of commanding an undead army more palatable.

"You should definitely take the necro-thing," Kellen interjected nonchalantly as he stood beside him. "Elleya has ranged abilities with her arrows; it makes sense for you to add something else to go with that flame sword," he added.

Evan bit his lip, processing his words. "Alright," he said, taking the necro-dagger and fastening it to his left hip. "What does this armor and shield do?"

"Those," answered the trader in his raspy tone, "give you two very important traits. Since you showed adeptness at being a counter striker, this armor allows you to make two sudden movements that leave you untouchable."

"Hmmm," Evan said. "So, I couldn't be cut during it?"

"Precisely," the trader answered.

"What about the shield?" Evan asked.

"It beats as the drum of the dagger," he replied. "When you use it so, it can stun most creatures with evil intent. It won't affect those you deem friendly. However, it's a trade between that and your dash."

"So, I only get one of the abilities?" Evan replied quizzically.

"You get both, but if you use one, the other becomes inert for several seconds. They cannot be used in conjunction," the trader stated.

"Is it the same for using one of them consecutively?" Evan asked.

"Yes," the trader answered emphatically. "If you beat the drum, you cannot beat it again for an extended period."

"How long exactly are we talking here? A minute? An hour?" Evan asked, arms crossed.

"Only twenty seconds of time in your realm. The weapons themselves will flash Duraté's glow when it's capable of being used again," he said, interlacing his skeletal fingers together.

"Are there limits on what I can control with this thing?" Evan asked him, holding up the spiky weapon.

The trader's eyes shot flames again as it contemplated his question. "It is something you must test for yourself. It is not an item Duraté has given to anyone since this realm's magic was corrupted."

"You mean, there might be someone out there on the surface with one of these things?" Evan wondered aloud.

"Perhaps," the trader replied.

Evan shrugged, collecting his wares and walking to the other side of the room to put on the new armor. Myrkor approached the table as the trader waved his hand over it, revealing new items chosen for him. He'd lost everything in the last trial and was eager to find replacements.

"Whatcha got for me?" he asked the trader, hands proudly on his hips. "Care to share what my choices are?"

The trader's head lowered, smiling an eager toothy grin. He pointed to a satchel that had the same look and size as Myrkor's previous one. "This bag contains a large amount of crafting equipment. You'll be able to make much better potions than what you had before."

Myrkor let out a long, labored grunt. It was something he hadn't processed yet. The entire team's additional items were lost in the last trial. He swallowed back the lump in his throat as he waited for an explanation for the second one.

"While the first bag is based in alchemy, this one has everything you'll need to create more of those explosions that freed you from the last trap. Duraté was not too fond of how you disobeyed her with your last decision," the trader scolded, eyeing him with a harsh stare. He lifted his chin thoughtfully. "However, she is always ready to reward someone willing to cultivate their own path."

Myrkor nodded to the set of hammers on the table. "And these?"

The trader smiled. "One is capable of enhancing weaponry. The other rends whoever is struck with an additional spark," he said, holding up his palms. "Think of one as a blacksmith's forge and the other as a pyromancer's lighter."

Myrkor rubbed his chin quietly for several seconds, unsure which was the better choice. "Any chance these bags can hold other items like my last one?"

"Yes, but only if they're smaller than the hammer," the trader replied.

"Hmmm," Myrkor grumbled, still deciding on which was best suited for him.

Evan stepped forward with a hand raised, wearing his new armor. It looked similar to the set he had before. However, this one had silver metal scales along the arms and boots.

"Any chance you can make something that adds effects to the hammer itself?" he asked.

The trader turned his eyes to him, smiling. "Yes, the kit inside is capable of that."

Evan nodded, pointing to the alchemy set. "I think this could be great. Considering you have more knowledge of items than anyone else in our party. Well, maybe Elleya understands more, but we'll probably never know since she only answers with two words at most."

Myrkor laughed. "Ok then, bud. I think you're right."

He grabbed the alchemy hammer, inspecting it. The head of the weapon was the same size as his last hammer, but it had a much shorter handle. Measuring it against his arm, it went from his wrist just past his elbow. He flipped it around, testing its weight, and discovered each side had a different set of intricate weaving lines.

Nodding approvingly, he went to put it in his belt, then realized he didn't have a holster for it.

"Hey, why didn't I get any armor or something to attach this to my belt?" he gruffly asked the trader.

The trader placed his hands on the table. "While your ingenuity is appreciated, Duraté believes she deserves some recompense since you eluded consequence in the last trial."

"Wait!" Myrkor yelled. "You mean I have to walk around this place in these while everyone else got brand new gear?!" he bellowed. Tugging at his shredded shirt with a thumb.

"If you look hard enough, I'm sure you'll find something during the remainder of your delve," the trader replied with a bright, echoing cackle.

Myrkor's face curled with underlying rage at being mocked. Leaning in closer, he seemed to ready himself to snatch the trader. The last time Evan had seen him get hot like this, he'd tried to wring Barthélemy's neck.

"Hey, big guy!" Evan announced in a loud, jovial tone. "How about we go check on the others? Maybe they've found something we can use to make you an even better set."

Myrkor didn't budge despite Evan tugging on his shoulder.

"C'mon," Kellen called, standing at the bottom of the stairs. "We've wasted enough time here. Unless this guy has food for us, we need to push on."

A loud grumbling sounded from Myrkor's belly at the mention of a meal. He turned to his friend. "I'm sorry, I lost our rations as well," he replied solemnly.

"I know," Kellen said. "So quit sulking, and let's go find some."

"Sulking? You rat!" Myrkor snapped, marching after him.

Kellen walked up the stairs, an air of indifference in his posture. Before following them, Evan turned back to the trader, whose beady eyes stared intently at him. He wondered if what he'd said about their journey was true. Would Evan be their party's leader? He shook the thought free, knowing it was foolish to consider. After all, what was his status compared to that of a holy Aurëlian cleric? His internal arguing was interrupted by the surge of hunger biting the depths of his stomach. Taking his cue to leave, he traveled up the steps to join the others in search of something to eat.

CHAPTER TWENTY

A NEW PARTY

Looking up at the wall high above, Sunasa's face grew an eager smile. It had taken some time to find the remaining potions he'd needed to disguise his other men, but eventually, he'd found some. They'd drunk an elixir that changed their appearance to O'dachi, which was the closest-looking race to their own. Hiroyan's – even in the current state of the world – wouldn't be allowed inside Lysgahr. However, a band of O'dachi vagrants joining a party to seek riches in the dungeon was an easy sell. Taking the potion merely shrunk their ears, adjusted their cheekbones, and made their hair slightly thicker. The benefit was that even if they passed through something that removed magical enhancements, wearing a hood would conceal their true race long enough to reach the temple.

He'd chosen his best scout, who was an incredible archer, and the best two soldiers to join him. Neither of his brothers had the constitution to survive the trials, so he knew it was better to bring capable fighters instead.

In the corner of his eye, he noticed a young Kah'zyin boy approaching, rubbing his hands together. He couldn't have been more than ten, considering his horns were still nubs. Wearing a nervous look, he barely made eye contact as he spoke.

"Sir, I came looking for payment," he said hesitantly.

The night air was still, making it quiet enough to hear his meek voice.

"Yes, here you are," Sunasa answered, waving one of his men over, who handed the young boy a bag.

He opened the drawstring and looked inside, then raised his head to meet Sunasa's, perplexed at the contents. "There's only a pair of boots in here?"

Sunasa nodded. "And you're lucky to get them in addition to what I owe you."

"I... I don't understand?" the boy stammered.

"Your payment is buried in the dirt far from here. I've marked the tree with three cuts near the roots. If you head northeast now, you should make it before someone else has the chance to notice it's there. It's quite the rough hike, and those sandals you wear wouldn't last the night," Sunasa answered coolly.

"But... my family needs me in the square. None of them are able enough to find it, and I know they won't let me go alone," he shyly protested, eyes on the ground.

"Hmmm," Sunasa huffed, a slight laugh in his tone. "Then don't bother telling them and leave now. Once inside, I can update them on your status," he leaned in close. "If they love you as much as you think, I'm sure they'll find someone to come after you and help."

The boy swallowed, taking a deep breath to muster whatever courage he had. "You can have this, and I'll take the potions back."

Sunasa unsheathed his sword from his back and held it up, squeezing the hilt. A bolt of lightning zapped the ground at the young Kah'zyin's feet. The child leaped back, falling on his hip as his eyes grew wide with fright.

"You made the deal," Sunasa said, lowering his sword so the glowing blue light highlighted the anger in his eyes. "A deal done to secure money for your ailing family. Do you lack enough conscience that you're willing to go back on your word?"

The boy sat in shock, unsure how to respond to the mixture of lecture and threat.

"Nothing to say, now?" Sunasa continued, grabbing him by the arm and yanking him to his feet. "Start walking. After the second large hill beyond this one, you'll see a row of five withered trees. The marked one is in the center," he said, pointing the boy northeast of them. "Just keep walking this straight line, and you won't miss it," he finished, giving him a firm slap on the back. "Go."

The young Kah'zyin trundled off, tears welling in his eyes as he started his hike up the steep grassy hillside.

"And put on the boots when you crest the top!" Sunasa called to him, cupping his mouth.

The boy looked back and nodded, face twisted in an uneasy grimace, not sure why he responded to his directions at all.

Sunasa nodded and made a shooing motion with his outstretched hand. The boy raced to the top of the hill and over the other side.

"It was kind of you to give him the best route," one of his men said.

"I know, Francis," Sunasa replied calmly. "Although, I marked two trees. But I'm sure he's smart enough to dig under both."

"I see Rayleigh with our contact," Francis announced.

Sunasa turned, seeing a furry hooded figure walking beside his magically disguised subordinate. Taking a long breath, he sighed away his distaste of Rehnarians. Working with one was the only way he could get inside, and if what he'd heard was true, they'd found a lone cleric looking for a new party.

If he had a choice, they wouldn't partner with any of the wretched creatures, but it was the only way he'd pass through the outer wall. Their fortunes had been favorable, as they'd gotten word of a desperate one searching to find replacements after his group had disbanded. It was the perfect mark for their plan. Someone needing help who didn't have better options. Someone who wouldn't pry too hard at their answers. He wasn't worried about his skill inside the dungeon; he just needed this cleric to get him inside the temple. Once they reached the dungeon entrance, this Rehnar became completely discardable.

'I'll finish him off myself if I have to' Sunasa thought.

As he drew closer, Sunasa noticed his robes were emblazoned with gold and red markings he'd rarely seen. He hoped it meant that this cleric was of high station or greater power than most.

"Your man here says you wish to delve for Duraté's gift?" the cleric said.

Sunasa nodded. "Yes, we migrated south from Bako after our section of town was overrun by tainted corpses."

The cleric held a harsh gaze, surveying Sunasa from head to toe. "What reason do you have to search for the fruit?"

Sunasa held his hands out cordially. "We need a place to plant roots. If what I've heard is true about the items and wealth inside, it would give us the tools needed to settle a new territory. One we could cultivate for generations."

"Where's the rest of your kin?" the cleric asked.

"We've setup camp in some uninhabited land near Lake Fera. After approval from the eldest, we received permission to come here," Sunasa lied.

The cleric squinted, leaving the air breathless and still. Tension thickened like a heavy cloud at each passing second of silence.

Finally, he spoke. "So, you plan to sell what you find to build a new life for your family?"

Sunasa nodded, a calm smile cresting the corners of his mouth.

"Hmph," the cleric grunted. "That reason is better than most," he looked each one in the eyes before continuing. "If you're actually being honest."

When Sunasa stepped forward to speak, the cleric held up a hand, halting him.

"I really don't care if you're truthful; I just need to know one thing?" the cleric asked.

It took every inch of muscle in his body to hold himself back from ripping his lightning sword free and slicing the arrogant creature's head in two. He swallowed down his rage at being interrupted by a lesser being, knowing the friendly façade was his only means to broker this deal.

"What is it?" Sunasa asked.

The cleric chuckled. "I knew O'dachi pride runs strong, but you almost had a vein burst from your neck at being cut off. Let's toss the pleasantries aside and be real about what you're signing up for."

Sunasa exhaled a heavy sigh through his nose, waiting for the cleric to continue.

"The last group had a family with them, and as soon as one fell to the trials, they fled out the first door they found," he pointed to Rayleigh. "If one of your family here gets sliced to a thousand bits, do you have the guts to push ahead?"

Rayleigh glanced at Sunasa, who tilted his head in a shrug, allowing him to answer. He turned his head back to the cleric. "We've seen plenty of death after the Cataclysm. None of it was pretty. After finding my wife being eaten by the living corpse of her father, nothing in the dungeon will deter me."

Sunasa's brow rose, impressed he was willing to divulge that. His story was not fiction or embellished; his motivation afterward made him the most relentlessly effective scout in his guard.

The cleric smiled wryly at Rayleigh's intense eyes, like a knowing parent observing a child's temper.

"I take it the rest of you have a similar sad tale to share, but I don't want to hear them," he said, waving them to follow. "We'll go to the city before daybreak, as the night watch is less picky about who I bring in."

"They would question a cleric?" Sunasa asked.

"It's not often, but enough to annoy me. One of the day-watch has an axe to grind with me and likes to make anyone I bring inside uncomfortable," the cleric answered.

"I know you had a party before; how far did you delve before they quit?" Sunasa asked.

"We reached the second trial before they turned back," he answered.

Sunasa's eyes bulged. His father truly was watching over them. He looked to the sky, saying a silent thankful prayer. Rayleigh had met with countless people who'd traveled outside the city in his attempt to make contact with one who could get them in. All of them had claimed no one had gotten past the maze. Now, his group had found the one Rehnarian who had. He halted. Had this cleric been the one who'd freed that Kah'zyin they'd captured? Did he have the map? And if this cleric was already looking for ways to get them in with the least friction from officials, they couldn't have dreamed of a better contact. He smiled, continuing to follow the cleric as they rounded the curved border wall towards the front of Lysgahr.

"We're going to enter after we pass that turret," the cleric said over his shoulder, pointing to a tower inset in the stone wall. It came to a point several stories above the wall itself.

After a few more yards trekking through the tall grass, the cleric faced them, bringing the group to a stop.

"I'll open this section here, which leads to an area just outside the square. We can get some food and discuss what gear you'll need," the cleric instructed.

Sunasa nodded. "I appreciate how prepared you are. We're fortunate to have found you. However, all this time talking and I haven't introduced myself or my brethren," he said before pointing to the rest of his men. "You've already met Rayleigh. This is Francis and Dubhán," he said before extending his hand. "I'm Riagán," he finished, lying to their new teammate, having given a fictitious O'dachi name for him and his soldiers.

The cleric shrugged casually and returned his polite gesture, putting his furry hand in the disguised Hiroyan's.

"I'm Barthélemy," the cleric replied.

CHAPTER TWENTY ONE

THE TRADER'S TRIAL

"I APPRECIATE THE HOSPITALITY, but does he have to stand there staring at us like that?" Evan asked, nodding to the cloaked figure looming one floor above them.

"He wishes to see us enjoying the abundance Duraté has given," Elleya answered, taking a bite from a large berry.

The five of them sat around a chest overflowing with food. Once all of them had reached the center of the circular room, the trader had reappeared, standing in one of several arched openings overlooking their floor. Raising his hands, the metal fire pot had disappeared, and a chest of goods sat in its place. Most of it was small enough to fit in Myrkor's new pouch, and he wasn't shy about stuffing it with an assortment of cured meats, cheeses, and fruit. He also wasn't shy about stuffing his face either. Evan was worried he'd eat everything before anyone else could reach in, but the wooden box refilled itself with more once half of it was taken.

In many ways, it was more fortunate than receiving the weapons since they wouldn't have survived much longer without something to eat. And he assumed there was very little inside the dungeon that was edible.

"I bet if we went back through one of the spots, there would've been some fruit," Grymjer said between bites of a large hunk of dry-aged steak. "I saw some trees planted in the maze, and I bet there were fish in that river you were in," he said, looking to Kellen.

"It's common to find food in sections of the trials," Elleya said. "Usually, it's not handed out like this, though. Most of the council have cultivators in their guard who scour for food. It takes a lot to feed one, and no matter how much is brought in, you'll always need more."

Evan looked to the wall as he drank water from a gold chalice. Each of them had one appear next to them as soon as they started eating.

"Has something seemed off to you about this delve?" Evan asked her.

She looked at him, unsure where he was going.

"It seems like we've been given more opportunities than usual," he continued. "It seems like she's more desperate for someone to find the gift."

Elleya took a slow breath, pondering his statement. "It may be the corruption of magic after the Cataclysm. But honestly, nothing has seemed far from what I've heard about the dungeon."

Evan looked to the trader, unsure what to make of the new weapons, armor, and food. Even Myrkor was allowed to stay despite the trader mentioning he'd somehow dodged a consequence of his trial.

"What exactly happened with that castle?" Evan asked him.

"Well," he answered after chewing through a hefty bite of smoked fish. "I had to complete a puzzle to escape. When I failed, I started glowing and heard a voice tell me I was going to be taken back to the surface," he continued, wiping crumbs from his face with the back of his hand. "There's no way I was getting sent back to the surface and leaving you guys stranded, so I put together an explosive and blew the top off!" he finished, giving a loud belly laugh.

"Is that how you lost your shirt?" Elleya asked, pointing to his shredded attire.

He grunted, unhappy at being reminded that his armor was torched. "No, I went to a safe spot downstairs, then came back up and jumped out the opening. Once I landed, I started taking lashes from something, but I couldn't see what," he shook his head. His face wore the beleaguered expression of someone who'd escaped torture. "Every step I took towards the exit, I got another one," he shrugged. "Maybe if I'd gone back, they would've stopped. But I'll be damned if I was going to quit with victory staring me dead in the eyes."

Grymjer patted him on the shoulder, a broad smile on his face. "We're glad you made it here, Myrk!"

His head snapped to Grymjer, wearing a deep scowl. "Don't call me that!"

Grymjer laughed, waving off his threat as he stepped closer to the chest and grabbed a brick of cheese. Myrkor continued glaring as he watched the jovial little Gremling munch on the savory morsel.

Evan held his chin in his hand. "You failed, and yet it planned to send you back. The second trial only took one life but sent everyone else back as well."

Elleya listened intently as Evan mused aloud.

"I just can't shake the idea that Duraté is much more eager for someone to find the All-Giving Fruit," Evan said. "Don't get me wrong, I still don't take anything lightly in here, nor do I assume we're safe. It's just something I wanted to share since we should take any advantage we can get," he looked to the trader. "If I thought he'd give me an answer, I'd ask him."

Elleya gnawed at her lower lip. "It's good to point out, but even if it's true, we'll still have to reach the end on our own merit."

Grymjer stood up, stretching. "How much longer do you want to stay on this floor before we move on?"

Myrkor stopped stuffing his face suddenly, concern growing over him. "Have any of you seen an entrance to the next stage?"

They each looked around the group, none of them able to provide an answer.

Evan stood up quickly. "Do you have everything you need?" he asked Myrkor, pointing to the chest.

He nodded back, climbing to his feet.

"Now that you've had your fill…" the trader called down in his creaky voice. "I'll see you at the bottom," he finished, cackling loudly.

His hollow laugh echoed as the floor fell, taking the party with it. Each of them fought against the rush of gravity, steadying themselves on hands and knees as the platform plummeted. Eventually, the speed began to slow, giving them time to regain their footing. It was now falling at an easy pace, enough so that they could see the walls around them. Rather than the blur it was before.

"Push everything towards the middle," Evan said, taking the large satchel he'd gotten from the trader and throwing it in the middle.

The chest had disappeared, leaving vacant space they could use. Everyone took his idea, putting their heavier items in the middle of the group.

"Over there!" Kellen yelled, pointing above.

Several armored skeletons leaped from arched openings like the one the trader had occupied. As they landed in front of him, Kellen slashed through each one.

"Circular formation!" Evan called, each member backing shoulder to shoulder with another.

"This is a good chance to try our new gear," Grymjer announced, lifting his glove as a moss green scythe formed in his hand.

Stepping forward, she slashed through an armored zombie's torso, causing it to split in two. Its upper half fell off the platform while the legs toppled over.

After dispatching with a few himself, Evan looked around to see how the others were faring. All of them were destroying the monsters with ease. It was the first time since they'd entered that he actually felt complete confidence during a trial.

Oddly, a tinge of envy poked him as he watched Elleya form a large hand from the end of her wand, which she used to smack incoming enemies away. Everyone wielded their latest weaponry except him. While he wanted to test the necro-dagger, he knew this fight wasn't the best opportunity for it. He imagined himself and the others surrounded by several clumsy zombies

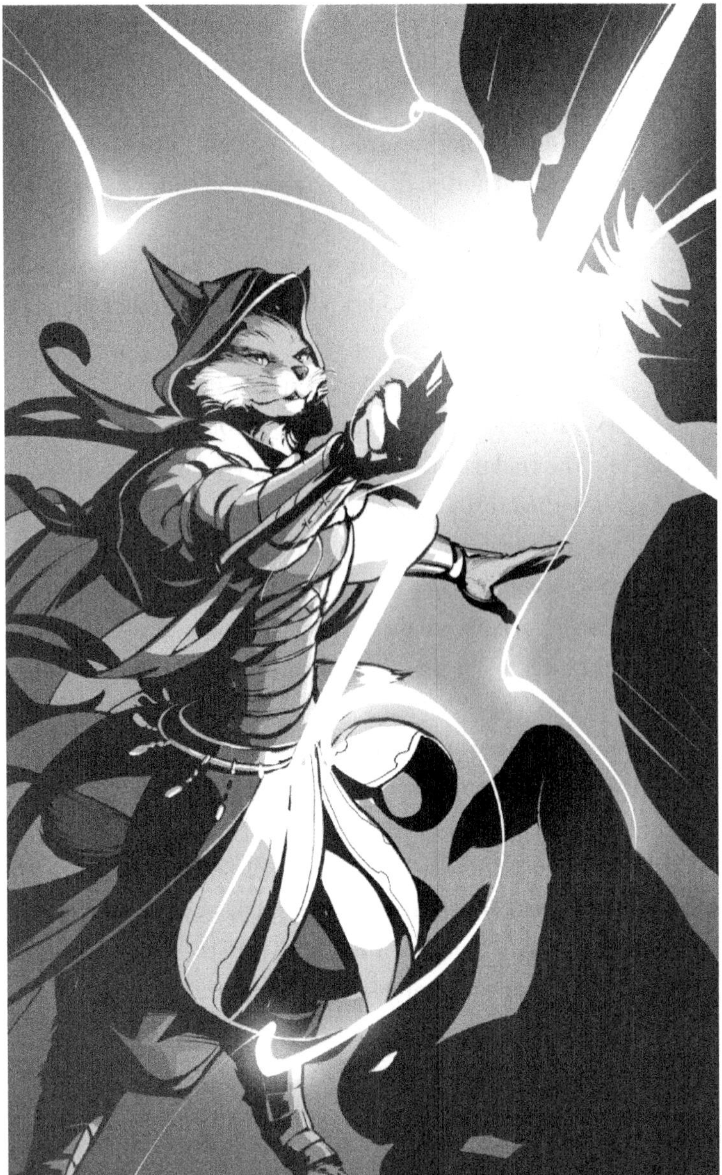

under his control. By his estimation, the floor was likely fifteen feet in diameter. Added help from undead minions was better left to somewhere less cramped.

"Damn, I wish I had my old hammer right now!" Myrkor bellowed, smacking a zombie between the eyes.

Evan bit his lip to avoid laughing, realizing his situation could be worse. He smiled, telling himself that as soon as he got the chance, he'd test out the dagger.

Sharp ringing of grinding gears sounded around them as the floor slowed to a crawl. None of them lowered their guard, even as the floor came to a stop. Undead bodies were piled underneath them. Peering over the edge, Evan believed they were at least four feet above the next floor.

"Pretty impressive!" Grymjer said happily, hands on his hips. "There's gotta be close to a hundred of those things under us."

Elleya whipped her wand about, a cloud of blue dust cascading over them. "This spell removes anything poisonous that might be on your armor."

Myrkor raised an eyebrow, crossing his arms. "That's quite the spell they gave you."

She smiled. "I'm very thankful for it."

"It looks like there's a few rooms down this hall," Kellen said, hopping from the platform.

Elleya grabbed her items from the center and joined him, wanting to see what came next. The other followed soon after and were met by a long hallway with a few wooden doors on either side. The walls were made of dark rocky surfaces, like the inside of a cave. It was a stark contrast to the organized stone or exquisite marble buildings they'd been in before.

"Maybe we'll find you a new shirt, Myrkor," Evan chided, opening one of them.

"Hmph," Myrkor grumbled. "Whoever finds one my size gets first choice of food."

"Deal," Evan replied, walking over to a chest and opening it.

"Hey," Grymjer called, waving Myrkor over. "I've got an idea.

As Myrkor approached, Grymjer held the door open for him. Inside were several pieces of clothing and equipment laid out on a long table.

"I got an extra armor set," Grymjer said, pointing to the table. "And I know Evan kept his spare. So, you should test out that crafting kit and make something with them."

Myrkor rubbed his beard, pondering the idea. "I did want a chance to test this thing out," he said, placing the pack on the table next to the clothes.

Talking to himself, he pawed through the bag, lifting a few pouches and vials and holding them up to read their contents. After several minutes of digging, he had one tiny leather purse and three small glass bottles lined up.

"Ah, I knew they had to have one," Myrkor said, lifting a short, curved knife with a sharp hook on the end. "There's no way I could make this work unless we had an alchemist knife."

Kellen walked in, having finished inspecting the other rooms. "I didn't get anything useful in the other rooms. I'm guessing you found something?"

"He's going to make a new set of armor," Evan said.

Kellen huffed. "He's decent at mixing potions, but he can't forge to save his life…"

"Hey!" Myrkor objected. "I helped fix that sword of yours the last time."

"Only because I needed your big hands to hold it in place while I used the forge stone," Kellen replied.

"Since you're so good at critiquing my work, you should teach me some of your tricks here," Myrkor retorted. "This kit was given to me, so I'll have to be the one to use it," he looked back at Kellen. "Even if it's blacksmithing."

Kellen smiled; eyebrow raised. "I'll be sure to teach you a thing or two, Myrk."

Myrkor frowned, turning back to the table. Evan nudged Kellen, giving him a knowing stare to take it easy on the big guy for a beat. Kellen rolled his eyes but retained his half-smile, approaching the table next to his friend.

"Did your set have magical enhancements, too?" Kellen asked, looking at Grymjer.

"Yes, mine was built to withstand any sharp weaponry from piercing it," Grymjer answered.

"Alright," Kellen said, lifting up the chest plate to study its makeup. "You'll definitely be able to retain that skill no matter how you carve it up with the alchemic knife. But, saving that shield ability Evan had will be a fifty/fifty chance at best. You'll want to use the least abrasive chemical first, then work your way up."

Myrkor looked at him. "That defies the conventional wisdom of potion craft. The light ones will be canceled out by the stronger ones."

Kellen placed his hands on the gear. "You let me handle it that way at the shop."

"If I had known..." Myrkor grunted.

Kellen held a finger up, politely interjecting. "It's what I learned blacksmithing for the military. It's something we don't share with normally share with others. But since the world's come to an end, I think I can trust you four with that secret."

Evan puffed a short laugh. "Considering he's made armor that allows scales through, I'd trust him, Myrkor."

Myrkor shrugged. "That's a fair point," he looked over his shoulder at Evan. "You want to add your spare set to the pile?"

Evan walked over, slinging his shoulder pack off and emptying its contents on the table. Myrkor took the shirt, pants, cuffs, and boots, laying them out orderly.

"I bet if we take a piece of each section, we can keep that shield skill," Myrkor said, surveying one of the boots.

"It's the best shot since you're obviously not fitting into these," Kellen replied, running a finger along the metal sections of the chest plate.

Myrkor opened the small velvet purse and sprinkled some dust on the alchemic knife. "Let's make me some new armor."

CHAPTER TWENTY TWO

ADVANCES

After completing the second trial with ease, Barthélemy was becoming impressed with his new party members. He'd assumed these O'dachi had some combat skill, as he'd heard all their men were instructed in basic sword fighting. However, they were polished well beyond his expectations. They also had a knack for understanding group placement in combat, and the most vocal of their family had strong instincts with the puzzles.

'Riagán must clearly be a leader back home,' he thought, musing how these men fit into the dynamics of their family on the surface.

He didn't spend too much time wandering down that path, knowing the closer he got would only lead to pain. Or worse, making a mistake that cost them a trial. Standing in front of the next entrance, he took a moment to process what he witnessed. It flashed several locations, all of them appeared to be in the same place, since they all had the same color foliage and overcast glaze to their sky.

"Which one do you think is best?" Sunasa – still disguised as Riagán – asked, pointing to the shimmering visions of the next trial.

Barthélemy rubbed the side of his neck, squinting in concentration. "None of them show signs of being advantageous over the others. We should see if it will let us go in groups. If you and your men want to choose which pairs you want, I can go ahead."

"Which one would you take?" Sunasa asked.

Barthélemy shrugged. "I'll take the garden with the statues. I assume it could have a puzzle requiring knowledge of Rehnarian history."

"Hmm," Sunasa grunted affirmingly. "I think you're right. Rayleigh and Francis will take the maze and I'll go on the bridge with Dubhán."

"See you on the other side," Barthélemy said over his shoulder.

"Wait," Sunasa said, holding up his hand. "Do you think that other party you mentioned is there?"

Barthélemy halted, then turned to face him. "I'd imagine they'd be close to the end by now, but if any of them are still alive, I don't believe they'll be hostile."

Sunasa's eyelids narrowed. "How can you be so sure?"

Barthélemy replied, "As I said before, I ran into them on this stage and they weren't looking for a fight. I got close to combat with one, and the others looked to diffuse the situation," he sighed. "Their easily gained trust will be their downfall. The dungeon looks to exploit your weakness, not coddle it."

Sunasa bit his lower lip. "If I tell them we know you, will that increase our chances that they'll be friendly?"

Barthélemy nodded. "I believe so," he said, throwing his hood on and turning to the fog.

The four deceitful Hiroyans watched him as he passed through to the next trial.

"Is that the actual plan?" Rayleigh asked in a low tone, stepping close so Sunasa could hear him. "And should we deal with him after the trial?"

"I've changed my mind," he replied, looking to the fog. "Considering that other party he mentioned reached this stage, we should use his expertise as long as possible."

"What if our true race is revealed?" Rayleigh asked.

Sunasa held up a finger. "There's four of us and one of him. He's quite the fighter, but not enough to deal with us. His knowledge will be paramount in catching up to that other party, if they're still alive."

"Well," Rayleigh replied. "I can go with Francis now."

Sunasa extended his hand in front of him, halting his path. "I believe there's another trick to this. Look at it now."

The other three stared intently as only four scenes took turns appearing and disappearing in the mist cloaked doorway.

The Hiroyan going by Dubhán stepped back, posture straightening. "It's going to make us take each one on our own!?"

Sunasa laughed. "It seems so."

"We should still try one together," Rayleigh said, slapping Francis on the shoulder in a sign to join.

Sunasa shook his head. "Feel free to try, but I can already tell that it wants us to have one each. There were only as many locations as there were members of our party."

"But didn't the Rehnarians march armies through the entrances before?" Rayleigh objected.

Sunasa pointed to the mist. "I'm sure it would have adjusted in some way to separate large groups. This Dungeon was the creation of a living god, our limitations do not apply here."

Rayleigh sighed, approaching the arched entrance.

"I'll enter the maze," he said, speaking to the ceiling.

When it answered his request, he turned and saluted the group before stepping through.

"Hmph," Sunasa huffed. "Good to know we don't have to wait for a particular one."

He stepped forward, frowning in consideration as the locations shimmered in front of him. "Actually, I'll take the dock," he stated, stepping through the threshold.

In a flash, his body fell to wet shore. It was dark and gritty, with large pebbles rather than fine grain. Turning in a circle, he noticed a beam of light descending onto a tower far from his position. A cliffside covered in ivy stood between himself and the tall building. It was clearly the destination, and if he were lucky, he might find some of his soldiers along the way. Approaching the vines, he grabbed and pulled, testing if it would hold his weight. He waited for several minutes, further assessing it for tricks. When something poked his skin, he yanked his hand back, understanding it was another mirage.

"Alright," he said, looking over his shoulder to the river rushing underneath the dock. "It clearly wants me to take that path instead."

Standing at the edge, he knelt down and ran his hand along the water's surface, noticing it was neither cold nor warm.

"What a peculiar place," Sunasa noted aloud.

A sloshing sound licked across the river a few yards away. Looking up, he saw an armored corpse climbing to its feet. He drew the lightning sword he'd taken from Evan and squeezed the hilt. A few bolts snapped from the blade, electrifying the water. The corpse-knight jittered about as the current ran through. Its skin eventually cooked; it fell with a splash before it was washed away.

Eyes focused ahead; Sunasa waited as more of them came trudging across the river. Using the same technique, he burned through the small group. Once they floated away, he stepped into the river and sheathed his sword. Retrieving two daggers from his hip holsters, anticipation tingled up his spine. Seeing a few more corpse-soldiers waddle through the knee height water, his anticipation grew to excitement. Solving puzzles and traps didn't fulfill his spirit like dispatching an enemy face to face. He stalked toward the creatures, eager to unmake them with his own hands.

CHAPTER TWENTY THREE

THE TRADER'S SERVANT

"Looks like you're not the only one who can make a decent set of armor," Myrkor said, turning his arm to form a translucent shield.

After an hour working with his new crafting kit, he turned the extra sets of clothes into a sleeveless shirt and padding for his thighs and knees.

"Hmph," Kellen replied, rolling his eyes.

Clearly his assistance helping Myrkor make the set had gone unseen.

"Good tips with the potion order," Evan said thankfully, patting Kellen on the shoulder. "With him adding a shield, I doubt we'll be defeated in the dungeon."

Kellen eyed him, nodding appreciatively before walking to the door. Evan watched Myrkor practice a few strikes with his hammer while holding the tall shield. It seemed to adjust its height to fit the wielder, as the shield covered Myrkor, despite him being much larger than Evan. He'd also enhanced his hammer with frost magic. They'd debated which of the many elixirs and potions was best, and finally decided being able to slow or freeze enemies gave them the best tactical advantage. It was also an element in their group that none of the other party members had.

Finished trying out his new wares, Myrkor strode proudly from the room, eager to test them in battle. The other three followed, exiting into the long hallway. Trekking ahead, Myrkor and Evan took lead in the formation, flanked by Elleya and Grymjer, while Kellen watched their backs. They'd decided on this setup as the best way to travel any unknown sections of the dungeon.

Several yards down the arched stone walls they came to an opening. It was another circular section like the room in the last fight they'd had, but much larger. Staring above, Evan noticed more floors with openings that overlooked them. In the center loomed a large figure crafted from white marble.

It was at least five times larger than Myrkor, standing two stories tall. Its head was comprised of six long snakes, yet it had the torso, arms and legs of a corpulent man. The weight of its massive belly was shown by the bottom half of its torso resting on the ground with squatted legs. Like an obese feline resting on its haunches.

"Wait," Evan said, ensuring the group didn't cross the threshold. "Clearly we're going to deal with this once we cross this line," he said, pointing his unsheathed dagger to a section of tile between them and the room. "Anything about this monster stand out to any of you?"

After a moment of contemplation, Elleya broke the silence. "This isn't a creature I've faced before, nor seen in my studies of the dungeon."

"I've heard of beasts with multiple heads before, but usually their bodies resembled the extinct dragons rather than a man's form," Myrkor replied.

Evan looked about, waiting for any additional opinions. When he received none, he waved the group forward. As soon as the last one crossed the line of pale-green tile, a cloaked figure emerged on the overlooking floor above them, at least fifty feet above their station.

The trader lifted his arms and the platform plummeted down. It came to a sharp stop and after regaining their balance, they saw the trader appear in the door of another surrounding floor above them. Their floor was free from any walls and peeking over the edge, Evan noticed a series of stone walkways crisscrossing the circular pit below.

"The last platform tested your endurance against several, but can you defeat one of many?" the trader said as flames shot from his beady pupils.

The snake-head eyes on the monster suddenly burned with the same flame, like a candelabra igniting.

"Spread out!" Elleya called, each of them circling the large beast.

It stretched its arms wide, splitting and shedding its marble exterior like a serpent's skin. A snake head turned to each of them and belched a straight flame, making them all scatter from their positions. After completing his roll, Evan noticed the sixth head remained in a trance, eyes glowing red. Still running from the chasing flame, he glanced at the trader, whose eyes glowed the same color.

"Anyone with ranged attacks, shoot for the trader!" he yelled.

Grymjer and Elleya lobbed arrows and green globs of lava at the balcony. The trader disappeared and the blows smacked the wall where he'd stood. Elleya's arrow bounced off the stone, while Grymjer's burning ooze slid off it, leaving no signs of damage. The cloaked trader reappeared on another side; Evan watched as the eyes lit red again.

"He loses control when you shoot at him," Evan announced. "Keep your aim on him and we'll go for the monster while Myrkor watches your back."

Myrkor charged over to Elleya, who was closest to him, and activated his shield as she fired another arrow. Grymjer scrambled for them, sliding in the nick of time behind the massive shield as a line of fire licked his heels.

Evan shot a glance at Kellen, who nodded in kind. They dashed to opposite sides of the beast, slashing at its legs. To their dismay, each cut seemed to heal quickly. Evan shoved the dagger back in its sheath on his hip and reached over his back for his sword. A heavy arm took a swipe at his midsection, making him leap away. Running to the same side as Kellen, he decided on another strategy, taking out his flame sword as he approached.

"Let's hack the same spot," Evan said, swinging his flaming blade at its knee.

Kellen did the same, taking turns between dodging incoming slashes and fire. Eventually, they had a gaping wound in its leg and were close to severing the limb. Howling in anger and pain, the monster jumped off its good leg and threw its weight head first at the shielded trio. Myrkor snatched Grymjer's arm and lunged to the side.

Their collective stomachs dropped as screams echoed from the cavernous pit beneath them. As the viper-headed behemoth stood, they no longer saw Elleya, confirming their worst fears.

"All at once for its legs!" Evan yelled, charging for the monster. "Even you Grymjer, we need that scythe's power!"

A chorus of battle cries rang out as they sprinted towards the viper-head beast. Kellen slid under a punch, which shook the floor as it struck, then began slashing at the back of its ankles. Grymjer and Evan ran around the creature on opposite sides, barely avoiding shots of orange fire. Myrkor, who didn't have their speed, used his shield to deflect a flurry of flame spat at him.

After a few strikes it yanked the leg back and tumbled to one side, rolling away from them. Soon fearful bellowing rang out as another of their party was taken.

"Damn you!" Kellen yelled, rushing the beast.

Leaping high in the air, he flipped his sword in a downward grip. He landed among the thrashing snake heads and plunged his weapon into the upper torso they shared. Green blood erupted from the wound causing it to shriek in agony. The vipers snapped at his scales, but the teeth were unable to break through. Myrkor lobbed a few flames for the same spot as Evan raced ahead. He jumped and landed on the opposite shoulder Kellen was on, his new armor enhancing his agility.

As he went to stab, several of the heads wrapped themselves around Kellen. Raising his sword, he changed his hand hold to slash at their necks. The one remaining wrapped around his arm, stopping his swing. He reached for his dagger, but was cut off as a massive hand snatched his ribs. The creature walked to the edge, tossing Kellen off first. Evan watched his armored body bounce off several stone bridges as he fell.

Fear gripped his chest, instincts kicking in as he slammed his free fist against the nearest knuckle. His attempts to buy time were fruitless, as he was hurled from the platform. He watched the floor grow farther away as he descended to his death. Quickly looking to his side, he reached an arm out, hoping to catch something. Unlike Kellen, he hadn't hit any of the walkways. His mind working quickly, he twisted his body, hoping to face his fall and make it easier to find some means of landing safely.

'My armor!' he realized, closing in on a stone catwalk.

Closing his eyes, he tensed his muscles, activating his dodge. His body flicked in white light as it hit the bridge. He waited, bracing for any signs of pain beyond his sore ribs from the monster's grasp. Feeling nothing new, he slowly stood, unsure what surviving this fall meant. Had any of the others made it? How far from the bottom was he? And even if he made it back up, could he survive another fight against that thing by himself.?

"Any of you up there?" a gruff voice called from below.

Looking over the side, he saw a green figure waving at him.

"That you, Myrkor?" Evan yelled back.

"Yea!" Myrkor replied. "The shield saved me, but I'm not sure which way to go?"

Evan looked about, hoping he'd see signs of anyone else. Each end of his bridge had a faintly lit opening. He cupped his hands and called up, begging for an answer.

Silence.

Hanging his head, he took a deep breath before looking back over the edge to Myrkor. "Does your path have doors?"

"It does, but I'm not sure where they lead," Myrkor answered.

Eyes rising to the platform, he noticed it was at least ten stories above. Looking over the ankle height ledge, Myrkor was only three stories down.

"I can jump to you and we'll go together," he instructed. "I just have to wait for my armor to regenerate its ability."

"Alright," Myrkor replied. "I'll wait here."

"...*evan*..." a faint echo sounded from above.

His eyes darting up, he saw the side of a helmet bedecked head one story above on a bridge left of himself.

Scales retracted on Kellen's armored head before he spoke. "You see anyone else..."

"Myrkor's below us, any chance you can make it to me? I could help you the rest of the way," Evan answered eagerly. Thankful Kellen was saved by his natural trait.

"I... I can't," Kellen replied, head rolling back onto the walkway out of Evan's view.

"Just stay there and we'll come to you," Evan said, leaping off the side to another bridge only a few yards beneath him.

He continued his descent until he reached Myrkor's position.

"Which one should we take?" Myrkor asked the moment he touched down in front of him.

"This one," Evan replied, pointing to the first one he faced. "We have a coin-flip's chance of being right. At worst we just head back and try the other one."

Myrkor tilted his head and shrugged before reaching into his satchel. He handed a thin vial to Evan. "Take it now if you want, I have plenty in here if we need more."

Evan took the vial and stuffed it in a pouch on his belt. "Thankfully, I wasn't hurt from the fall, but I'm sure I'll need it eventually."

"Here then," Myrkor added, tossing him another vial with a gold liquid. "This one should allow you to use your ability more than once."

Evan started, unsure what to make of the new item. "How…"

"When I dug around in the kit, something came over me. Visions of what I could do and what I had in here," he replied, patting his pack with a meaty hand. "It imparted all its contents to me. Some were ingredients, others were items. I wasn't sure how this one would come into play until I thought about what you're capable of. It also makes your dagger's control of the dead last longer."

Evan stuffed it in the same pouch. "Any chance you can make more?"

Myrkor nodded. "After we find the others and reach somewhere safe, I can craft a few.

Evan swallowed back the lump in his throat. "Myrkor, I'm not sure they…"

He held up a hand, cutting him off as he walked past. "Kellen's still up there and if he couldn't make it down, clearly, he's badly hurt. The other two might be in worse shape. They need us," he said waving Evan to join him.

Evan steadied himself and followed after, feeding off Myrkor's unwavering optimism. He knew at least one of them was still alive. He'd hold onto that spark of hope.

"Everyone's gone!?" Grymjer yelped, ducking under another swipe from the monster.

He'd been on the run for several minutes and the adrenaline of fear was wearing thin, letting exhaustion creep in. the beast shot fire at his back, but his new gear made the flames roll off like running water.

Over his shoulder, he noticed something. A slender figure lying on a bridge below. Wanting a better look, he lobbed a flame ball at the trader, momentarily removing his control.

"Elleya!" he shouted, peering over the edge.

Close to fifteen feet below, her body rested on the stone, her head surrounded by a pool of blood.

"Oh no…. no, no, no…" he stammered.

Distracted for too long, something hard smacked his back, knocking him from the platform. Before he hit the stone several feet down, he tucked his arms and legs to protect himself. Despite it being a short fall, the speed at which he was slapped off the stage made him bounce against the bridge.

"GYAAAA!!" he shrieked, feeling his leg snap.

Skidding to a stop, he clutched his knee instinctively, knowing the bone had snapped below the shin. Thundering stomps signaled the viper-headed mammoth had followed him down and was closing in. Frantically searching, he looked for anything to aid him. A fanged head interrupted his search, forked tongue darting eagerly at its next kill. His heart pounding, he looked past his feet, noticing the bridge ran underneath the raised floor. Digging his nails into the stone, he pulled himself ahead in a vain attempt to reach safety. Fire belched from the serpent and he threw his gloved hand overhead.

He was still alive. Eyes wide, he saw the fire deflecting off the glove towards the wall behind him. A sudden thought struck him. Twisting his hand, he directed the barrage of flame back at the monster. It shrieked in anger as the head was severed from the neck. Filled with renewed energy, he scooted with everything left, knowing it was his only chance to flee from death's door.

The monster's cries sounding hollower, he looked overhead and realized he'd reached his destination. Sucking wind, he felt the pain return to his leg now that he'd survived.

"Should I get back up there and kill it?" he wondered aloud. "Maybe if I finish it off it will save everyone like the second trial?"

He bowed his head, knowing that was a death sentence. Finding a trick to hurt the beast was one thing, actually climbing back up there and defeating it – with a broken leg no less – was impossible.

"Elleya!" he remembered, digging in his belt pouch for a potion.

Broken glass pricked his skin as he lifted the remnants of a broken vial.

"That's why I always keep a spare," he said, determined to find a solution.

Grasping the next vial, he inspected it and saw the vial was undamaged from the fight and fall. He looked to his leg, realizing he had two choices, each with severe consequences. He could drink it himself and gamble she still had something to heal herself, or he could climb down and hope his splintered leg wouldn't cause him to misstep and fall in a way that broke the vial.

"There's always another way," he told himself, uncorking the vial, but only drinking a third.

The wound around his leg and the scrapes and nicks running along his face healed. He shook his leg, realizing it hadn't healed his fractured bone.

"Dammit!" he cursed to himself, unsure what to do next.

Seeing his boot gave him an idea. He took the one off his good leg and removed his knee-high sock. Placing the thick, flat sole at the broken point, he howled. Gritting through the surge of pain, he curled the rest of the boot around his leg and tied it with the sock. Thankfully the boots he'd received were a flexible leather beyond the base.

Inhaling deeply, he steeled his nerves and crept to the edge. Looking down the pit, there were two stone walkways between himself and her. Each one was about four feet below the other, meaning if he dropped down them correctly, he could reach her.

Sitting on the edge, eyes shut tight, he hopped to the first bridge, trying his best to land on his good leg and roll. The harsh ground stung his foot, but he tilted his body enough to fall through the landing without causing more harm to his injured leg. Leaning on his elbow, he muscled himself over to the next edge and followed the same sequence. The sting in his foot grew sharper, and he felt something snap.

"YAAAAAAAH!" he screamed, clenching his teeth as every bit of him winced at the newly broken bones.

"It's just your foot, Grym," he told himself, sliding to the third and final drop.

Dropping again, his instincts betrayed him and he crumpled to the ground using both legs. He didn't scream this time. The agony was so intense that he sat there for several moments while his body shook so hard, he thought his chattering teeth would splinter. Finally, one arm after the next, he crawled over to her limp body. Each second, he prayed for any sign of life. Placing his ear next to her mouth, they perked as his eyes grew wide.

He could hear faint, shallow breaths. Frantically snatching the vial, he opened her mouth and poured in the potion. Soon, the seeping wounds on her head closed as the scrapes on her body disappeared. Tilting her head to face him, he gently shook her shoulder, begging to hear her voice. His concern grew when she gave no answer. Her eyes were half open and only a dim light remained.

"I knew that wouldn't be enough potion!" he shouted, slamming his hand on the ground. He shook his head, unwilling to accept her comatose state. "There has to be a way…"

On her arm he noticed the emerald tip of her wand peeking out from under her sleeve. He ripped it back and yanked at the wand, but it was fastened to a holster around her inner arm. Clumsily unbuckling it, he tossed it aside as he held up the wand.

'How'd she, do it?' he thought, mind casting back to when she'd sent the healing cloud over their party.

He waved it overhead. "Heal!"

Nothing happened.

He tried several more swishes in the air along with other shouted incantations.

They were all fruitless.

He fell on his back next to her covering his face, tears welling in his eyes. Guilt and shame covered his spirit like a soaking wet quilt. A few tears trickled out the sides of his eyes as a blank expression took hold of his face. He sat up in an instant. There was no way he was letting her die here. Or even worse, leaving her unresponsive but breathing body to rot in this place.

"She's still breathing," he assured himself. "Her wounds are healed. I just need one more spark to make that heart beat strong again."

Lifting the wand once more, he closed his eyes, envisioning her crafting the same spell. Waving it in the best imitation he could muster, he prayed to her god for help.

A cloud of blue speckled mist puffed out, falling over both of them. An odd sensation tingled his broken foot as the bones reset. Unfortunately, his snapped shin still remained split. As the rest gently fell over Elleya, her eyes closed. Seeing any change filled his chest with the warm glow of hope. Clasping his hands, he continued praying to Duraté, knowing her god was the only one capable of answering him in the depths of this dungeon.

GASP!

Elleya shot to a seated position, lungs heaving as she regained life. Grymjer wrapped his arm around her in a tight squeeze.

"Thank Duraté, you're alive!" he yelled. Letting go of his embrace, he held her shoulders as she turned her eyes on him. "How're you feeling?" he anxiously asked.

She held her chest as her eyes blinked rapidly. "I f...feel fine."

Still holding one shoulder, he held her wand in front of her. "I used that spell you did back there, the healing one. I didn't think it would work, but it saved you."

She squinted, befuddled at his statement. "That's... impossible."

"Maybe Duraté answered my prayers," he argued jovially. His face in a broad smile. "Whatever it was, this thing did just enough to bring you back. I couldn't do it quite the same as you, but it gave me just enough after the potion..." he continued rambling, unable to hold back.

A wide appreciative smile spread across her face and she hugged him tight, interrupting his happy yammering.

"Thank you," she said, holding him tight.

As she let him go, he patted her on the shoulder. "I do have a small favor?" he asked, pointing to his leg. "Can you fix this?"

CHAPTER TWENTY FOUR

RECLAIMING GROUND

THE TWO OF THEM MADE their way down the faintly lit flight of stairs. All the fixtures had gray flames that despite their size, barely cast viewable light. After reaching a room with no access to a higher floor, they decided to double back and take another path.

"I've been meaning to ask you this?" Evan said as they filed down the steps. "Do you know what those ashen markings are that Kellen had on his face?"

Myrkor bit his lip, unsure if he should answer. "I..."

Evan held a hand up. "I don't plan to pry deeper if you can't say."

"It's fine," Myrkor replied. "He won't tell you, but he wouldn't care if I did."

"I've only known a couple O'dachi in the capitol, but I find their culture fascinating," Evan said.

"Why's that?" Myrkor asked.

"They have a strong sense of order about them and keep strong ties to their family. I appreciate that," Evan said.

Myrkor eyed him. "Did your family survive the strike?"

Evan shrugged. "I don't know. Until I was asked to chase that Chyterian, I hadn't left Yohme's center city. I was honestly hoping I could earn enough to by a horse and go after them. It's funny that owning one has become more valuable than most weapons I found."

"I plan to remedy that," Myrkor stated firmly. "With this kit, I think I could make a horseless carriage."

Evan eyed him, brow curling in confusion. "I'm not sure how to answer that," he said with a laugh.

Myrkor rolled his eyes, shrugging. "When I reached in that bag, one of the recipes sparked an idea, but it's one I can't act on in the dungeon. As far as your first question, the markings are usually made from the soot of your burned relatives. The slashes were markings of a burial." He tapped the side of his forehead, saying, "I'd rather not ask whatever he saw during that trial. I have no idea how or why he'd do that in this place."

Evan held a thoughtful gaze, remembering he had a new sword as well. Mind circling around several possibilities, he put it on the list of things he'd ask his party once they returned to the surface.

His party?

It sounded so strange that he instinctively worded it that way. Those were the trader's words; ones he couldn't disagree with more. How could he possibly lead the group after his tactics got them tossed down a pit.

"Quick, over here!" Myrkor shouted, waving Evan to follow.

After topping a set of stairs, they finally reached the bridge Kellen was on. Myrkor hurried to his side and retrieved a potion from his bag. He flipped the cork off with a meaty thumb and tipped Kellen's head back by the chin.

"I can p...pour it myself, you lunk," he laughed through ragged breaths, grabbing the thin bottle and guzzling it.

Myrkor chuckled, extending a hand to his surly friend, who snatched it, taking the assist to his feet. Now healed, he recoiled his scales and twisted his neck. Each stretch was met with a series of loud pops as the vertebrae adjusted.

The proud O'dachi looked to the platform, which appeared a mile away. "I'm cutting every head off that thing when we return," he stated in a heated tone.

"Let's go find the others," Evan said, patting him on the shoulder as he walked past.

The two of them sat around a small fire Grymjer had built, sharing their observations of the trader's beast. Each of them bounced ideas back and forth, all of them involving the entire party. Neither of them was willing to say their greatest fear out loud.

'What if we're it?' Grymjer thought. *'Is there a reason to push on? Would Elleya even want to continue?'*

They'd been resting by the fire for some time, though inhabiting the depths of the dungeon meant they weren't sure how long. Grymjer's stomach rumbled. It was the second time they'd lost their food supply in one delve. However, this time he'd put a few scraps of dried meet in a pocket. He'd hoped planning for the worst meant it wouldn't happen. This place was the exception to that rule.

'Plan for the worst because you're going to bleed out on a filthy floor,' he cursed under his breath.

"What?" Elleya asked, inquiring about his murmurs.

"It's nothing," he replied, getting up from his seat.

He ripped another dusty wooden shelf off the wall then set it at an angle and stomped it in two. Sitting back down, he tossed scrap in the fire and held his hands up to warm them.

"I had another question about your church," he said.

Elleya's head perked up from the flames. "Please tell me I won't have to divulge another mistake from my past?"

He chuckled. "No, nothing like that. I was just curious how you maintained order in Lysgahr? You've had an answer for everything. It's not common after the world ends, ya know?"

She smiled, tilting her head at the complementary question. "Think of it this way. All that remained of our governing structure were clerics and priests. If you think of us like a military, we're the foot soldiers. Our entire life is regimented around doctrine and rules. When the temple housing our entire leading structure fell, all we could do was continue our mission."

Grymjer leaned on one hip, another question coming to mind. "I get that, but it's still impressive. The entire power vacuum losing them creates. I'd assume you'd see someone looking to take the empty reigns."

"If the dungeon was destroyed, I see that possibility," she replied, a calm half-smile crossing her mouth. "But having the gift here gave us one focused goal. We clerics thrive chasing a holy calling."

Grymjer rolled to one knee, then stood in a big stretch. "Makes sense. Tell me though…"

BLAM!

The door burst open and an undead bedecked in blue armor staggered in. Grymjer scrambled back to the wall, readying a flame in his gloved hand.

"WAIT!" a voice cried out from behind the zombie. "It's me guys!" he said, waving a hand

"Evan?" Grymjer said, dumbfounded.

Looking past the creature's shoulder, he could see him waving a short spiky blade.

"I used my dagger on the enemies we ran across," Evan continued. "I can keep them under my control now."

"For how long?" Grymjer asked. His immediate fear of the thing outweighing seeing his friend return.

"Thank Duraté you're alive," Elleya said, a warm smile on her face as she ran past the monster and hugged him.

"We chopped liver?" a gravelly voice said behind him.

As Myrkor and Kellen sidled in the room, Grymjer's heart wanted to leap out of his chest.

"Everyone made it?!" he yelped, jumping to his feet as he ran to the them. He hopped and punched Myrkor on the arm. "If I survived, I knew you all had to be out there somewhere."

"It's great to see you too, buddy," Evan said to Grymjer, giving his shoulder a firm squeeze.

"You too, friend," Grymjer replied in a quiet, appreciative tone. "How long are they hanging around?" he asked, pointing the zombies and crystal eyed knights lining the hallway outside the door.

"I only have so long to control them," Evan answered. "But Myrkor gave me this potion that enhances that power. If I pour it on the dagger, it extends the time I can control them."

"Can?" Grymjer wondered aloud.

"Don't worry," Evan replied, flipped the blade in his hand. "There's a glow I can see that dims as my time runs out. It's at its brightest right now, but I'm going to take them a few rooms back and hide them until we're ready."

"You think they won't follow you back?" Elleya asked.

Evan waved them off. "It'll be fine, I'm going to barricade the door which will hold until we're done. Myrkor and I tested a few tricks along the way, and they don't seem to remember where I've taken them. They'll just linger around until they see one of us."

"If you say so," Grymjer replied, tilting his head in acceptance.

While Evan led the pack of monsters away, the rest of them took turns sharing stories. Recounting their falls from the platform, and how they each made it to the room. Myrkor, who thankfully still had his supply, handed out food. He then took a small drawstring purse from his bag and poured it into a large silver bowl he found on a shelf Grymjer hadn't burned yet.

"Light this," he instructed Grymjer.

Once the flame licked the powder, it dissolved into a deep red liquid.

"When heated it melts into lingberry juice," Myrkor said proudly.

"Is that bag infinitely supplying you?" Elleya asked, taking a small silver cup from Myrkor before taking a drink.

"It's filled to the brim with supplies, but they don't replenish," he answered with a sigh. "I was telling Evan that when I reached in, it told me all its contents and several recipes. Most of them consist of elements on the surface, so I'll be able to make more, just not down here."

The door opened and Evan strode in with no creatures in tow. "What'd I miss?"

Myrkor chuckled. "Grymjer was the last one standing on the platform," he said holding an upturned palm near the smaller Gremling. "He got smacked off the thing and saved Elleya, but not before he discovered his glove can deflect that creature's flame. It ricocheted off and burned itself," Myrkor finished, wearing a wide smile.

"That's pretty damn impressive!" Evan replied.

"Well," Myrkor said, hands on his hips. "What's next?"

Evan walked over to the fire, sitting on the opposite end from the group. He waved them over, waiting for them to join before he spoke.

"We all survived that fall," he said, leaning forward. "But if it weren't for each other, none of us would be here. It took Myrkor and I to help Kellen, and you two saved each other," he continued, pointing to Grymjer and Elleya. "Unfortunately, for the trader and his pet, none of us are gone," he continued, holding a solitary finger up. "There's a reason we've made it this far. We were destined to reach the end of this dungeon. We've got another shot and I know we can create a winning strategy."

The rest of the group was leaning closer, attention locked on Evan as he spoke. Renewed vigor filled them.

He continued. "I've got some ideas, but I'd like to hear what each of you think first."

Kellen spoke first. "Grymjer and I are immune to its flames, I say me and him team up this time and go in first."

Elleya spoke next. "I need to use my healing, rather than offense this time. If we can each hold potions of our own, then Myrkor can focus on offense. That beast is flame based, so I think his frost hammer is a crucial component in defeating it.

"Anything else?" Evan asked the group.

Grymjer held up a finger. "I've got an idea on how to deal with the trader, but we'll need that undead army of yours."

Evan smiled, excited to put them to use. "Consider it done."

CHAPTER TWENTY FIVE

UNEXPECTED COMPANY

LEADING THE PARTY INTO the hallway, deep-seeded doubt washed over Evan. Despite his speech, returning here created a sense of bubbling, acidic dread in his stomach. He gulped back the fear creeping up his throat.

'Just stick to the plan,' he reassured himself.

Another thought crossed his mind, one he was surprised hadn't appeared before.

'Why would the pit have a way back?' he pondered, rubbing his neck.

Would a god play favorites? Were they really destined to reach the end? He could ask himself a million questions, but he knew none came with answers. There was no way out of all the groups that ventured inside, they were somehow chosen to win. He knew their victories weren't luck, and even the other cleric they'd met had survived losing a trial.

'I wonder if he found another par...' his thought trailed off as he saw a cloaked figure with two pointed ears peeking out the top of his hood.

"Barthélemy?" Evan called to the shadowy figure. The rest of the party fanned out around him as he called to the cleric.

The Rehnarian spun around, facing him with his staff held high. "It's you..." Barthélemy said softly, clearly surprised to see them.

A few more men walked out of the rooms lining the hallway to join Barthélemy.

"Is this the other party?" one of them said, stepping forward with his arms crossed.

Squinting through the dancing torchlight mounted to the walls, the man's appearance at first looked O'dachi. Something about his voice felt familiar to Evan, but he couldn't place it.

"It is," Barthélemy said, stepping to the front of their group. "I'm surprised we'd surpassed your position, considering how long it's been since we've seen each other."

Elleya started, ready to speak of their actual achievements, but Evan extended a hand before her, cutting her off. His eyes met hers, he saw her perturbed objection at allowing her former ally to believe he'd bested her. Deep down, she knew it was best they didn't share any details if they wished to retake the lead. Turning her head away, she folded her arms and looked to the wall, showing clear uninterest in further conversation.

"We'll be leaving now," Evan said, striding towards the Barthélemy's party, since they stood between them and the trial.

"Why not work together?" the familiar voice asked.

Evan squared up to the man. "I appreciate the offer, but the one who led you down here turned us down already," he answered, pointing to Barthélemy. He raised his hands, begging off any tension. "We have no ill-will, but we're going to keep our group as-is. I like to have familiar allies when I'm about to face an unknown enemy.

"Really?" the O'dachi man said, smiling wide. "And what if we insist?" he asked, testing Evan.

Evan huffed a short laugh, raising his arm to the side and pointing his dagger down the hallway. It glowed an amber gold as several corpses marched toward them.

The familiar man reached over his back to unsheathe his weapon, but was stopped by Barthélemy. "You can control them?!" he inquired, voice an octave louder.

"Yes, this batch is with me," Evan confirmed. "And if there's no interference, we'll be leaving," his own party stepped aside to let the group of seven monsters through. Evan dropped his arm and they halted. "I can let them go first, then if we run into an enemy or trap, they'll take the heat."

Barthélemy bobbed his chin. "I think that's best. However, since there's only one way, and we've only a few rooms left to check, we'll be right behind you."

Evan swirled his dagger in a circle, and three of the undead walked past the other four in his group, positioning themselves to block any chance of treachery. "That works for me."

Barthélemy and his party stepped aside and let Evan's party pass through. Looking behind him, Evan noticed the other party waited for them to be several yards ahead before they followed. Finally reaching the end, they noticed there were two openings and two stone beasts standing on separate platforms. The dungeon had created a trial for each party.

"Neither looks any different," Myrkor said. "Want to take the one on the right?"

Elleya looked over her shoulder, then back to the group. "They're waiting some distance behind us, so they'll start right after us."

Evan nodded. "Alright. Even a few seconds is a decent head start. We know what we're getting into. Let's move."

He confidently strode into the large antechamber with his party and undead minions. The trader appeared and the platform dropped once more. Turning back, he saw Barthélemy's party race to the second opening.

The trader emerged on the walkway overhead, eyes glowing. "I see once wasn't enough," he cackled, placing his arms on the railing.

"Take your paltry greetings and toss them in the pit where they belong. We're here to fight, not listen to you yap," Evan snapped, readying his sword.

The trader laughed, eyes glowing red as their monster shed its marble skin to start the fight anew.

"Now Myrkor," Evan commanded, waving his minions toward his teammate.

Ripping open the drawstring on a bulky pouch, he heaved a powdered mixture onto the group. Despite having a skull for a face, the trader somehow contorted it in confusion watching them. Kellen and Grymjer charged in next, the small Gremling deflecting flames as the tall O'dachi jumped and slashed at the slithering necks.

Elleya waved her wand until a large hand emerged, which wrapped itself around three of the armored-undead. Evan called the other four creatures to his side, charging the monster as well.

"Ha!" Myrkor bellowed. "Look at that!" he announced, seeing his powdered concoction in action.

He'd crafted a mixture that reduced the creatures' mass, making them easy to lift. Elleya, now carrying them towards the edge closest to the trader, tossed them onto the balcony. The trader squealed as they lumbered towards him, caught completely off guard. He freed himself from controlling the creature, turning his attention to deal with the undead mob.

Myrkor charged in, leaping into the air with his hammer held high. Everyone else continued slashing at the beast as he landed on its shoulder, slamming his hammer into an arm. Frost covered the limb just before Kellen slashed his sword through it, shattering the appendage. The creature screamed, staggering back. Myrkor launched a frenzy of hammer strikes at the base of each serpentine neck, freezing them with one blow before stomping them to bits after. All the heads gone at once, it fell to its back, thundering against the ground with a massive thud that shook the floor.

"Your tricks only delay my judgement!" the trader yelled from on high.

Having taken care of the three minions, he slammed his hands on the railing. His eyes shot red flames once more and six more snake-heads burst from its upper torso. Everyone looked to each other as the behemoth climbed to one knee, readying itself to provide another onslaught.

Evan glared at the hideous thing, undeterred. "It's not meant to die here," he announced pointing to the edge. "We need to send it off to the pit."

Elleya shot a cluster of glowing red arrows for the trader, who barely ducked the volley. "I'd be happy to give that creature such a fitting demise."

After a moment, her arrows popped in a burst of sparks, making the trader leap for cover. The rest of the group attacked the monster in the same formation, each using the tactics they'd proved effective. This time, after clearing all its heads, Myrkor dusted it with some of his powder. As he hopped off, the rest of the group shoved the toppled beast until it fell over the side, tumbling in a blubbery mass to its death. The trader slowly reached his feet, staring at the group. Their weapons still held at the ready, refusing to lower their guard.

"You've done well, enjoy your spoils before the next trial," he announced to them.

As he lowered his arms, the platform shot skyward taking them to the top of the tower at a fiendish pace. As it slowed to a stop, they looked up, realizing they were standing in the beam that lit the island. Evan wondered how all of the interior they traversed fit inside a singular structure, but he knew better than to linger on that quandary. Feeling the light wash over him, he enjoyed its healing touch as his body slowly vanished, taking him to the next stage.

CHAPTER TWENTY SIX

A FRESH START

As HIS BODY REAPPEARED, Evan took a moment to ensure he wasn't alone. Thankfully, his party surrounded him in the same spots they'd stood on the tower. Twisting his neck and stretching, he noticed that he felt lighter all of a sudden.

"Oh no... there's no way," he stammered under his breath.

His skin broke into a cold sweat as he patted his hips and back, realizing his weapons were gone. His teammates' frustrated yells followed, leading him to the conclusion they'd suffered the same fate.

BOOM!

An explosion in the distance arrested their attention. To their side was an enormous set of stairs with a massive boulder rolling down it. The party split off and hid behind two walls bracketing the steps as the massive rock rumbled by.

"I'm going to get a look at what our best path is!" Myrkor shouted as more blasts followed.

Activating his shield, he ran up a few steps before retreating to the wall with Evan.

"We'll come to you," he called to the trio on the other side.

They waited for another boulder to pass before they ran across the gap, skidding to a stop next to the rest of the party.

Grymjer thumbed over his shoulder. "We're not the only ones taking on this trial."

Evan looked past them and saw another large stage like their own several yards away. Surrounding the massive floors was a red molten liquid, which bubbled and popped like boiling water. He wondered how the other group beat the last trial in the same time as his party. Barthélemy's band must be so adept that they'd made it all the way to the snake-headed monster's trial while Evan's group traversed the pit-bridges. He assumed it must have let them skip the first trial, since Barthélemy had beaten it before. Believing there was no other way they made up that much time.

Shuffling over, he could see the side of the other large staircase and decided he could use the view to their advantage.

"It looks like each quarter of the way are more spots like this to hide," Evan said, pointing to the other staircase. "But there are enemies lurking around them. We'll need to take them out as we ascend."

"I'll go in front," Myrkor said, "I still have my shield."

"Wait..." Evan said thoughtfully. "We all still have our armor, which means I can pass through one as well. So, I'll take the lead of another group. Grymjer, did it let you keep your glove?"

The short Gremling shook his head. "It left me with the rest of my gear though."

"Ok..." Evan thought aloud, rubbing his chin. "You're still flame resistant anywhere you're covered."

Grymjer nodded.

"Alright," Evan continued. "You'll lead the second group then."

"I'll join him," Elleya said, raising her palm.

Grymjer stuck his fist out, smiling, and she punched it firmly with her own. Kellen stepped next to Evan, understanding his pairing.

"Alright," Myrkor said. "Follow me," as he finished, he switched his shield on and ran for the center of the stairs.

As the hulking Gremling raced up the stairs, the rest of them followed behind in a single line. Keeping his eyes ahead of Myrkor, Evan noticed they were closing in on the first set of walls.

"After three more steps, split off and take cover!" he yelled as another blast of explosives echoed.

The groups split into sets of two, Myrkor ran to his left, unable to look behind and take his eyes off the incoming barrage of massive cannon balls. Kellen and Evan took the right side, grabbing the first enemy they saw and shoving at it until it fell of the side of the structure to the magma below.

They didn't have time to see exactly what the creature was, but it appeared humanoid except for the beak on its face. On the opposite side, Myrkor shoved another of the bird-faced monsters, sending off the side as well. Looking down, Evan noticed something long and sharp glinting on the ground.

"Take this," he said, snatching the spear and handing it to Kellen. "This will work well dealing with the next set." After seeing his confused expression at someone giving away a weapon, Evan continued. "You're the quickest fighter and I still have invulnerability in my back pocket. I'll take the lead and bait whatever comes next. When they go through me, you can step in and catch them off-guard."

"Hmph," he grunted with a raised brow, realizing the tactic was sound.

"HEY!" a grumbly voice bellowed from the other side. "You two ready?" Myrkor asked, waving to them.

"On your count!" Evan called back, cupping a hand to this mouth.

As Myrkor held up his hand to signal his count, he noticed Elleya held a spear as well. Seeing the large green hand drop, the two raced to fall in behind the other three, continuing their campaign to reach the top. After cresting several more stairs, they saw four of the bird-men on either side. A cannon fired from the upmost floor, sending another lead ball hurtling toward them.

"Move!" Myrkor shouted taking the right side this time.

He rammed shield-first into the closet enemy, knocking it into two others, the last one jumped to its side, narrowly avoiding being sent to the lake of lava below.

As it ran, lifting an axe for Evan's head, he flinched. Its swing slid through his body and smacked into the concrete stair. Kellen stepped in, ramming his spear through the bird-beast, before kicking it in the chest. The quick combo sent it flying off the side. As the two continued to fight with the remaining three assailants, Myrkor ran to the other side to help Grymjer and Elleya, who'd been on the defensive since the split.

Charging in, he knocked one off the edge, evening the odds. Elleya took another down with her spear as it readied its axe for Grymjer. Picking up the recently dropped weapon, Grymjer ran for one of the last two beasts. Being much shorter than it, he swung for the thigh, slicing both legs clean through. Toppling head over heels into the center of the run, it was crushed by an immense boulder making its routine downhill tumble. Looking over his shoulder, he saw Myrkor and Elleya toss the last of the attackers away.

Taking the lead position again, Myrkor readied the group for another move. Evan and Kellen raised an arm, signaling their readiness to join. The group took their formation once more, it now being second nature.

Looking for the next set of enemies, Evan smiled, seeing there were only two of the bird-like humanoids watching the next walls. His grin faded when they screeched and sprouted wings, flapping themselves away, high above their reach, toward more of their kind.

"Let's circle up and take one side," Evan instructed. "We'll follow you Myrk!"

Seeing the skin on the back of his friend's neck turn from green to red made him smile. He wanted the angriest Myrkor he could muster to fight these things. He followed his massive teammate to the right side. As one of the monsters swooped in for them, Myrkor leapt into the air and snatched its leg. Landing on one knee he slammed it into the ground. Its head popped like ripe tomato as it hit the sharp edge of a stair. Before Evan could stop him, he went after the other, leaping to snatch it and smash it as well. On the opposite side now, he slowly turned to face the group. His chest heaved with the effort he'd expended and ebony blood dripped from his face. The rest of the party moved to form a circle on his side, but were cut off by a massive cannonball.

"I'll be fine," Myrkor said between pants.

Looking up, Evan noticed Myrkor's aggressive tactic had scared the other two monsters. They retreated to higher ground by taking to the air above them, feverishly flapping about. Kellen shrugged and launched himself up, tossing a spear through one while Elleya took down the other.

"I appreciate improvising, but if we break formation again, it'll get us killed," Evan instructed.

"You're the one that called him Myrk," Kellen said coolly.

"I guess we all made mistakes then," Myrkor said with a smirk, running to meet them.

"He just wanted to build a little rage behind those soft eyes," Grymjer chided with a chuckle.

Myrkor shook his head, laughing. "Only you can get away with that."

"I've got an idea for the next run," Elleya stated, ripping a spear free from a fallen bird-man. She pointed to the cannon in the middle. "Kellen, grab the other spear and let's both lob them behind it. We need to distract whoever's loading it."

He obliged, retrieving a spear from another corpse before coming to her side. As they sent the sharp volley through the air, Myrkor led Evan and Grymjer up the stairs with their axes at the ready. After rounding the cannon, they found several bird creatures who had taken cover as the spears dropped on them. The explosive weapon was so huge that the beings couldn't see around it. The trio assaulted the gaggle of surprised bird-beasts, chopping at each one they saw. Kellen and Elleya came right behind them, working with Myrkor to shove more off the side. After an exhausting few minutes destroying every last enemy, a two-story set of stone doors descended on the opposite side of the landing. As they opened, the voice of Duraté called from the dark entrance.

"JOIN ME IN MY HALL FOR THE FINAL TRIAL."

CHAPTER TWENTY SEVEN

THE FINAL TRIAL

STEPPING THROUGH THE darkness, their party was met with a room wrapped in greenery and decadence. Gold marble columns engulfed in deep-green vines stretched to the ceiling. The ceiling sat at least fifty feet above them and was decorated with painted images of battles, gods, and Rehnarians.

"Wait," Grymjer said, pointing to them. "They're moving?"

The rest of the party stared at the living artwork as the lines swirled and morphed, showing different scenes throughout history. Turning his attention to the other end of the room, Evan saw a throne built to seat someone at least ten times his size. But it was empty.

'I wonder if the comet took her as well?' Evan wondered.

A flash of light followed to their right, as Barthélemy's party was transported inside. At the throne, a mass of vines snaked up the seat and formed a feminine figure wearing robes that cascaded to the ground. The vine exterior shed and the face and clothes appeared human like in shade.

"YOU WILL BOTH HAVE YOUR CHANCE AT ABUNDANCE," Duraté said, her voice still strong but not bellowing as it had before. Her words interrupted the tense stares between the rival parties.

All of them spun to face her. She reached both hands up and a crown with elongated antlers appeared, which she placed gracefully on her head.

"FIND THE KEY AND IT WILL OPEN THE DOOR TO MY ORCHARD," Duraté instructed.

Two sets of gates half the height of the room appeared with loud slams as they hit the shiny marble floor. A set of chains wrapped themselves around the bars and a huge lock clanked each set shut.

"ONE OF MY SERVANTS HOLDS IT," Duraté said, waving a hand aloft.

As the glittering dust fell from her hand, it created two mobs of creatures. Eyeing the lot, Evan noticed they were spaced enough to clearly show each party had their own group to deal with. Each set comprised many monsters they'd faced before. The bird-men flapped in the air above rows of crystal-eyed knights and armored zombies. At the rear stood something they hadn't yet seen – a colossal monster wearing robes like the trader – wielding a pointed spear with two curved axe-blades at the top. His head was a curling mixture of branches and half sprouted flowers. It seemed to have replaced the viper-hydra they'd fought on the platform.

"BEGIN," Duraté announced.

A moment later the massed horde charged toward them.

"Move as one line!" Elleya shouted.

Their party stormed into battle, weapons at the ready. Their faces all wore a beleaguered mixture of fear and determination, knowing they were in for the fight of their lives.

"Mobs like this want to swallow you up," Elleya said, sending a bolt of blue light through the head of a zombie. "Make sure you don't get pulled to far from the group."

Evan slammed his dagger through the chest of a crystal-eyed knight, then shoved his boot into its waist so he could yank the blade free and back-fist it through another.

"I'll add some new members to our party," he said, sweat dripping from his brow.

After felling a few more he lifted his dagger, calling the living dead to join him in battle. The group of undead minions came to the aid of Elleya, who'd been smacking monsters away with her wand's whip spell.

"Hey, we should finally use these!" Myrkor said, tossing a leather holster to Kellen. "You're the fastest, dole them out to the group."

Glancing into the container, Kellen saw that it held four vials filled with glowing gold liquid. He drank one, feeling his organs stretch although his body remained the same size.

"It's the same stamina potion we found after the second trial. I made them a while back when I found the recipe in my pack," Myrkor yelled, slamming his hammer into the shoulder of an oncoming enemy. Evan leapt in and stabbed through the fallen monster, adding it to their zombie ranks.

Kellen raced over to Elleya, stuffing a vial in her belt, then ran to Grymjer and Evan, providing them with the same item. The group continued their best efforts to funnel enemies to Evan, letting him feed his dagger with new souls to control. After sending the newest recruits at the robed tree-beast, Evan turned his gaze to the other party, wondering how they fared.

Their strategy seemed to be working too. They'd create a circle around sections of the monsters, allowing the rear group to take them out while protected from future assaults by the three in front. It was a sound formation used to slowly decimate troops and lower their numbers. Something odd struck him after seeing a blade covered lightning slash through a sizeable group of spear wielding bird-soldiers. Then he saw that the one member at the back of their formation wore a feathered cloak.

"You bastards!" Evan yelled. "You're not O'dachi!"

"Cover us," Elleya said, using a blast from her wand to propel herself to his side. "I need to coordinate with Evan."

"They have my gear," he growled angrily. "I knew I recognized that voice, it's Sunasa," he growled, keeping his voice low so as to not distract the rest of the party or alert their competition.

"Barthélemy would never allow him in," she said sternly, eyeing the other party.

"That's because he doesn't know he's working with Hiroyans," Evan replied. "Any chance you have a spell that would remove their disguise?"

She shook her head. "But maybe Myrkor has something. I'll check with him."

Soon the beefy Gremling landed with a thunderous slam by his side, his jump to Evan not as graceful as Elleya's.

"Need something?" he asked Evan.

He pointed to the other party. "I believe everyone with Barthélemy is actually a disguised Hiroyan. Any chance you've got something in that bag that could expose them?"

"I'd rather spend time chasing the key ourselves," Myrkor argued. "We're close to that giant tree-wizard that's controlling them. I'm sure he has the key."

Evan patted him on the shoulder. "I understand, but they're closing in as well and this could be a distraction that gives us the advantage."

As Myrkor thought it over, Evan could see white lines scrolling across his eyes.

"That pack lets him see its entire contents!?" Evan mused aloud. "I'm going to miss finding gear in the dungeon," he added with a chuckle.

Myrkor met his stare with a confident smirk. "I've got a recipe, but I'm going to need you all to cover me while I make it. Once it's done send Kellen or Elleya over to deliver it."

Evan saluted as he ran back to join the others, who'd chopped and hacked their way a few rows closer to the tree-wizard. It was good timing, as they were being swooped upon by a new contingent of flying bird-soldiers. Evan launched his dagger at one that was in a tug-of-war with Elleya for his spear, since she'd grabbed it with her wand's whip. It struck the flying beast in the stomach. As it flinched, Elleya yanked it to the ground and Evan pounced on it to yank his blade free. Another stab and it was under his command.

"Grymjer, toss a fireball at one and I'll send this guy in!" Evan called.

The move would allow his winged minion time to fly in and knock more down that he could take. Without the distraction, it would've been gobbled up by a murder of the crow-faced creatures. After collecting his bounty of new help, Evan looked back to Myrkor. He was still knelt on the ground mixing vials and powders. Thankfully the other party was too distracted to notice or care what their alchemist was up to.

However, the wizard leading the assault caught on. He whisked his spear overhead, creating more of the same dust Duraté had used earlier. A new contingent of flying humanoid creatures covered in armor and black feathers dove for Myrkor. Evan raced over to his teammate, but couldn't reach him in time. Myrkor tried to dodge, but was caught in the shoulder by a black spear. He howled, clutching his arm as he rolled away from the aerial assailants.

"Elleya!" Evan yelled, racing to Myrkor's side.

"I can't leave or they'll overrun us!" she shouted back.

"I'll be fine, switch out with her," Myrkor said, uncorking a short glass bottle with his teeth and throwing it overhead with his good arm.

A burst of violet sparks scared the creatures off, buying Evan time. He raced back to Elleya's side and slapped her back, alerting her to take his place. Turning on her heel, she launched herself to Myrkor's position.

'I have to trust they'll execute it in time,' Evan told himself as he joined Grymjer and Kellen in the push toward the branch-headed warlock.

After felling several more waves, he heard a burst of unbridled laughter from across the room. Barthélemy's party had defeated their warlock and Sunasa – still disguised – had snatched the key. His men formed a line between their king and Barthélemy, who clearly looked confused at the betrayal.

"Dammit," he said, sending his flying minions after the ones assaulting Elleya and Myrkor. "We have to switch plans!" he called to them.

They obliged, running to meet him at the front lines. The entire party together, they smashed and slashed their way viciously through the last line of monsters, finally reaching the flowery warlock. Evan stood defiantly, pointing his dagger ahead. He'd lost a few minions in the frontal assault, but still had plenty left to deal with the final nemesis.

"Take him!" he bellowed, ordering the remainder of his undead army after it.

They scrambled and flew feverishly, ripping, tearing, gorging - gobbling up the colossal robed servant of Duraté. Their work done; a key appeared before the party.

"ONLY ONE MAY GO," Duraté announced.

The party instinctively looked to each other, ensuring they had a consensus on who would take the call.

Evan sheathed his dagger and stepped forward. "I have unfinished business with Sunasa. I'd like to go in."

Myrkor nodded. "I'll work on the potion, and once it's done, I'll need you guys to help me use it."

Elleya looked to Barthélemy, who was in a shoving match with two members of his party, while the other was assisting Sunasa as he used the key to unlock the gate.

"I may have to help an old friend before you finish the elixir," she said, stalking over to Barthélemy.

"Grymjer, can you help her?" Evan asked. "I think Kellen should work on the elixir with Myrkor since he's got experience cra…"

"You got it," Grymjer interrupted, shooing him off. "Now go open the gate."

Evan snatched the key and shoved it in the over-sized lock. It took a few moments of jiggling it around before it clicked. The chains fell to the floor and disappeared, allowing the gates to swing open. He took a deep breath and sheathed his dagger before snatching his flaming sword. Stepping through the murky fog, an invigorating sense of purpose filled his chest. He discarded his feelings of revenge for Sunasa, understanding this mission was more about fulfilling a promise to his friends. He'd collect Duraté's gift for them, there was no other option.

CHAPTER TWENTY EIGHT

THE STRANGLING ORCHARD

Holding his flame sword aloft, he hoped it would help him see better through the mist. The metal that once held a torchlike flame was no longer lit. Hearing a crunching sound to his right, he noticed Sunasa traversing the same foggy landscape.

"I see this place shows your true nature," Evan said to him.

The Hiroyan king unsheathed his sword and held it high, squeezing his hand on the hilt. When nothing happened, he laughed before sliding it back in its holster.

"It seems it took away any magic we once had," he said, hands arrogantly on his hips. "Tell me, did you decide to come here in search of vengeance?"

Evan scowled, remembering how he'd been stuffed in a cage waiting to be tortured. "Unlike you, I seek the gift to restore order to the Kingdom of Yohme."

Sunasa laughed. "Enjoy your noble mission then," he said, turning on his heel and walking away. "I'd banter with you more, but I have a godly item to acquire." He waved as he strode into the thick fog. "I'll make sure to let you know what it tastes like after I find it."

Evan grunted, starting after him. He halted, realizing he was surrounded by rows of scraggy-branched trees bearing nothing. Clearly one of them held what he sought and he'd have to find it before Sunasa. Flinching, he pushed his feet hard against the earth, planning to propel himself using the additional agility his armor gave. But he only completed a standard hop. Duraté had given them powerful items, but she'd taken them away. Whoever found the fruit was going to do so by their own innate ability.

Taking a deep breath, he tested his lungs to see if the stamina potion was still active. When he felt a normal breath emerge, he shook his head. It truly was a test of personal fortitude. He ran down the nearest row, puffy gray mist parting as he took each step. Eventually, he heard the jingle of a tiny bell as he passed one.

Surveying it, he saw a tiny gleaming silver hint of light on the top branch. Facing it, he took a step toward it and the sound rang louder. Taking a step in a few other directions made it ring in a softer tone.

"That's how it works," he said, running by the tree until he heard another similar sound.

He continued the game, running quickly from bell branch to bell branch, following the musical clues until finally he found it. The mist parted to reveal a solitary tree growing from a patch of green mossy earth. On the lowest of its gangly branches hung a large piece of golden pear-shaped fruit.

Eyes growing wide, he raced for it. As soon as his toe touched the mossy ground, brown scaly vines ripped through the earth and snatched his feet.

"What in Varkin?!" he shouted, tugging his feet to free himself.

He soon heard footsteps to his right. Sunasa stood a few feet away, watching him sawing his sword against the vines to free himself.

"Ha!" the Hiroyan king belly laughed. "I see why it's known as the strangling orchard."

He stopped one boot length from the moss, taking a moment to kneel down and study it. Running a finger on it, nothing happened. Evan struggled against the ensnaring roots, watching his nemesis take off his boot and sock. Then he ran a bare foot along the moss, but wasn't met with the same fate as Evan. He hollered in uproarious laughter again, removing his other boot.

"Your yowling gave me the answer – thanks for showing me how to avoid the trap," Sunasa said with a sardonic grin. He took a deliberate pace, ensuring his hypothesis was correct before he spoke again. When nothing shot up get him, he glanced back at Evan. "I'll keep my promise and let you know how it tastes," he raised a finger. "And one more thing, I'll make sure your next cage gives you a nice view of your cleric friend. I'm assuming she's the one who saved you?"

Evan didn't answer, still struggling against the ensnaring vines in a futile attempt to free himself.

Sunasa looked to his feet, smiling again. "This is a nice precursor to the way you'll feel under my rule. I'll make sure you

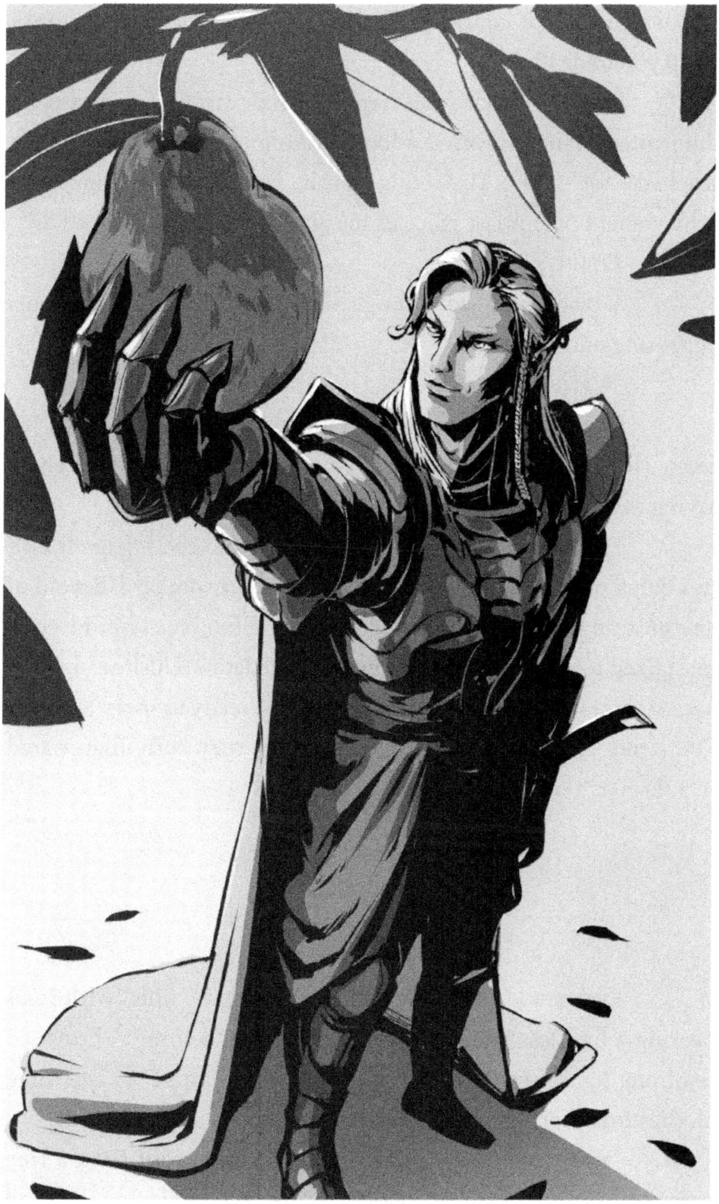

can watch each of your friends' slashed throats bleed out before I whip you to death."

Turning back to the tree, he strode firmly forward until the fruited branch hovered a foot before him. The vengeful king reached for the All-Giving Fruit, anticipating the final achievement of this last piece of his plan.

THWOK!

A blade plunged through the fruit, exploding beige guts peppering onto Sunasa.

"WHAT!" he screamed.

Evan's eyes narrowed as a thankful grin grew across his face. He'd only had one chance to launch his sword through it, saving everyone from Sunasa's inevitable victory.

The vines disappeared around him and the fog dissipated in a quick puff. The two now stood in an empty orchard, devoid of any meaningful spoils. Sunasa growled, yanking his sword free as he stalked toward Evan like a vengeful predator. Unsheathing his own sword, Evan clutched it in both hands, ready to parry Sunasa's first strike. Before their blades could meet, they both disappeared in a flash of glowing light.

Evan stood in another orchard; this time filled with trees bearing a limitless bounty of the fruit he saw before. A crowned feminine figure strode to greet him. It was Duraté, in the same clothes from her throne room, but she'd assumed human size.

"You've freed me," she said, plucking a fruit from a tree before taking a dainty bite. She closed her eyes, enjoying the taste of each successive chew.

Eyes darting around, he noticed it was only them. Sunasa had not been brought on the journey to whatever this place was.

"I...I don't quite understand," he finally answered.

Her face flashed with strobing light as she greedily consumed the rest of the crop. She tossed cores behind her and as they landed, a new tree grew in that place.

"I was trapped in here, forced to share my abundance with the Rehnarians. It's a pity that my own creation turned against me," she said solemnly, running her hand across another branch.

He squinted, unsure how to respond. But he couldn't stop himself from speaking, he had to know more. "How is that possible?"

"I brought them to life," she answered. "And they grew beyond my control. They never gave me a reason why they cursed me to stay. I assumed it was my brother Bailen's doing. But none of his Hiroyans ever came here."

"One almost took your gift," Evan replied evenly.

"Really?" she said, her voice taking an oily-smooth tone.

In this place, her voice had changed from the harsh high tone, to something silky and appealing.

"The king of their people planned to take your gift and use it to rule over Yohme," Evan replied. "In the end, I guess the Rehnar were no different."

"Hmm," she smiled neatly at him, plucking another fruit free and tossing it to him. "For freeing me, you may take whichever blessing you desire. But you won't be able to trap me like they did. I culled that crop from the orchard," as she finished, a smattering of trees vanished.

"Would you be able to restore Yohme to the way it was?" Evan asked.

She sighed, running her hand along a tree trunk. "I can't change what the comet has done."

Evan ran a hand over his face in frustration before placing both fists on his hips. "The only thing I want is to bring order back to this continent."

Her head snapped up, soft pale red eyes watching him admiringly. "If that's actually what you seek, I think there's a gift here for you."

Swallowing back his trepidation, he walked over to her as she plucked a fruit from a tree – this one shaped like a small red plum – and handed it to him.

"What will this do?" he asked.

"Give you the order you seek," she stated flatly.

Licking his lips, he took a deep breath and bit a massive chunk out, getting a third of it between his teeth. His eyes shot wide open as he was sent rocketing from the orchard. He fell to his knees on thin air looking down over the Kingdom of Yohme.

"You've given my abundance to all," she said, stepping beside him while placing a dainty hand on his back.

He wanted to scream, to flail, as he hovered in the sky miles above solid ground. Her caress melted his fears away and washed a sense of satisfaction over him. Climbing clumsily to his feet, he saw her standing proudly as temples similar to the one she'd been captive in, grew across the continent.

"As you saw before entering this place, the people make order around my offerings. So, I've spread them to the world. You can find more of my gifts and treasures inside them," she grabbed his shoulder. Holding him firmly for the first time since they spoke. "After I leave, you'll be given this world to enjoy. One that will move beyond the plague to something new."

Evan gulped, unsure what to make of this revelation. "Did you remove them?" he asked. "The tainted corpses?"

She shook her head. "That was done by a force greater than me, I can only give you something to combat it. None of the corrupted can take what I've given, I assure you."

Her speech concluded, she waved a hand in front of them and he felt himself dissolve again. When his eyes opened, he stood in the large antechamber where the last trial had been. Opposite him, Sunasa was on bent knees.

"You destroyed it!" Sunasa bellowed at Evan, leaping up and rushing him with his sword raised high.

SWISH!

An arrow snapped from Barthélemy's bow, piercing Sunasa's side. He fell face first on the floor, skidding to a stop a few feet past Evan. Loud crunching steps caught their attention as the giant-sized god rose from her throne. Looming over them, she stood for a moment as Sunasa staggered back to his feet.

He spat in her direction. "Bailen shall be the only god I worship," he seethed, looking about the group. "It doesn't matter what trickery she employs, standing over us like this. It's all a façade, like the rest of this place. If she were a real god, like my father, that fruit wouldn't be destroyed!"

SQUELCH!

A fist the size of three horses slammed to the ground, bursting Sunasa against the bright marble floor. Seeing their leader splattered to bits, the other disguised Hiroyans backed away, hoping to avoid execution.

Barthélemy spun to them, raising Aurelia's staff and swirling it in a circular pattern. Three tiny daggers made of glittering gold light shot at the group, piercing their foreheads. As their bodies struck the ground, Barthélemy took off his hood. Evan noticed he had a long scar running behind his left ear that matched the one across his eye. Turning his attention back to Duraté, he watched her approach the giant throne, running her fingers along one of the stone armrests.

She turned her head. "I hope you find the order you seek."

With that, her body turned to bits of ivy-green dust, wisping skyward. A new opening appeared beside her throne; its doors ajar. A bit of light peeked through, and from Evan's estimation, it appeared to be sunlight from the surface instead of the twinkling dungeon fog they'd become used to. Barthélemy and the party turned to Evan, wondering what she meant. Instead of answering, he calmly paced to the double doors and pulled one open.

He glanced over his shoulder. "I'll tell you when we reach the surface."

CHAPTER TWENTY NINE

THE NEW COUNCIL

"I BELIEVE YOU SHOULD BE the new leaders of our people," Elleya stated firmly.

A group of six other Rehnarians, a mixture of clerics and priests, stood around her. A group which included Barthélemy. She hadn't expected killing the leader of their rival race would be the reason for their mutual forgiveness, but stranger things had occurred since the Cataclysm. After Evan's recounting of his meeting with Duraté, they both understood there were more important things to worry about than past grievances.

"You say our council had trapped Duraté in the dungeon all this time?" a bald priest asked.

"Yes, Durthéley," Elleya replied. "She confided to the one in our party who reached the All-Giving Fruit. At some point, the council deemed it necessary to keep her here and feed off her power. It may have something to do with the war against the Hiroyans. Our theory about them was correct. Bailen was a fallen god as well."

Durthéley rubbed his chin, contemplating her response.

A priestess in the group raised her hand, adding her thoughts. "And now Duraté's gone? What are we to make of the trials, now our way of life is gone?"

"It's only spread, Layala" Barthélemy said. "The one in Elleya's party who accidentally freed Duraté was shown a vision of new temples and dungeons throughout Yohme, well beyond Lysgahr."

Layala crossed her arms, brow furrowed in worry. "If it weren't coming from both of you in this place, I wouldn't believe it."

After calling this new council together, Elleya had taken them straight to Duraté's former resting site in the dungeon. It had been easy to achieve, since the door remained open between the god's former quarters and the temple entrance. Deep in her heart, she believed it had been a parting gift from her god. One that let her prove the words she spoke.

"So, it's settled," Elleya said, walking to the door and opening it for the others. "We'll announce the creation of the second council to our people."

After looking to each other and seeing none object, the clerics took their leave through the magical door. The only one who remained was Barthélemy. Elleya stood silently, waiting to see if he'd exit as well.

Finally, after an extended pause, she spoke. "I appreciate you accepting my offer."

"You're the rightful one to lead after finding the gift," he said.

Neither of them spoke further as awkward emptiness filled the immense room.

She exhaled, knowing simple banter wouldn't suffice anymore. "I don't blame you for letting Sunasa in. He would have fooled me if I was still looking for a way inside."

Barthélemy grunted appreciatively. "I don't blame you anymore either. I wanted to say it when I saw you on the second stage. But once you were there in the flesh, for the first time since…"

"It's ok," she interrupted. "You don't need to explain anything to me. I was young then, and my emotions overcame me. If I could go back, I'd have told you myself instead of leaving a piece of parchment to do it for me."

"Hmm," Barthélemy temporized, eyes shimmering as they welled up.

He wanted to say more, but couldn't find the words. He'd never been much for them before, and it seemed that trait had carried on after the comet fell. She smiled softly, seeing an old habit in him that was endearing. In a peculiar way, it was as if this tiny bit of familiarity took her back to when they were young, racing through the academy halls. A time when their hearts and dreams weren't hardened from the expectations and outcomes of life beyond childhood.

She swallowed, finally asking the question she'd been dying to since she first saw him. "Is Aurelia still alive?"

Barthélemy looked to the door. "I don't know, but I plan to go find out. I was going to start by scouting the last temple she was stationed at," he turned his eyes back to her. "Will you come with me?"

She wore a wide grin. "I'm afraid I promised the party we'd search another dungeon near the Whispering Peaks." When he started to hang his head, she walked over and wrapped him in a tight embrace. "But I'll find you as soon as we're done." Stepping back, she held her hands firmly on his shoulders. "You're part of the council now, so I'm obligated by holy decree to see you at least once a year."

He laughed, placing a hand on her arm. "After I reach Aurelia, I'll find you first."

They walked through the door together, enjoying the peace they'd finally found.

EPILOGUE

GEARING UP

Evan smiled as he entered the quaint building. It had taken quite a trek to reach Julien's shop from Lysgahr, but he needed to see his old friends. Nearly a month had passed since he'd left.

"Evan?" a gruff voice wondered, seeing him walk in.

"Hey, Gillium," Evan replied. "I wanted to introduce you to my party."

The surly Koln's eyes curled to thin slits, studying the pack of four standing behind his friend.

"New customers!" Julien stated excitedly. "It's been some time since we had anyone in here able to buy something decent."

Myrkor sidled past the group and approached the counter, wanting to see what the merchant had in stock. "What minerals ya got?"

As the two chatted about wares, Gillium hopped off his stool to get a closer look at the rest of the group.

"Quite the lot you brought in here, Evan," he said, hands on his hips as he eyed them.

"Well," Evan replied. "It's some story and I'm happy to catch you up, but I'll need a favor first."

"Hmph, what's that?" Gillium asked.

"I need you to tell us the story behind this," Evan said, waving his necro-dagger.

Shuffling feet announced a tainted corpse carrying a heavy anvil. Gillium started to raise his wand, but Evan stood between them, cutting off his attempt.

"Don't worry," Evan said, holding up his newly acquired weapon. "He's with me."

Leaning over, the zombified knight placed the object on the floor near a table and chairs, then left the shop on Evan's command.

"I... you... how..." Gillum stammered, pupils darting between the anvil, Evan, and the door.

Evan sheathed the dagger and raised both hands. "Like I said, I can explain. But first I'll need you to help with this," he strode past the anvil and took a seat next to it. He pointed to a series of markings on the side of it. "You're the only Koln I trust, and I need you to tell me what this means."

Gillium squatted down, running his finger over the etched grooves in the dark shiny anvil.

He looked up at Evan in awe. "These are from the lost period in my people's history. Where did you find this?"

Evan smiled, leaning an arm on his knee. "It was buried in a cave near the Whispering Peaks. We think it leads to a dungeon."

"A dungeon?" Gillium asked, eyes glowing with curiosity.

"So, you can decipher that?" Evan replied quizzically.

Gillium stood; arms crossed emphatically. "I prided myself on ancient texts when I was a youngling. I know the story behind these words." He held up a finger. "But you'll have to share the story of how you found it first, and also how these ones fit in," he stated, pointing to the rest of the party.

"Good," Evan began, sitting upright. "You guys want an ale or something?" he asked, looking about the group. "We've got time, right?"

Grymjer's eyes shot to him. "They've got ale?"

"The best you'll find," he answered.

The short Gremling raced to the counter as Kellen followed. While they pressed Julien on his drink selection, Elleya took a seat at the table.

"When I really think about it," Evan continued, crossing one leg over the other. "It all started when Grymjer and I found a map."

AFTERWORD

Thanks for reading! If you enjoyed this tale, please leave a review on whatever platform you purchased this from. It helps more readers find my work. If you'd like to stay up to date on new releases, please visit my website, AsherNovel.com. I hope to see you soon.

- Bryan Asher

Printed in Great Britain
by Amazon